What Can I Do Now?

Radio and Television

Second Edition

Books in the
What Can I Do Now? Series

Art
Computers
Engineering, Second Edition
Fashion
Health Care
Music
Nursing, Second Edition
Radio and Television, Second Edition
Safety and Security, Second Edition
Sports, Second Edition

What Can I Do Now?

Radio and Television

Second Edition

Ferguson
An imprint of Infobase Publishing

What Can I Do Now? Radio and Television, Second Edition

Copyright ©2007 by Infobase Publishing

All rights reserved. No part of this book may be reproduced or utilized in any form or by any means, electronic or mechanical, including photocopying, recording, or by any information storage or retrieval systems, without permission in writing from the publisher. For information contact:

Ferguson
An imprint of Infobase Publishing
132 West 31st Street
New York NY 10001

ISBN-10: 0-8160-6032-0
ISBN-13: 978-0-8160-6032-0

Library of Congress Cataloging-in-Publication Data

What can I do now? Radio and television.—2nd ed.
    p. cm. — (What can I do now? series)
  Includes index.
  ISBN 0-8160-6032-0 (hc : alk. paper)
  1. Broadcasting--Vocational guidance. I. J.G. Ferguson Publishing Company.
  PN1990.55.W43 2007
  384.54023'73—dc22   2006031756

Ferguson books are available at special discounts when purchased in bulk quantities for businesses, associations, institutions, or sales promotions. Please call our Special Sales Department in New York at (212) 967-8800 or (800) 322-8755.

You can find Ferguson on the World Wide Web at http://www.fergpubco.com

Text design by Kerry Casey
Cover design by Takeshi Takahashi

Printed in the United States of America

VB Hermitage 10 9 8 7 6 5 4 3 2 1

This book is printed on acid-free paper.

All links and Web addresses were checked and verified to be correct at the time of publication. Because of the dynamic nature of the Web, some addresses and links may have changed since publication and may no longer be valid.

Contents

Introduction   1

Section 1: What Do I Need to Know About
   the Radio and Television Industry?   3

Section 2: Careers   17
  Broadcast Engineers   18
  Broadcasting Executives   27
  Radio Producers and Disc Jockeys   35
  Radio and Television Anchors   43
  Reporters and Correspondents   50
  Screenwriters   59
  Sportscasters   68
  Television Directors   76
  Television Producers   84
  Weather Forecasters   91

Section 3: Do It Yourself   101

Section 4: What Can I Do Right Now?   109
  Get Involved   110
  Read a Book   130
  Surf the Web   140
  Ask for Money   146
  Look to the Pros   160

Index   164

Introduction

If you are considering a career in radio or television—which is presumably the reason you're reading this book—you must realize that the better informed you are from the start, the better your chances of having a successful, satisfying career.

There is absolutely no reason to wait until you get out of high school to "get serious" about a career. That doesn't mean you have to make a firm, undying commitment right now. Indeed, one of the biggest fears most people face at some point (sometimes more than once) is choosing the right career. Frankly, many people don't "choose" at all. They take a job because they need one, and all of a sudden 10 years have gone by and they wonder why they're stuck doing something they hate. Don't be one of those people! You have the opportunity right now, while you're still in high school and still relatively unencumbered with major adult responsibilities, to explore, to experience, to try out a work path—or several paths if you're one of those overachieving types. Wouldn't you really rather find out sooner than later that you're not cut out to be a news anchor after all, that you'd actually prefer to be a broadcast engineer? Or a producer? Or a reporter?

There are many ways to explore the radio and television industries. This book gives you an idea of some of your options.

The section What Do I Need to Know? will give you an overview of the field—a little history, what's happening in the field today, and promises of the future, as well as a breakdown of its structure (how it's organized) and a glimpse of some of its many career options.

Section 2, Careers, includes 10 chapters, each describing in detail a specific radio or television specialty: broadcast engineers, broadcasting executives, radio producers and disc jockeys, radio and television anchors, reporters and correspondents, screenwriters, sportscasters, television directors, television producers, and weather forecasters. These chapters rely heavily on firsthand accounts from real people on the job. They'll tell you what skills you need, what personal qualities you have to have, what the ups and downs of the jobs are. You'll also find out about educational requirements—including specific high school and college classes—advancement possibilities, related jobs, salary ranges, and the employment outlook.

Section 3, Do It Yourself, urges you to take charge and start your own programs and activities where none exist—school, community, or the nation. Why not?

The real meat of the book is in Section 4, What Can I Do Right Now? This is where you get busy and *do something*. The chapter "Get Involved" will clue you in on the obvious volunteer and intern positions, the not-so-obvious summer camps and summer college study, and other opportunities.

While the best way to explore radio and television is to jump right in and start doing it, there are plenty of other ways to get into the broadcasting mindset. "Surf the Web" offers you a short annotated list of radio and television Web sites where you can explore everything from job listings (start getting an idea of what employers are looking for now) to educational and certification requirements to on-the-job accounts.

"Read a Book" is an annotated bibliography of books (some new, some old) and periodicals. If you're even remotely considering a career in broadcasting, reading a few books and checking out a few magazines is the easiest thing you can do. Don't stop with our list. Ask your librarian to point you to more radio- and television-related materials. Keep reading!

"Ask for Money" is a sampling of radio and television scholarships. You need to be familiar with these because you're going to need money for school. You have to actively pursue scholarships; no one is going to come up to you in the hall one day and present you with a check because you're such a wonderful student. Applying for scholarships is work. It takes effort. And it must be done right, and often a year in advance of when you need the money.

"Look to the Pros" is the final chapter. It's a list of professional organizations that you can turn to for more information about accredited schools, education requirements, career descriptions, salary information, job listings, scholarships, and much more. Once you become a college student, you'll be able to join some of these organizations. Time after time, professionals say that membership and active participation in a professional organization is one of the best ways to network (make valuable contacts) and gain recognition in your field.

High school can be a lot of fun. There are dances and football games to attend, and maybe you're in band or play a sport. Or maybe you hate school and are just biding your time until you graduate. Whoever you are, take a minute and try to imagine your life five years from now. Ten years from now. Where will you be? What will you be doing? Whether you realize it or not, how you choose to spend your time now—studying, playing, watching TV, working at a fast-food restaurant, hanging out, whatever—will have an impact on your future. Take a look at how you're spending your time now and ask yourself, "Where is this getting me?" If you can't come up with an answer, the answer is probably "nowhere." The choice is yours. No one is going to take you by the hand and lead you in the "right" direction. It's up to you. It's your life. You can do something about it right now!

SECTION 1

What Do I Need to Know About the Radio and Television Industry?

Why did you pick up this book? Are you a sports fan, interested in a career that will allow you to watch basketball games for a living? Or maybe you're a music fan, and you're anxious to skip to the chapter on radio producers and disc jockeys. Or maybe traveling the world is more your speed, and you're hoping to read "How to Become a Reporter in 10 Easy Steps." Though this book doesn't outline anything as simple as 10 easy steps to success, it will introduce you to people working as producers, sportscasters, writers, and others involved in putting together the thousands of programs aired on radio and TV across the country on any given day. And though there are some tales of overnight success in the broadcast industry, you won't read too many of them in this book. The people featured here are people who have worked hard in the highly competitive radio and TV industry—not in the pursuit of fame or wealth, but because they love the work.

GENERAL INFORMATION

In the movie *Contact*, scientists receive a transmission from intelligent life on another planet. This transmission doesn't feature some scaly alien saying "Greetings, Earthlings;" it is a transmission originally from our own planet, from the opening ceremony of the 1936 Berlin Olympics. At first startled and upset by the appearance of Adolf Hitler on the monitor conducting the ceremonies, the scientists eventually determine that the message is actually a friendly one. "By sending back that broadcast," Jodie Fos-

ter's scientist assures everyone, "they're saying 'We heard you.'" This scene demonstrates the significance of the sounds and images broadcast around the world for the last several decades, and the role that radio and television have played in our lives. The scene also shows us the power of a single image, or a single voice.

For centuries, people have desired to send their messages quickly around the world. The twentieth century, with its broadcast technology, was influenced by this desire unlike any other time in history. The power and mystery of the radio broadcast was evidenced by a number of events: In 1938, Orson Welles' live radio broadcast of *The War of the Worlds* was so realistic with its simulated news coverage that many Americans sought refuge from a Martian invasion. Also in the 1930s, Franklin D. Roosevelt's fireside chats, for the first time, brought a U.S. president's voice and spirit close to the public he served. During World War II radio-transmitted voices of Tokyo Rose and Axis Sally were used as psychological warfare to disturb American soldiers with taunts about the girlfriends and wives they left behind. And today the public has access to a steady stream of broadcasts via radio, satellite, television, and even the Internet.

Instantaneous worldwide communication had first become a reality in 1895 when an Italian engineer, Guglielmo Marconi, demonstrated how to send communication signals without the use of wires. In the early 1900s, transmitting and receiving devices were relatively simple,

Lingo to Learn

AM broadcast Amplitude modulation system of radio transmission using power of 25 to 50 kilowatts, the maximum power permitted by the FCC.

analog A signal that varies continuously in frequency or amplitude. Digital transmissions of data, which can be compressed for better quality, are replacing analog.

Arbitron ratings These ratings are provided within local markets to identify how many people are listening to the different radio stations within the market as well as to further identify who those people are—their age, sex, and buying patterns.

broadcast journalism Journalism that conveys its information electronically via radio or television.

demographics Specific data about a group of viewers, such as the viewers' gender, age, and other identifying factors.

digital A transmission, by a computer, composed of a discontinuous signal; replacing analog signals in telecommunications.

edit Assemble video, audio, and graphics into news, information, or entertainment segments for broadcasting.

FCC Federal Communications Commission; a board of the U.S. government that regulates broadcasting and other communication.

FM broadcast Frequency modulation method of radio broadcasting; it produces a clearer signal than AM.

format The style or general policies of a radio station. Music, news, and advertising must fit within the specified format.

frequency The number of cycles per second in a broadcast signal; by broadcasting on different frequencies, many radio and TV stations can serve a single area.

HDTV High definition television; linked to satellite, cable, and computer networks to provide better resolution than current systems.

market The geographic area that a station serves.

and hundreds of amateurs constructed transmitters and receivers on their own and experimented with radio. Ships were rapidly equipped with radios so they could communicate with each other and with shore bases while at sea. In 1906, the human voice was transmitted for the first time by Reginald A. Fessenden. Small radio shows started in 1910; in 1920, two commercial radio stations went on the air, and by 1921, a dozen local stations were broadcasting. The first network radio broadcast (more than one station sharing a broadcast) was of the 1922 World Series. By 1926, stations across the country were linked together to form the

National Broadcasting Company (NBC). Four years later, the first radio broadcast was made around the world.

Though the advent of television changed the kind of programming available on the radio (from comedy, drama, and news programs to radio's current schedule of music, phone-in talk shows, and news updates), there has been a steady growth in the number of radio stations in the United States. The United States alone has more than 13,000 radio stations. However, until the government lifted restrictions in the mid-1990s, allowing companies to own more stations in one market and garner greater advertising revenue, some radio stations suffered because of a smaller audience, and therefore, less advertising. With larger broadcast companies continuing to buy up smaller companies, the radio industry should survive as cost-effective competition against TV and the Internet.

Modern television developed from experiments with electricity and vacuum tubes in the mid-1800s, but it was not until 1939, when President Franklin D. Roosevelt used television to open the New York World's Fair, that the public realized the power of television as a means of communication. Several stations went on the air shortly after this demonstration and successfully televised professional baseball games, college football games, and the Republican and Democratic conventions of 1940. The onset of World War II limited the further development of television until after the war.

Since television's strength is the immediacy with which it can present information, news programs became the foundation of regular programming. *Meet the Press* premiered in 1947, followed by nightly newscasts in 1948. People who bought early TV sets just for the novelty of it, or to gather everyone around the tiny, snowy screen to see a favorite niece sing on a locally broadcast talent show, were soon rewarded by the rapid expansion of the industry in the 1950s. The Federal Communications Commission lifted a freeze on the processing of station applications, and the number of commercial stations grew steadily, from 120 in 1953 to the 1,740 broadcasting television stations of 2004.

It was in the 1960s and ensuing decades that television's power became most apparent: together the country mourned the death of President Kennedy; witnessed the murder of his alleged assassin, Lee Harvey Oswald, by Jack Ruby; and formed opinions on the Vietnam War based on live TV news footage. The successes and failures of NASA programs brought viewers together, from the first steps on the moon, to the famous, near-fatal mission of Apollo 13; to the first space shuttle launch; to the tragic explosions of the *Challenger* and *Columbia.* In recent years, Americans were captivated and horrified as they watched the terrorist attacks (and their aftermath) unfold in New York City and Washington, D.C., on September 11, 2001.

But the big three networks (NBC, ABC, and CBS), which, along with PBS, reigned for many years as primary sources of information and entertainment for millions of people in the United States, have

More Lingo to Learn

media TV, radio, newspapers, and other forms of wide-reaching communication.

Nielsen ratings A listing of TV programs according to the number of viewers; compiled by Nielsen Media, ratings are used in determining advertising rates.

NPR (National Public Radio) A network of about 789 noncommercial, nonprofit stations.

playlist The list of the recordings to be played during a particular radio program or time period.

ratings The audience of a radio program as estimated by survey.

satellite A device that orbits Earth and transmits television and other communications signals.

satellite radio Radio programming that is broadcast via satellite. Satellite radio, unlike traditional radio broadcasts, can reach listeners over thousands of miles.

telecommunications The transmission of signals across a large geographic area, by television, radio, and other stations.

TelePrompTer A monitor that displays the script for reading on air by a newscaster or other TV presenter.

television market The business of television broadcasting. Top TV marketplaces are New York, Los Angeles, and Chicago.

transmitter A tall tower that sends a radio station's signals to its listening area.

FOX, UPN, and WB, from developing and competing. And although more and more people are looking to the World Wide Web as a source of information, people still rely on television and radio as reliable, trustworthy sources of news and of quality entertainment. In addition, television and radio stations are using the Internet as another tool to provide information and entertainment to the public. Today, most television and radio stations have a strong presence on the Internet.

STRUCTURE OF THE INDUSTRY

Keep track of the number of hours you and your family spend in front of the TV and compare the figure to the national average—seven hours and 40 minutes a day for each household. With so much time spent watching television and listening to the radio, a person can learn a lot about the structure and history of broadcasting; no wonder so many people pursue work in sportscasting, newsscreenwriting, and other broadcasting careers. In any given hour, a cable or satellite viewer may have a choice of more than 100 programs; this number is increasing as more specialized cable channels develop original programming. And as we channel-surf with ease, sitting back with our remote controls, thousands of people are hard at work to bring us these programs. Approximately 327,000 people are employed in various ways by radio and television, at both the local and national levels.

Some people in radio and TV, such as disc jockeys, talk show hosts, news

consistently lost viewers to cable, satellite TV, the Internet, and movie rentals. This hasn't stopped new networks, such as

anchors, and sportscasters, are prominent around the nation or in their local community, their voices and faces familiar to large audiences. Others work behind the scenes, putting together the many programs aired on radio, public TV, and cable on any given day. There are also engineers maintaining the broadcast equipment and salespeople selling airtime to advertisers to keep the station profitable. In television, large stations located in metropolitan centers can employ several hundred people, whereas a small station in a small city may employ as few as 35 people. In radio, the smallest station may employ only four or five full-time people. And some programs are put together by people working on a freelance basis—producers, directors, and writers employed by a station or a production company from project to project.

Obviously, your local FOX channel doesn't have the resources to put together an episode of *24*. So how does the show manage to find its way piped into your home by a local station? Many television and radio stations are affiliated with one of the national networks (such as FOX, ABC, CBS, and NBC). An affiliate station is not owned by the network, but merely has a business contract; the network then supplies the affiliate station with a large amount of programming. Shows like *24*, along with most of the original comedies, dramas, and news magazines in prime-time television, are supplied by the networks; the affiliate stations put together local daily news broadcasts, coverage of local sporting events, and specials of regional interest.

Ever been frustrated by the sudden cancellation of a favorite TV show? Or had the radio talk show you listened to every morning suddenly replaced by a music program? Well, you may have been the only fan of these programs; ratings systems determine what people are watching, what radio stations they're listening to, and when. Maybe you've even served as a Nielsen family, filling out a diary, listing the programs you watched during a specific week. With numbers compiled by Nielsen ratings surveys, networks and affiliates determine what to charge advertisers for airtime during their programs. The highest-rated programs don't always have the highest ad rates, however; the Nielsen surveys also provide numbers about the kind of audience (such as young or old, women or men) watching a specific program, and some advertisers prefer to target specific age groups and genders. Because commercial radio and TV stations rely on advertising revenue to stay successful, much in the broadcasting industry (scheduling, staff, salaries) is determined by ratings.

Cable television networks operate under some of the same arrangements as commercial television stations. Some cable networks are advertiser supported. Although one cable station may seem to rely entirely on reruns of *All in the Family*, *The Love Boat*, and other recycled commercial television, others create their own programs. Cable networks that focus on specific subjects of interest, such as the Travel Channel and the Food Network, create special programming for their audiences. Other cable networks (such as HBO and Showtime) are subscriber supported, and run motion pictures, sports or entertainment events, and movies or series produced specifically for cable.

Even the worst program on TV takes up its fair share of space in the air as it's transmitted along electromagnetic waves. So, in an attempt to keep things in order in a variety of ways, there is the Federal Communications Commission (FCC). Congress established the 1927 Federal Radio Commission, which in 1934 became the FCC. The FCC is involved in many aspects of broadcasting, from business matters to the content of programs. The FCC supervises and allocates airspace, makes channel assignments, and licenses radio and television stations to applicants who are legally, technically, and financially qualified.

The commission also sets limits on the number of broadcasting stations that a single individual or organization can control. These limits were relaxed, however, in the mid-1980s: broadcasters today no longer must perform as many public affairs and public service functions, the license renewal process is easier, ownership requirements are more lax, and it takes less time to buy and sell a station. In 1992, FCC regulations were relaxed even more, so a single company could own up to 6 stations in one city and 60 stations nationwide. Previously, an owner was limited to one AM and one FM station per city, and twelve nationwide. This new leniency has paved the way for large station and network mergers in recent years. The Telecommunications Act of 1996

created even more leniency, allowing phone companies to enter wider cable markets; this is expected to result in heavier competition among cable companies for the TV viewer.

CAREERS

In what other industry could you have a career playing your favorite music all day, or giving the play-by-play of a baseball game, or organizing the day's newsworthy events into a broadcast with the power to influence thousands, maybe millions, of people? Of course, not all jobs in the broadcast industry are ideal—some involve a great deal of stress at low salaries; and many broadcasts, even on the national level, only reach small audiences. In many small stations, jobs may be combined; an announcer may shoot news film, a secretary may write copy, an on-the-air sportscaster may serve as a salesperson.

Though some people achieve great wealth and fame in radio and TV, others seek out less competitive positions within the industry and settle into them. A sports lover, uninterested in working her way up into a position with a network sports department, may make a living as a camera operator for a local station; a radio disc jockey may prefer to work in a small town where he has more control over the playlist than he would in a larger station.

TV sitcoms, news broadcasts, radio talk shows—all involve the collaboration of a number of professionals from the initial planning stages to the actual broadcast of the final product. Many of these professionals can work in both radio and television, while other careers are industry specific. You will also discover that there are many more off-air careers than there are of the on-air variety—so don't tune out opportunities as a supporting player in these fields.

Off-Air Careers

Management. The job of *general manager* requires a unique combination of business ability and creativity. General managers are almost always people who have had successful experience in sales, programming, or engineering. Their responsibilities include the handling of the daily problems of station operations in consultation with program managers, sales managers, and chief engineers. They determine the general policies for the station's operations and supervise the execution of those policies. They normally handle the station's relations with the FCC and other government bodies and participate in many community activities on behalf of the station.

Program directors plan a program schedule and integrate programs to give the station a broad audience appeal. The program director of a station, in collaboration with the general manager, determines and administers the station's programming policies and plans the most effective program schedule for the station. He or she works with the *producers* and *directors* (who plan and supervise the production of programs, both in rehearsal and during broadcast), on-air personalities, and other members of the department in developing new programs or improving old ones.

The traffic department is little understood but serves a vital function in a broadcasting station. It is the heart of the station's administrative operations, through which all instructions regarding programming and sales must be cleared. The department maintains the logs of the station's daily program activities, which are used by the programming, sales, and accounting departments. This job is generally the responsibility of a *traffic manager,* who may be assisted by one or more traffic clerks.

Preproduction, Production, and Postproduction. Preproduction consists of the planning and organization it takes to get a radio or television show up and running. A radio or television show must be scripted, budgeted, and scheduled in order for it to be a broadcast. Actors and actresses must be hired, and props, sets, and costumes must be prepared. Production consists of the actual shooting of the television show or newscast, and in radio, the broadcasting of the show. Postproduction consists of the work necessary—such as editing, recording, and graphic production—to get a recorded television or radio show into final broadcast form. Here is a list of the major careers in these areas:

A variety of workers help create the proper setting of a television show, newscast, or movie; other workers help actors and actresses create a physical appearance that is appropriate for a broadcast. Many television stations employ *graphic artists* or *scenic designers*, who plan set designs, construct scenery, paint backdrops, and handle lettering and artwork.

Props workers create the physical aspects of a scene for television and motion picture productions. Some larger stations have *makeup artists* and *costumers* who work with the art staff. *Costume designers* help create the look of a television show, be it a Western set in the 1800s or a modern-day medical drama set in an inner-city hospital. They research clothing styles and design or plan each actor's and actress's wardrobe. Makeup artists and *hairstylists* make sure that actors and actresses look the right way for a scene or broadcast.

At radio stations, *music librarians* are occasionally employed because of the heavy reliance on recorded music. This individual evaluates and often selects the music to be used for a particular show, and catalogs and stores the musical recordings.

Writers fall into different categories in broadcasting, depending on their area of work. *Screenwriters* work on actual programs, developing the words and ideas for each show. In the news division, *newswriters* may be responsible for writing the entire news section of a broadcast, or, in longer programs, they may write the introduction to news segments developed by *reporters* and *correspondents* (those who collect the local news and transmit live coverage). Most local television news stations have writers who write the newscasters' scripts and correspondents who write their own pieces. *Continuity writers* script commercial announcements, public service announcements, and station promotional announcements.

Animators and *cartoonists* create animated images in movies and on television shows such as *The Simpsons*.

Television producers work behind the scenes of television programs and newscasts; they write scripts, hire staff, and bring together the many different elements of production to create a successful show. *Casting agents* are responsible for auditioning actors and actresses for television shows (and also motion pictures). Sometimes they hold open auditions; other times they may contact people they feel might be particularly good for a role.

Radio producers help to determine a radio station's identity. They research the marketplace and create radio shows to interest and entertain the targeted audience. While a disc jockey is on the air, producers keep the radio show running behind-the-scenes by keeping track of commercials, screening callers, and arranging the appearances of on-air guests such as celebrities and sports figures.

Television directors control the decisions that shape a television program, from live production and local newscasts to dramatic TV movies and sitcoms. *Directors of photography* make sure that each shoot goes as planned. They check anything that might affect the quality of a shot, such as weather conditions or lighting. *Program assistants* coordinate the various parts of a show by assisting the producer or director. They arrange for props and makeup service, prepare cue cards and scripts, and usually time rehearsals and shows. *Floor staff* work on the studio floor, arranging sets, backdrops, and lighting, and handle the various moveable props used on the show.

Lighting directors make sure that lighting is appropriate for the mood of a television show or broadcast. *Electrical technicians*, sometimes known as *gaffers*, assist the lighting director. The *grip*, sometimes known as the *best boy*, assists the gaffer with setting up the appropriate lighting and cameras for each production.

The *floor manager* directs the performers on the studio floor in accordance with the producer/director's instructions by relaying stage directions and cues. Using a headset, he or she is in touch with the director in the control room at all times.

In the technical nerve center of a station, surrounded by racks of electronic equipment, the *broadcast engineer* brings together the various elements of the show, switching from the camera in the studio to a slide projector, then to a videotape player or a live remote, and finally to the network program usually originating in New York or Los Angeles. Broadcast engineers are supervised by the program director. Broadcast engineers also work at radio stations.

On the studio floor, *engineers* handle the camera and microphones as the show progresses. At the transmitter, often miles away, the *transmitter engineers*, who have final technical control over the program, monitor and adjust the complex electronic gear to ensure the strength, clarity, and reliability of the signal sent from the transmitter. All of the technical work is supervised by the *chief engineer*, a fully qualified engineer with considerable experience as a working technician. In radio, this person may be the only engineer; in television, he or she may supervise as many as 40 people. The work of the chief engineer is to plan and coordinate the engineering requirements of shows, including the scheduling and assignment of crews. The chief engineer is responsible for the operation and maintenance of the equipment, makes decisions about purchasing new equipment, and often designs and develops special equipment for the station's needs.

In television production, the *video director* supervises the video editors who time, cut, splice, and clean tape. This person also supervises the advance screening of the videotape to determine its suitability for broadcast and participates in the decisions involving the purchase of taped shows.

Promotions, Sales, Marketing, and Community Affairs. Promotion departments publicize the station's programs, image, and activities. Headed by a *promotion manager*, such a department typically plans and directs advertising campaigns, arranges for public appearances of on-air personalities, and designs other promotional activities aimed at the station audience. The promotion department may also develop sales promotions that include the planning and layout of advertising for trade journals and production of sales brochures and other material used by sales department personnel.

Commercial radio and television stations are supported by the money received for commercial announcements and programs. *Salespeople* secure these advertising revenues. Local sales are the responsibility of the *sales manager*, who sets the general sales policy for the station and supervises the daily activities of the sales force. The sales manager develops sales plans that will appeal to sponsors, and also plans special campaigns to tie in with seasons of the year and special events.

Marketing workers help radio and television stations advertise themselves to the viewing or listening public. People working in marketing might develop a catchy phrase, like NBC's "Must-See TV," an instantly recognizable song, an eye-catching logo, or anything else that will help identify the station and attract viewers or listeners.

Local stations closely identify with their communities. *Community affairs directors* plan and execute a station's services and programs that are meant to respond to the needs of the community. These include public service announcements, public affairs programming (often undertaken in conjunction with the news department), and special events and public service campaigns that deal with community-related issues.

On-Air Careers

On-air performers, such as announcers, newscasters, sportscasters, reporters, weatherpeople, disc jockeys, and actors and actresses are the workers that the public knows best. Their work, and their personalities, help a station build a listening- or viewing-audience. Here are some of the most recognizable on-air careers:

Radio and television anchorpeople, sometimes known as *anchors*, analyze and broadcast news received from a variety of sources. They help select, write, and present the news.

Television and radio reporters and *correspondents* gather, write, and report on news events for broadcast audiences. They may conduct on-air interviews, help edit recorded footage, and report live from remote sites. They may occasionally work as anchors.

Television and radio commentators offer their personal opinions about current events, politics, sports, and entertainment on radio and television newscasts. *Food critics* present reviews of restaurants and food-related events for television and radio stations.

Weather forecasters compile and analyze meteorological information in order to prepare weather reports for daily and nightly newscasts. They help create graphics, write scripts, and explain weather maps to audiences. They also provide special reports during weather emergencies.

Sportscasters cover and report on sporting events for radio and television newscasts; they write, produce, and edit feature segments for broadcast.

Talk show hosts oversee daily or weekly news, comedy, or variety shows on television and radio. *Game show hosts* supervise contestants who compete for prizes such as cash, trips, and merchandise. *Comedians* are entertainers who make people laugh. They appear as members of ensemble casts on television shows like *Saturday Night Live*, on sitcoms, on talk shows, and on radio shows.

Actors and actresses play parts or roles in dramatic productions on television, on the radio, on the stage, and in motion pictures. *Stuntpeople* fill in for actors and actresses when a dangerous stunt is required, such as a chase atop a moving train, a fall from a building, or a barroom brawl.

Disc jockeys introduce songs and news reports, field phone calls, and discuss current events or other topics on radio stations.

EMPLOYMENT OPPORTUNITIES

The best place for a beginner to look for a job in radio and television is in one of the many smaller stations throughout the country. Between 2004 and 2014, employ-

> ## Historical Facts
>
> - When the concept of television was discussed in the 1880s, it was referred to as "seeing by electricity."
>
> - The first TV camera and TV tube were patented by Vladimir K. Zworykin in 1923 and 1924, respectively. These inventions, along with the first practical model of a TV in 1938, earned him the title "father of television."
>
> - Television was given a public demonstration by John Logie Baird (1888–1946) in London as early as 1926. He televised a ventriloquist's dummy.
>
> - The first people to appear on TV were those involved in Baird's experiments. In 1926, Bill Taynton, a 15-year-old office boy, was the first person to be televised, followed in 1930 by Irish actress Peggy O'Neil at a home exhibition. Television sets were then known as televisors.

ment in the broadcasting industry is expected to grow by 11 percent—a rate that is slower than the average for all industries combined, according to the U.S. Department of Labor. Competition will be stiff—especially in larger markets. Jobs should be easier to find in radio because more radio stations hire beginners. Internships are an excellent way to gain experience; work at a high school or college station is also valuable.

Large stations normally require a considerable amount of broadcasting experience for nearly all jobs in the programming, engineering, and sales areas. Employees of large-market stations generally belong to unions, and thus earn higher salaries than their nonunion counterparts.

Smaller stations, particularly those in smaller communities, are often willing to hire individuals with less experience. Many people establish roots in smaller communities and develop highly satisfactory careers. Others, after they have acquired an understanding of radio and television operations and skill at their particular job, move on to larger stations in larger communities where the financial rewards are greater. It is possible to get a beginning job at a network, but networks have many more applicants than openings. Although they may occasionally hire inexperienced people, it happens very rarely.

Much of the production work for TV and radio programs is taken on by freelance workers; directors, producers, writers, and others hire on with networks, stations, or independent production companies to cover sporting and entertainment events, to create radio programs, or to create documentaries and news specials.

INDUSTRY OUTLOOK

Are you ready for DentistryTV? Or the All Jell-O Channel? This may be in the future of television, as advancements in technology allow for more cable channels than ever—between 200 and 500. Even a network TV program as popular as *Lost* doesn't draw as many viewers as a top-rated network program of 10 or 15 years ago; this is the result of competition for the TV viewer, a competition that will continue to determine the state of the broadcast industry. As more cable channels develop, so will more network television affiliates, all vying for the fickle attention of the viewing public. This, obviously, will provide more work for people in broadcasting. "Narrowcasting" is also likely to increase, offering job opportunities for people in radio and TV. Narrowcasting involves producing programming for a specific community, such as educational programs for schools, or health programs for hospitals and doctors' offices.

The broadcast industry is also expecting heavier competition from the home personal computer; approximately 68 percent of Americans use the Internet, and this percentage is increasing. Many in the industry aren't that concerned about a loss of viewers—they see the Internet as a way to better reach their viewers and listeners. Currently, thousands of radio and television stations have Web pages.

The emergence of satellite radio—fee-based, radio programming that is broadcast via satellite—has created hundreds of new stations. Additional opportunities will be available to disc jockeys, producers, and support workers as this industry continues to grow.

Though the number of women and minorities working in the broadcast industry has increased, and will likely continue to increase, analysts are not expecting big changes in the next decade. Women and minorities still face discrimination and prejudice in the workplace—many women earn lower salaries than men in the same careers. Ideally, the percentage of minorities working in the industry would reflect the percentage of minorities in the general population; unless the industry radically changes its hiring practices, this balance won't be struck anytime soon. Some organizations are attempting to bring more minorities into the industry: The National Association of Broadcasters (http://www.nab.org) offers financial assistance to minorities looking to buy into broadcast properties, and also offers job placement services. The Broadcasting Training Program (http://www.thebroadcaster.com) assists minorities by offering valuable training opportunities.

SECTION 2

Careers

Broadcast Engineers

SUMMARY

Definition
Broadcast engineers operate and maintain the electronic equipment used to record and transmit the audio signals for radio and the audio and visual signals for television. They may work in a broadcasting station or assist in broadcasting directly from an outside site.

Alternative Job Titles
Broadcast operators
Broadcast technicians

Field technicians
Maintenance technicians
Video control technicians
Video-robo technicians
Video technicians

Salary Range
$15,000 to $29,000 to $63,000+

Educational Requirements
Some postsecondary training

Certification or Licensing
Voluntary

Employment Outlook
About as fast as the average

High School Subjects
Computer science
Mathematics
Shop (trade/vo-tech education)

Personal Interests
Broadcasting
Building things
Figuring out how things work
Fixing things
Travel

"Five . . . four . . . three . . . " The director counts down to show time, the anchors seated on the set and poised to begin the show: ". . . two, and one . . . roll and up . . ." The darkened screen comes alive with the graphics and music of the local news program broadcast live across the city. ". . . camera two—focus it . . ." With that direction the video-robo engineer moves camera two into position and brings its image, a close-up, into sharp focus. ". . . take two . . . " The technical director switches to the second camera, from the close-up to a shot of both anchors. To achieve a smooth cut the anchor looks into the second camera at exactly the right moment: ". . . and roll." The video recording engineer begins a prerecorded videotape that has been precisely timed to run as long as the anchor's copy.

WHAT DOES A BROADCAST ENGINEER DO?

Broadcast engineers, sometimes known as *broadcast technicians*, set up and operate the equipment used to record and transmit television programs. They install the equipment, keep it in working order, and repair it when necessary. Broadcast engineers work in particular departments, such as news or sports, or for an individual program. Depending on their assignments, engineers work in studios and other controlled environments, or they may go out into the field. For anyone interested in a career in broadcast engineering, there are several different specialties to choose from.

With the introduction of robotic cameras, stations no longer need to employ an engineer for every camera. Instead, a *video-robo technician* will direct the camera's movements via computer. Video-robo technicians are also responsible for the "look" of the broadcast image. Using a video panel with joysticks assigned to each camera, the engineer pans and tilts the camera and fine-tunes its focus.

Often it is necessary to broadcast live from a "remote"—a site outside the studio. Reporters may also need to record material at a remote site for later broadcast. Shooting outside the studio is the responsibility of the *field technicians*. Once at the remote site, the technicians transmit to the station through telephone wires. After the transmission is connected, they connect any microphones or amplifiers that may be needed. If the engineers cannot use telephone wires, they will set up and operate microwave transmitters to broadcast to the station.

No matter how advanced the equipment becomes, there will always be a need for competent maintenance support.

Maintenance technicians are responsible for ensuring that every camera, microphone, transmitter, amplifier, and any cables used by the station are in working order. Assisting the maintenance technicians are the *technical stock clerks* who order all the necessary equipment.

Video technicians continue to work in the control rooms of stations that are nonautomated, and they are responsible for adjusting the visual quality of the picture. Using a control panel for each camera and monitors in the control room, a video technician adjusts the focus and sharpness of the picture before it is broadcast.

During a live broadcast, such as a news program, videotapes recorded at an earlier time may be aired. Usually, these tapes have been recorded by technicians; however, with the increasing accessibility of video and digital recorders, tapes recorded by the public are often used. *Video recording technicians* work with the producer to ensure that the recorded tapes play at the appointed time during the live broadcast. For example, while a news anchor reads the copy, the video recording technician plays the recorded material accompanying that story. These technicians often create their own sound and special effects.

Working in the master control room, the *transmitter operator* monitors and logs the transmitter signals sending out the actual broadcast. Every broadcasting station is assigned a specific frequency, and it is the responsibility of the transmitter operator to supervise the station's transmission. The *chief engineer* is responsible for the station's entire technical operations, including the station's technical budget. A successful chief engineer will often have several years of experience, as well as an advanced education. Working with a scheduling assistant, the chief engineer assigns projects to the technicians and is responsible for making sure that the station is running smoothly. The chief engineer is also responsible for hiring new employees and supervising the work of the entry-level technicians.

WHAT IS IT LIKE TO BE A BROADCAST ENGINEER?

Breaking stories, last-minute edits, screaming producers: these are the highly stressful elements of producing broadcast news. For Tony Palos, a video-robo engineer in Chicago, Illinois, these elements have become part of a daily routine.

At the beginning of his shift at 3:00 P.M., Tony checks the working order of the robotic cameras. He also works with the lighting crew to determine the best position for the cameras, taking into consideration the different anchor personnel who will be reporting that day's news.

Once the cameras are set, the technicians begin to record videotapes needed for the 4:30 P.M news program. The videotape and accompanying copy are timed by the producer and video recording technician to ensure that the newscast has the correct running time. After the script has been written, the director will decide what type of shot will be used with each news story and then formulate a rundown for that day's show.

The director is in charge of calling the shots, while the technical director puts the commands into action, actually push-

---

Lingo to Learn

amplifier A device used to boost the strength of an electronic signal.

analog A form of transmitting information.

bandwidth A measure of spectrum (frequency) use or capacity.

broadcasting Process of transmitting radio or television signals via an antenna to multiple receivers.

broadcast quality May refer to both technical specifications and artistic quality.

channel A frequency band in which a broadcast signal is transmitted.

digital Conversion of information into bits of data for transmission; allows simultaneous transmission of voice, data, or video.

page An individual preprogrammed computer screen assigned to a camera and used to control the camera's movements.

panning Rotating a camera horizontally.

remote A broadcast being taped outside a station's studio.

rundown A second-by-second breakdown of a program's schedule.

tilting Moving a camera vertically.

transmitter An electric device consisting of circuits that produce a radio or television electromagnetic wave signal.

ing the buttons that change the broadcast picture. From the several monitors in the control room during the program, the directors choose the specific shots to be used. The director's orders are carried to the various engineering rooms by a speaker system.

As the video-robo engineer, Tony sits in a separate control room from the technical director and director. With the different monitors in his office, he checks the studio floor, the camera shots, and the picture being broadcast live. He controls the three robotic cameras with a computerized touch screen. The camera's movements are manipulated by preprogrammed screens, called pages, that are assigned to each camera.

Standing approximately six feet tall, with automated legs, the robotic cameras resemble characters from science fiction movies. Each stands on black-and-white tiles called "home base," and all movements are determined relative to that spot on the floor. For example, during a news broadcast one camera will have to move away from the anchor table to the area where the weather forecasts are taped. To move the camera, Tony hits the button on that camera's computerized page to move it in the required pattern. By manipulating joysticks on the video panel, Tony moves the camera in a pan or tilt action. He is also responsible for the quality of the broadcast image and uses the panel to adjust the focus, shadow, and scope of the image.

With the introduction of the robotic technology, the engineering staff has been reduced from 180 to 100 people.

Before its introduction, a camera operator and a video engineer were needed for each camera. Because of the sophistication of the technology and proficiency of the video-robo engineers, quality has not suffered.

Tony has worked in the broadcasting industry for many years. Prior to working in the control room as a video-robo engineer, he worked for NBC Sports as a field technician, a job he describes as a "blast."

Indeed, for someone who enjoys traveling a great deal, working as a field technician can be very exciting; for Tony that excitement took the form of covering Super Bowls and other major sporting events. The engineering crew often stays at the same hotels as the athletes and can share in the festivities.

On the other hand, fieldwork can be physically demanding. "A lot of the glamour that people think is there, really isn't," Tony says. To cover a football game that starts at noon, the engineering crew's day begins at 5:30 in the morning. In stadiums designed without cable modification, technicians run all the wires as well as construct and mount the camera equipment. Because a camera operator may be assigned to cover a particular player on both the offense and defense (for replay and close-up purposes), he or she may spend the whole day taping a game and never see a minute of live action. The day doesn't end until all of the camera equipment has been taken down; by then the stadium is almost empty. "It would be us and the cleaning crew," Tony says.

To Be a Successful Broadcast Engineer, You Should . . .

- pay strong attention to detail
- be a team player who can also work independently
- be able to handle the stress of working in all kinds of environments
- enjoy working with highly technical electronic and computer equipment

DO I HAVE I WHAT IT TAKES TO BE A BROADCAST ENGINEER?

It takes a team effort to successfully broadcast televised news. Each team member needs to be a professional with years of experience. "You can't do it twice," Tony says. "The news is live."

Manual dexterity and excellent vision and color perception are important to broadcast engineers; successful broadcast engineers must also be extremely dedicated to their careers. As they struggle to air the latest-breaking news before the competition, producers and directors can become short tempered and quick to criticize. Experienced engineers don't let the yelling get to them. In fact, a smart engineer will view these experiences as opportunities to learn, in order to avoid the wrath of the producer and director in the future.

Also, television stations are like hospitals: they never close. Someone must always be there as long as the station is broadcasting programs. Even though Tony has worked at his station for many years, he is still occasionally scheduled to work holidays. "You can have 40 years here and you'll be working Christmas Day," he says.

Tony takes great pride in his work, and has a lot of respect for his coworkers. He knows they are dedicated professionals who share his commitment to produce the best work possible.

HOW DO I BECOME A BROADCAST ENGINEER?
Education
High School

The aspiring broadcast engineer needs a high school diploma. Video classes were not offered when Tony was in high school. Today, however, many high schools have video production classes and even have their own radio and television stations. Anyone interested in broadcasting should take advantage of these opportunities.

As recording equipment has become more accessible to the public, it has become easier for video students to gain experience. With much of the broadcast equipment computerized, computer programming classes are important. High school students interested in broadcasting should take basic mathematics courses through geometry, as well as any electrical courses or physical science courses offered.

Postsecondary Training

Competition in the field has become more intense, so it is important for a broadcast engineer to have a degree from a junior or technical college. When Tony decided that he wanted to pursue a broadcasting career, he entered DeVry Institute of Technology and received a degree in electronics. At a technical college, students take courses in direct and alternating current, technical drafting, and electronic principles. Any engineer hoping to move into a supervisory or managerial role will need a bachelor's degree in electronics or electrical engineering.

In addition to possessing a technical education, students need to strengthen their communication skills. For Tony this meant earning a degree in English literature from Loyola University. Because he was working with highly educated professionals, Tony wanted the confidence to express his ideas to his superiors in moments of extreme stress, a confidence he developed while pursuing a liberal arts degree.

Certification or Licensing

Engineers are certified by the Society of Broadcast Engineers after they have completed their technical training. Certification is seen as a mark of competence. The society is a nonprofit organization offering a national representation for its members. There are strict qualifications for joining the society. The society offers educational seminars, conferences, and industry tours to keep its members informed of new broadcasting technology.

Federal law requires a restricted radio/telephone operator permit for persons who operate and maintain broadcast transmitters in radio and television stations. No examination is required. The Federal Communications Commission (FCC) no longer requires people working with microwave to have a general radio/telephone operator license; however, some states may require a license.

Internships and Volunteerships

When choosing a school, look into the internship opportunities and job placement services available to students. Many radio and TV stations offer special training programs and may even hire the interns who demonstrate good working skills. Although some internships are paid, most are not, due to the number of people seeking them; if the internship is unpaid, your school may grant you a certain number of credits for the experience.

You may want to pursue your own internship, even before you begin a college program. Contact some local radio and TV stations and ask if they would allow you to work alongside the technicians for a few hours a week. In an unpaid internship, however, you may not be actively involved in the work; laws limit the amount of work that can be required from unpaid interns.

Labor Unions

Most of the stations in the larger markets are unionized. Tony belongs to one of the largest broadcasting unions, the National

Advancement Possibilities

Chief engineers direct and coordinate radio or television station activities concerned with acquisition, installation, and maintenance, or with modification of studio broadcasting equipment.

Producers plan and coordinate various aspects of radio, television, or cable television programs.

Technical directors coordinate activities of radio or television studio and control-room personnel to ensure the technical quality of picture and sound for programs originating in a studio or from remote pickup points.

Association of Broadcast Employees and Technicians-Communications Workers of America. Another union covering electronics is the International Brotherhood of Electrical Workers.

WHO WILL HIRE ME?

The most important and difficult step for the entry-level engineer is getting a foot in the door. Tony began working at his current employer as a part-time assistant in the guest relations department, where he answered telephones and took viewer comments. From guest relations he moved up to a technical porter's position, helping to clean up the minicam shop. He gained important experience the following year when he started working as a technical stock clerk.

Eventually, Tony was allowed to work part time as a cameraman. For four years he went back and forth between the stock room and the studio. When he finally decided he wanted a career in engineering, he applied to the DeVry Institute of Technology. The station helped him with the tuition.

For most entry-level engineers, their careers begin in the smaller markets. Beginning engineers may deal heavily with maintenance, but because smaller stations are often nonunion, their responsibilities could cover several different areas.

Working in smaller markets is considered an excellent opportunity for entry-level engineers to discover their own strengths and weaknesses and to help them decide in which field of broadcasting to specialize. There is less intense pressure on the technical crew in smaller markets, and the beginning engineer can learn how programs are produced, including the proper use of lighting, the most effective use of camera angles, and the interrelationship of the various departments in a television station. Once an engineer understands the production process, he or she can anticipate the demands that the producer may have in the future.

The chief engineer of the station carefully supervises the work of the new engineers. However, once their competence has been proven, new engineers work independently or even supervise the newer engineers.

When broadcast engineers want to advance in their careers, they send out tapes of programs they've worked on, tapes that demonstrate their skills with lighting, shooting, or editing. The field is very competitive, and it takes persistence on the part of the broadcast engineer to break into the larger markets. Success depends on the engineer's qualifications, dedication, and enthusiasm. "If they really have their heart set on it they will probably do all right," Tony says about ambitious people pursuing work as broadcast engineers. "Someone who really has the desire will find a place."

The Society of Broadcast Engineers (http://www.sbe.org/) and the National Association of Broadcasters (http://www.nab.org/) offer job listings at their Web sites.

WHERE CAN I GO FROM HERE?

Experienced engineers can move on to positions as supervisory technicians or chief engineers. A college degree in engineering is generally required to become a chief engineer at a large TV station. Other possibilities for advancement include becoming a technical director or a producer.

WHAT ARE THE SALARY RANGES?

Larger stations usually pay higher wages than smaller stations, and television stations tend to pay more than radio stations. Also, commercial stations generally pay more than public broadcasting stations. The median annual earnings for

> ### Related Jobs
>
> - audio recording engineers
> - cable television technicians
> - camera operators
> - communications coordinators
> - electronics service technicians
> - videographers
> - wireless service technicians

broadcast technicians were $29,130 in 2004, according to the U.S. Department of Labor. The department also reported that the lowest paid 10 percent earned less than $15,190 and the highest paid 10 percent earned more than $63,180 during that same period. Experience, job location, and educational background are all factors that influence a person's pay.

WHAT IS THE JOB OUTLOOK?

Employment for broadcasting engineers is expected to grow about as fast as the average for all occupations, according to the U.S. Department of Labor. The number of new radio and television stations appearing will slow as the industry continues to consolidate and the pace of employment opportunities will be affected by the development of new equipment technology. Despite this prediction, qualified engineers with a diverse skill set will be in demand, especially in smaller towns and cities.

Some engineers may find work outside of broadcasting. As the new technology becomes more accessible, new industries are discovering the usefulness of visual communications. More and more corporations are creating in-house communications departments to produce their own corporate and industrial videos. Videos effectively explain company policies ranging from public safety (aimed at their customers) to first aid (aimed at their employees). Also, videos of high quality can introduce a company to potential clients in the best light.

In addition to industrial work, videographers are in great demand today for the production of commercials, animation, and computer graphics. The field of videography is changing rapidly with the introduction of new and cheaper computer systems and desktop software packages. Maintenance workers will always be in demand, even with techological advances. Someone will always have to be on hand to fix broken equipment and to keep new equipment in good working order.

Broadcasting Executives

SUMMARY

Definition
Broadcasting executives are responsible for a wide variety of managerial tasks that allow radio and television stations to operate successfully.

Alternative Job Titles
Radio and television executives
Radio and television managers

Salary Range
$8,000 to $50,000 to $300,000

Educational Requirements
Bachelor's degree

Certification or Licensing
None available

Employment Outlook
More slowly than the average

High School Subjects
Business
Mathematics
Music
Speech

Personal Interests
Broadcasting
Current events
Film and television
Music
Selling/making a deal

When Jay Zollar, a broadcasting executive in Green Bay, Wisconsin, was 16 years old, he walked into a local television station and asked if they could give him a tour. "Even then," he recalls, "I was captivated by the influence of television on the human race. It amazed me how households customized their living rooms around the television set. Listening to people talk about what they saw on television the day before showed me the influence this medium was having on people. Being able to watch the Olympics live from halfway around the world was an amazing thing to me. The seed was planted back then. Without knowing it, I was developing a desire to become involved in something that I saw having tremendous influence on people.

"As I grew older and entered college, the desire deepened as I came to a realization that I wanted to be in a position where I could participate in decision making as it related to how a local television station interacted with the local community it served."

WHAT DOES A BROADCASTING EXECUTIVE DO?

Broadcasting executives are key professionals in the radio and television industries. They manage staff and budgets, determine station programming, sell advertising, manage promotions, and interact with members of the community who have suggestions or complaints regarding programming.

General managers are almost always people who have had successful experience in sales, programming, marketing, or news. Their responsibilities include the handling of the daily problems of station operations in consultation with program managers, sales managers, producers, and chief engineers. They determine the general policies for the station's operations and supervise the execution of those policies. They normally handle the station's relations with the Federal Communications Commission (FCC) and other government bodies and participate in community activities on behalf of the station.

Program directors plan and schedule program material for radio and television stations and networks. They work in both commercial and public broadcasting and may be employed by individual radio or television stations, regional or national networks, or cable television systems. The material that program directors work with includes entertainment programs, public service programs, newscasts, sportscasts, and commercial announcements. Program directors decide what material is broadcast and when it is scheduled; they work with other staff members to develop programs and buy programs from independent producers. They are guided by such factors as the budget available for program material, the audience their station or network seeks to attract, their organization's policies on content and other matters, and the kinds of products advertised in the various commercial announcements. In addition, program directors may set up schedules for the program staff, audition and hire announcers and other on-the-air personnel, and assist the sales department in negotiating contracts with sponsors of commercial announcements. The duties of individual program directors are determined by such factors as whether they work in radio or television, for a small or large organization, for one station or a network, or in a commercial or public operation. At small radio stations the owner or manager may be responsible for programming, but at larger radio stations and at television stations the staff usually includes a program director. At medium to large radio and television stations the program director usually has a staff that includes such personnel as music librarians, music directors, editors for tape or film segments, and writers.

News directors oversee news teams (reporters, producers, photographers, editors, writers, newscasters, and announcers) at radio and television stations. They are responsible for the look/sound and content of the broadcast, and they oversee its technical elements as well. Directors need a sense of dramatics, combined with the ability to weld together into a smooth and artistic production the creative talents of performers and behind-the-scenes personnel under deadline pressure.

The entire productive effort of commercial radio or television stations is supported by the money it charges for commercial announcements and programs. The *sales manager* is responsible for securing these advertising revenues. He or she manages sales staff and develops sales plans that will appeal to sponsors and plans special campaigns to tie in with the seasons of the year and special events.

In contrast, *marketing managers* work with their staff and other advertising professionals to determine how the station should be marketed to the public. They determine what marketing methods should be used (print ads, television, radio, billboards, the Internet, etc.), how the materials should look, where advertisements should be placed, and when the advertising should begin. Managers must keep staff focused on a target audience when working on the promotion of their station. For example, a marketing manager for an oldies music station would market his or her station to its target demographic—typically listeners between the ages of 45 and 65 who grew up with the music that is being played. Managers might choose to reach this audience via advertisements in local magazines or newspapers that are geared toward this demographic, buying ad time on a television station that caters to this demographic, or using other means to reach the audience.

The traffic department is a little understood but vital function in a broadcasting station. It is the heart of the station's administrative operations, through which all instructions regarding sales and programming must be cleared. The depart-

---

Lingo to Learn

adjacency A commercial announcement positioned immediately before or after a specific program.

coverage The percentage of households in a signal area.

dayparts Segments of the television or radio broadcast day.

fixed position An advertisement that must run at a specific time.

frequency The number of times an advertisement or promotion will run.

O & O Station A station owned and operated by a network.

PSA A public service announcement provided free by a radio or television station for an organization.

preemption The interruption of regularly scheduled programming.

rating Estimated size of audience.

simulcast Simultaneous broadcast of the same program on two different stations.

spot Purchased broadcast time.

storyboard Layout for advertisement or sequence.

sweep Television and radio survey periods when audience viewing listening habits are measured.

syndicated program A program offered by an independent organization for sale to stations.

---

ment maintains the logs of the station's daily program activities, which are used by the programming, sales, and accounting departments. This job is generally the responsibility of a *traffic manager* who may be assisted by one or more traffic assistants.

Most stations have promotion departments that publicize the station's programs, image, and activities. Headed by a *promotion manager,* such a department typically plans and directs advertising campaigns, arranges for public appearances of on-air personalities, and designs other promotional activities aimed at the station audience.

Community affairs directors plan and execute a station's services and programs that are meant to respond to the needs of the community. These include public service announcements, public affairs programming (often undertaken in conjunction with the news department), and special events and public service campaigns that deal with community-related issues.

Some stations and networks employ *public service directors.* It is the responsibility of these individuals to plan and schedule radio or television public service programs and announcements in such fields as education, religion, and civic and government affairs.

Networks often employ *broadcast operations directors,* who coordinate the activities of the personnel who prepare network program schedules, review program schedules, issue daily corrections, and advise affiliated stations on their schedules. They also employ other executives who are responsible for the overall operation of stations or particular departments regionally or nationally.

Broadcasting executives at small stations often work 44 to 48 hours a week and frequently work evenings, late at night, and weekends. At larger stations, which have more personnel, broadcasting executives usually work 40-hour weeks.

Broadcasting executives frequently work under pressure because of the need to maintain precise timing and meet the needs of sponsors, performers, and other staff members.

Although the work is sometimes stressful and demanding, broadcasting executives usually work in pleasant environments with creative staffs. They also interact with the community to arrange programming and deal with a variety of people.

WHAT IS IT LIKE TO BE A BROADCASTING EXECUTIVE?

Jay Zollar has been the vice president and general manager of WLUK-TV FOX 11 in Green Bay, Wisconsin, for seven years. "My responsibility at WLUK-TV," he says, "is to guide and direct the various station departments with the goal of WLUK being Northeast Wisconsin's 'overall favorite television station.'"

Jay's primary function as general manager is to oversee and participate in the day-to-day operation of the television station. He directly oversees a general sales manager, news director, marketing director, business manager, and chief engineer. Underneath this group there are close to a dozen middle managers and approximately 85 employees. "Ultimately," he says, "I am responsible for every one of them, but I focus my attention on the department heads and middle managers."

In order to be successful financially, all commercial broadcasting stations must sell advertising. "For us to generate as much advertising revenue as possible," Jay explains, "we need to provide as many viewers as we can to the advertisers. For this reason, my day really revolves around a few key things. I work daily with our news director and our marketing manager on what our news product will look like. Marketing and news content need to be aligned so that we are telling our viewers what they can expect. I review each station promotional spot to ensure that it sends the message I deem reflective of the station. I regularly participate in the morning editorial meeting held in our newsroom so that I have a sense of what is being covered in our news. I personally respond to viewer comments generated through e-mails or mail so that I can have a strong sense of what the viewers are thinking. I make certain that technically we have a good clean signal on the air so that our viewers are able to receive our picture and sound. I also work directly with the companies that sell programming to the station with the goal of acquiring programs that I feel will be attractive to the largest audience possible. I also create or participate in the selection of the community affairs programs that we participate in. All of this is done each day so that as a television station we can become Northeast Wisconsin's favorite station. If we become the favorite station that means our ratings are growing. The higher our ratings are, the more money we are able to ask for our commercial time."

In addition to the aforementioned duties, Jay also interacts with his sales department in order to ensure that it provides clients with the best service possible. "We rely solely on our advertisers paying us for commercial time," he says. "I need to make certain that our clients are satisfied with us. On a daily basis, I evaluate our programming, news, and marketing content so that we as a station have the best chance of growing our ratings. We sell ratings to our advertisers, so we need to generate as many as possible. I often call, write, or e-mail our clients asking for feedback and suggestions on how we may serve them better."

To Be a Successful Broadcasting Executive, You Should . . .

- be creative
- have the ability to work under pressure
- be willing to work long hours
- have excellent managerial skills
- be decisive
- have good attention to detail
- care deeply about the interests of your listeners/viewers

DO I HAVE WHAT IT TAKES TO BE A BROADCASTING EXECUTIVE?

Broadcasting executives must be creative, alert, and adaptable people who stay up to date on the public's interests and attitudes and are able to recognize the potential in new ideas. They must be able to work under pressure and be willing to work long hours, and they must be able to work with all kinds of people. Broadcasting executives also must be good managers who can make decisions, oversee costs and deadlines, and attend to details.

Jay offers the following advice to high school students interested in executive positions in broadcasting: "Entry into this career does not come easily. You will have to start as an entry-level worker, prove yourself by working hard, have incredible integrity in trying to 'do the right thing,' and passionately care about the people who watch your station. There is no room for arrogance or independence in television. It takes a strong team that really cares about the people in the local market."

HOW DO I BECOME A BROADCASTING EXECUTIVE?

Education

High School

If you are interested in this career, you should take courses that develop your communication skills in high school. Such classes include English, debate, and speech. You also should take business courses to develop your managerial skills; current events and history courses to develop your understanding of the news and the trends that affect the public's interests; and such courses as dance, drama, music, and painting to expand your understanding of the creative arts. Finally, don't neglect your computer skills. You will probably use computers throughout your career to file reports, maintain schedules, and plan future programming projects.

Postsecondary Training

Those with the most thorough educational backgrounds will find it easiest to advance in this field. A college degree, therefore, is recommended. Possible majors for those interested in this work include radio and television production and broadcasting, sales, communications, liberal arts, or business administration. You will probably take English, economics, business administration, computer, and media classes. You may also wish to acquire some technical training that will help you understand the engineering aspects of broadcasting.

Internships and Volunteerships

You will most likely participate in an internship at a television or radio station as part of your college education. Internships allow you to learn more about the field and work closely with professionals in the field. Most internships are unpaid, but many colleges convey course credit for their successful completion.

If your high school or college has a radio or television station, you should volunteer to work on the staff. You also should look

Typical Broadcasting Expenses

The National Association of Broadcasters asked its member stations how much each allotted for various operating expenses. Expenditures broke down as follows:

- Programming: 24.9 percent
- News department: 24.2 percent
- General and administrative: 19.2 percent
- Sales: 15.9 percent
- Engineering: 8.8 percent
- Advertising and promotions: 4.0 percent
- Production: 3.0 percent

Source: National Association of Broadcasters, 2003

for part-time or summer jobs at local radio or television stations. This experience will help you learn more about how a station works and give you an opportunity to make contacts with those in the field. If you can't find a job at a local station, at least arrange for a visit and ask to talk to the personnel. You may be able to "shadow" a broadcasting executive for a day—that is, follow that director for the workday and see what his or her job entails.

WHO WILL HIRE ME?

According to the *CIA World Factbook*, there were 2,218 broadcast television stations and 13,750 radio stations in the United States in 2006. Cable television stations add another option for employment. Large conglomerates own some stations, while others are owned individually. While radio and television stations are located all over the country, the largest stations with the highest paid positions are located in large metropolitan areas.

Broadcasting executive jobs are not entry-level positions. A degree and extensive experience in the field are required. While you are in college you should investigate the availability of internships, since internships are almost essential for prospective job candidates. Your college career services office should also have information on job openings. Private and state employment agencies may also prove useful resources. You can also send résumés to radio and television stations or apply in person.

Beginners should be willing to relocate, as they are unlikely to find employment in large cities. They usually start at small stations with fewer employees, allowing them a chance to learn a variety of skills.

WHERE CAN I GO FROM HERE?

Most beginners start in entry-level jobs and work several years before they have enough experience to become broadcasting executives. Experienced executives usually advance by moving from small stations to larger stations and networks.

WHAT ARE THE SALARY RANGES?

Salaries for broadcasting executives vary widely based on such factors as size and location of the station, whether the station is commercial or public, and the experience of the worker. Television broadcasting executives generally earn more than their counterparts in radio. According to a salary survey by the Radio-Television News Directors Association, radio news directors earned a median of $30,000, and salaries ranged from a low of $8,000 to a high of $100,000 in 2006. Television news directors earned a median of $75,000, with salaries ranging from $25,000 to $300,000. The U.S. Department of Labor reports that general and operations managers in radio and television broadcasting had mean annual earnings of $88,878 in 2004. Advertising managers had mean annual earnings of $75,680.

Both radio and television broadcasting executives usually receive health and life coverage benefits and sometimes annual bonuses as well.

WHAT IS THE JOB OUTLOOK?

According to the U.S. Department of Labor, employment in broadcasting is expected to increase 11 percent over the 2004–14 period, slower than the average of 14 percent growth for all industries combined. This slow growth rate is attributed to industry consolidation, the introduction of new technologies, greater use of prepared programming, and competition from other media.

Competition for broadcasting executive jobs is strong. There are more opportunities for beginners in radio than there are in television. Most radio and television stations in large cities hire only experienced workers.

New radio (including those created by the emergence of satellite radio) and television stations and new cable television systems are expected to create some additional openings for broadcasting executives.

Radio Producers and Disc Jockeys

SUMMARY

Definition
The work of radio producers and disc jockeys determines a radio station's identity. Producers and disc jockeys research the marketplace and create radio shows to interest and entertain the targeted audience. While on the air, disc jockeys introduce songs and news reports, field phone calls, and discuss current events.

Alternative Job Titles
Announcers
DJs
On-air personalities

Salary Range
$12,000 to $32,000 to
    $1,000,000+

Educational Requirements
Some postsecondary training

Certification or Licensing
None available

Employment Outlook
In decline

High School Subjects
Journalism
Music
Speech

Personal Interests
Business
Current events
Entertaining/performing
Theater

In addition to meeting interesting people and entertaining people in their cars, kitchens, and bedrooms across the city of Fargo, North Dakota, morning radio show host Tracy Briggs says that what makes her happiest at the end of the day is thinking that she has made a difference in the lives of her listeners.

"A couple of months ago," she recalls, "we heard about a fund-raiser a small elementary school here was doing to help the victims of Hurricane Katrina. We invited the principal on the show to talk about what he was doing. Apparently that day a woman was listening whose nephew (a native of North Dakota) was a schoolteacher in one of the towns affected by the hurricane. The principal ended up getting in touch with him, and they decided to take the money and formally 'adopt' his classroom. So the money from North Dakota is going to kids who really need it, many of them whose homes were lost to the storm. It was just nice to play a small part in making this happen."

WHAT DO RADIO PRODUCERS AND DISC JOCKEYS DO?

If you listen to your car radio when you drive, you've noticed how the conversations and opinions of radio disc jockeys dominate the airwaves. And you probably have a favorite station and morning show. Some disc jockeys may drive you crazy, while others entertain you and help you keep your sense of humor as you get ready for school or bide your time in a traffic jam—they even provide you with live traffic reports so you can avoid those jams. Where do you have your car radio or home stereo set, and why? Do you prefer a serious news report in the morning? A live interview? Jokes and discussions about current events? A sunny personality, or a dark one? Maybe you just want somebody to tell you the names of the songs they're playing, and nothing else. The identity and style of a radio program is a result of the collaborations of on-air and off-air professionals. Radio *disc jockeys* talk the talk during a broadcast, and *producers* walk the walk behind the scenes. But in many situations, particularly with smaller radio stations, the disc jockey and the show's producer are the same person.

Radio producers rely on the public's very particular tastes—differences in taste allow for many different kinds of radio to exist, to serve many different segments of a community. In developing radio programs, producers take into consideration the marketplace—they listen to other area radio stations and determine what's needed and appreciated in the community, and what there may already be too much of. They conduct surveys and interviews to find out what the public wants to hear. They decide which age groups they want to pursue, and develop a format based on what appeals to these listeners. This all results

in a station's "identity," which is very important. Listeners associate a station with the kind of music it plays, how much music it plays, and the station's on-air personalities.

Disc jockeys are generally well known within their community, and they frequently interact with their listeners. In addition to making many public appearances for promotional and charity events, well-known radio disc jockeys are often approached by their listeners on the street. These listeners express their opinions about what they want to hear in the program. Based on this feedback, and on market research, radio disc jockeys/producers devise music playlists and music libraries. They each develop an individual on-air identity, or personality. And they invite guests who will interest their listeners. Keeping a show running on time is also the responsibility of a producer. This involves carefully weaving many different elements into a show, including music, news reports, traffic reports, and interviews.

In addition to keeping in touch with the listening public, radio disc jockeys and producers also keep track of current events. They consult newspapers and other radio programs to determine what subjects to discuss on their morning shows. They also take phone calls from listeners, in discussions which are often broadcast live during a show.

Promotions are important to the staff of a radio station. The on-air personalities are often involved in community events to promote the stations. Radio producers write copy for on-air commercials. They also devise contests, from

Lingo to Learn

aircheck Tape recordings of radio broadcasts, to be used by disc jockeys and producers as samples of their work.

demographics Statistics that show a radio listener's age, income, and other data; this information is valuable to producers and advertisers trying to reach specific audiences.

digital broadcasting Broadcasting radio programs with the digital technology used in computers and compact discs. Provides higher-quality broadcasts.

mixing Blending sounds by editing and splicing; usually done with computer.

playlist A list of songs to be played throughout the day by a radio station, composed by a disc jockey, programmer, or producer.

satellite radio Radio programming that is broadcast via satellite. Satellite radio, unlike traditional radio broadcasts, can reach listeners over thousands of miles. XM Satellite Radio and Sirius Satellite Radio are the satellite radio service providers in the United States. Worldspace Satellite Radio provides satellite radio service to many countries in the rest of the world.

large public events to small, on-air trivia competitions.

Though a majority of radio stations have music formats, radio producers also work for 24-hour news stations, public broadcasting, and talk radio. Producing news programs and radio documentaries involves doing a great deal of research, booking guests, writing scripts, and interviewing.

WHAT IS IT LIKE TO BE A RADIO PRODUCER OR DISC JOCKEY?

Tracy Briggs is a radio morning show host at WDAY-AM, a news/talk station in Fargo, North Dakota. "I am one-half of the morning news/talk show that airs from 5:00 A.M. to 8:30 A.M. weekdays," she says. Tracy has been working at her current job since March 2005 after 17 years as a news anchor/reporter at WDAY-TV. "I got into radio after filling in for the previous morning host who was on vacation," she explains. "As a news anchor I worked in the same building and had name recognition, so I was an easy choice to fill in. I found that I absolutely loved it! It was so much fun. After years in news, I was able to do a little more ad libbing, show some personality, and even have an opinion or two. When the job opened up permanently, I jumped at the chance to do it, not only because it was so fun and interesting, but also because the schedule was perfect for me. I'm the mother of two small children, and working mornings enables me to be home by midafternoon so I can pick them up from day care and soon school."

With a slogan of "start your mornings with a smile," topics discussed on Tracy's radio show tend to be lighthearted. "We ask trivia questions," she says, "and have a 'question of the day' such as 'what's your favorite comfort food?' or 'what's your favorite Christmas movie?' The lighthearted show works well for us since the rest of the day tends to be a little 'harder,' with political talk shows. I work with a male partner [Paul Bougie] with whom I have a lot of fun debating the very important questions I mentioned earlier."

After the show is over, Tracy and her partner spend time prepping for the next day (booking guests, preparing for interviews, etc.), recording promos and commercials, and occasionally going on client visits (visiting businesses that are booking live ads with the show). "This allows us to know more about the businesses about which we'll be speaking," Tracy explains.

DO I HAVE WHAT IT TAKES TO BE A PRODUCER OR DISC JOCKEY?

Working as the on-air personality for a live show requires you to think fast and speak clearly. You should also have a love for radio and a commitment to radio listeners. Whether producing behind the scenes or juggling all the elements of a

---

To Be a Successful Disc Jockey, You Should . . .

- be creative
- have a strong, clear speaking voice
- be eager to learn
- be able to think quickly and remain calm during stressful situations
- love communicating and interacting with others
- be yourself on the air
- be willing to work at all times of the day

---

broadcast while live on the air, you need to have organizational skills. You must be able to remain calm in the face of stressful situations.

HOW DO I BECOME A RADIO PRODUCER OR DISC JOCKEY?
Education

Although she earned a bachelor of arts in journalism from the University of North Dakota and a master of arts degree in mass communication from North Dakota State University, Tracy says that she gained most of her training for her current position on the job. "Although," she says, "I also believe my formal education has been *so* valuable in preparing me for the career. I had a varied liberal arts background, which helped me learn how to process and think through many subjects."

High School

Writing skills are valuable in any profession, but especially in radio and television. Take composition and literature courses, and other courses that require essays and term papers. Journalism courses will not only help you develop your writing skills, but will also teach you about the nature and history of media. You'll learn about deadlines and how to put a complete project (such as a newspaper or yearbook) together. If your school has a radio station, get involved with it in any way you can. Check with your local radio stations; some may offer part-time jobs to high school students interested in becoming producers and disc jockeys.

To Be a Successful Radio Producer, You Should . . .

- be able to think quickly and remain calm during stressful situations

- be organized

- have a good understanding of all aspects of a radio station, from management to advertising to promotions to news and traffic departments

- be able to work well with many types of people

Business courses and clubs frequently require students to put together projects; starting any business is similar to producing your own radio show. Use such a project as an opportunity to become familiar with the market research, interviewing, and writing that are all part of a radio producer's job. For both the future radio producer and the future disc jockey, a theater department offers great learning opportunities. Theater productions require funding, advertising, and other fundamentals similar to a radio production. In training for a career as a disc jockey, you can develop improvisational and speaking skills.

Postsecondary Training

Most journalism and communications schools at universities offer programs in broadcasting. Radio producers and announcers often start their training in journalism schools and receive hands-on instruction at campus radio stations. These broadcasting programs are generally news centered, providing great opportunities for students interested in producing news programs, daily newscasts, and documentaries. News directors and program managers of radio stations generally want to hire people who have a good, well-rounded education with a grounding in history, geography, political science, and literature.

Someone interested in becoming a disc jockey may benefit as much from a part-time radio job as from a college program. Being directly involved in the workplace provides you with valuable experience and the chance to produce tapes of your work. On-air personalities are often hired on the basis of their personalities, and enthusiasm, perseverance, and good speaking skills are valuable to people looking to be part of a radio show.

Internships and Volunteerships

While in high school, you may have an opportunity to work as a summer intern for a local radio station. Though you may be selling advertising, fielding phone calls, or assisting the staff in various other ways, some stations may provide you with some on-air experience. AM stations that broadcast local high school sports events may use interns to give the on-air play-by-play. Any on-air experience, from reading a list of community events to giving a news report will allow staff members to hear your voice and to provide helpful instruction. In many cases, interns and part-time employees can get full-time jobs if they show initiative and interest.

If enrolled in a broadcasting program at a college, you may have many internship opportunities. Some colleges bring in internship recruiters from radio stations across the country. When gathering information about journalism colleges, make sure you ask for detailed information about their internship programs. If you must pursue internships on your own, call local radio stations and check the Internet for internship opportunities in other cities. If you have a favorite national radio program, contact them about internships; though competition for an internship with a national program will be fierce, the internship could prove very valuable to your career.

Labor Unions

In most smaller markets, on-air personalities aren't required to belong to the American Federation of Television and Radio Artists (AFTRA); the networks and the TV and radio stations in larger cities do require union membership. AFTRA, consisting of dues-paying actors, announcers, DJs, newscasters, editors, writers, directors, and vocalists, has more than 70,000 members throughout the country. The union acts as an advocate for better wages, working conditions, and benefits. It isn't necessary to join AFTRA until you have been hired on with a station that requires membership.

WHO WILL HIRE ME?

Radio producers and disc jockeys usually start work at radio stations in any capacity possible. After working for a while in a part-time position gaining experience and making connections, a dedicated young producer will find opportunities to work in production or on air. For staff positions, producers and disc jockeys submit taped samples of their on-air work to radio stations along with their résumé.

WHERE CAN I GO FROM HERE?

After working their way up within a station, some disc jockeys choose to move to bigger cities for the larger audiences and better pay. Or, with their experience in broadcasting, disc jockeys and producers can move into management positions. Tracy is very happy with her new position and has no plans currently to pursue other options. "I'm having so much fun with this job," she says, "that I honestly hope I'm still doing it down the road. I

Advancement Possibilities

Television news anchors lead the broadcast on camera; they read the news and introduce live and taped news segments.

General sales managers head the marketing departments of radio stations; they direct staffs of salespeople who generate station revenue.

Station managers lead all the departments of radio stations toward financial goals; they are actively involved in sales and promotions.

Related Jobs

- actors
- artist and repertoire managers
- broadcast meteorologists
- comedians
- public-address announcers
- public relations workers
- radio and television traffic reporters
- reporters
- sales workers
- sportscasters
- stage managers
- television directors

love this community and, right now, the schedule I have with this job helps me be a more hands-on mom."

WHAT ARE THE SALARY RANGES?

Because the size of radio stations varies greatly, so does the pay for disc jockeys and producers. A disc jockey's popularity also determines salary—some disc jockeys are credited with attracting the bulk of a radio program's audience, good ratings, and advertising revenue.

According to the U.S. Department of Labor, producers employed in all fields (including radio) earned salaries that ranged from less than $26,940 to more than $84,190 in 2004. Producers employed in radio and television broadcasting earned mean annual salaries of $55,400 in 2004. The salary range for radio and television announcers is extremely broad with a low of $12,940 in 2004, and a high of more than $1,000,000 for popular broadcast personalities. The mean annual salary for radio and television announcers was $32,070 in 2004.

WHAT IS THE JOB OUTLOOK?

In the past, radio station ownership was highly regulated by the government, limiting the number of stations a person or company could own. Recent deregulation has made multiple station ownership possible. Radio stations now are bought and sold at a more rapid pace. This may result in a radio station changing formats, as well as entire staffs. Though some radio producers and disc jockeys are able to stay at a station over a period of several years, people going into radio should be prepared to change locations at some point in their careers.

You should also be prepared for heavier competition for radio jobs. Graduates of college broadcasting programs are finding a scarcity of work in media. Paid internships will also be difficult to find—many students of radio will have to work for free for a while to gain experience. Radio producers may find more opportunities as freelancers, developing their own programs independently then selling them to stations. On the other hand, the growth of satellite radio has created additional opportunities for disc jockeys and producers.

Fewer positions may also be available to disc jockeys in the future due to voice-tracking, which is the prerecording of a radio show by a DJ for one or more shifts in one or more cities. Voice-tracking saves radio companies money by allowing the work of one DJ to be used in a variety of settings and time slots. Of course, voice-tracking cannot be used for talk shows, remote broadcasts, or live concerts. The industry is divided on how this new trend will affect the radio industry on the whole.

Radio and Television Anchors

SUMMARY

Definition
Radio and television anchorpeople analyze and broadcast news received from various sources. They help select, write, and present the news and may specialize in a particular area.

Alternative Job Titles
Announcers
Newscasters

Salary Range
$8,000 to $50,000 to $1,200,000

Educational Requirements
Bachelor's degree

Certification or Licensing
None available

Employment Outlook
More slowly than the average

High School Subjects
Economics
English (writing/literature)
Political science
Speech

Personal Interests
Broadcasting
Current events
Film and television
Reading/books
Writing

"Working in Rapid City, South Dakota, there are always interesting stories," says Lindsay Kruger, a news anchor/producer at KNBN NewsCenter1. "This is small market USA. People here care about farms, cattle, stock shows, and rodeos. When a new McDonald's is built, that's the only thing you hear about on the radio. When the local grocery store remodels, it's the talk of town. We recently just opened our very first Olive Garden; our news station went live from the front of the restaurant and interviewed the manager. It's funny and so interesting to see the news where I work as compared to Orlando [Florida] (where I'm from). Things we air here as our top stories wouldn't even make it on the evening news in most markets. Now, don't get me wrong, we do have more serious, crime-related news here. Just not as often as in larger cities. But it's not about comparison; it's about what's important to the people here. And that, for me, was a big thing to learn and realize. Once you get over the fact that a few stolen cattle is your lead story (and the reporter is going live), you can report anything out here!"

WHAT DOES A RADIO OR TELEVISION ANCHOR DO?
Radio and television anchorpeople announce the news during regular and

special broadcasts. While some of the people in this field simply announce, many do a wide variety of tasks, depending on the size of the station and the market.

Anchorpeople are faced with constant deadlines, not only for each newscast to begin, but also for each one to end. Each segment must be viewed and each script must be read at the precise time and for a specified duration during the newscast. While they must appear calm, professional, and confident, there is often much stress and tension behind the scenes.

Anchorpeople open and close each news show, identify the station, and announce the station breaks. They help to write the scripts, rewrite news releases, and identify which news should be covered in the broadcast. Anchorpeople may also report the news, produce special segments, and conduct on-air interviews and panel discussions. At small stations, they may even keep the program log, run the transmitter, and cue the changeover to network broadcasting.

Although they perform similar jobs, radio and television anchorpeople work in very different atmospheres. On radio, the main announcers or anchorpeople are also the disc jockeys. They play recorded music, announce the news, provide informal commentary, and serve as a bridge between the music and the listener. They announce the time, weather, news, and traffic reports while maintaining a cheerful and relaxed attitude. At most stations, the radio announcers also read advertising information or provide the voices for the advertising spots.

News anchors specialize in presenting the news to the listening or viewing public. They report the facts and may sometimes be asked to provide editorial commentary. They may write their own scripts or rely on the station's writing team to write the script that they then read over the TelePrompTer. Again, research is important to each news story and the news anchors should be well informed about each story they cover as well as those they simply introduce. Some news anchors specialize in certain aspects of the news such as health, economics, politics, or community affairs.

For television anchorpeople, research, writing, and presenting the news is only part of the job. Wardrobe, makeup, and presentation also need to be focused on, and getting physically ready for the day is an important part of the job. Many details such as which hairstyles and which outfits to wear are important to create an effective look for the news.

Some anchorpeople specialize in sports, on either radio or television. These people cover sports events, so they must be highly knowledgeable about the sports they are covering and be able to describe events quickly and accurately as they unfold. *Sports anchors* generally travel to the events they cover and spend time watching the teams or individuals practice and compete. They research background information, statistics, ratings, and personal interest information to provide the audience with the most thorough and interesting coverage of each sports event.

The Internet and the World Wide Web are changing the job of anchorpeople in radio and television. Many radio and television stations have their own Web sites where listeners and viewers can keep updated on current stories, submit comments and suggestions via e-mail, and even interact with the anchors and reporters. Also, the World Wide Web has become another resource for anchors as they research their stories.

Because their voices and faces are heard and seen by the public on a daily basis, many radio and television anchorpeople become well-known public personalities. This means that they are often asked to participate in community activities and other public events.

WHAT IS IT LIKE TO BE AN ANCHOR?

Lindsay Kruger has been a news anchor/producer at KNBN NewsCenter1, an NBC affiliate in Rapid City, South Dakota, since October 2004. "Broadcast journalism wasn't my first career choice," she says. "I initially went to school with hopes of becoming a bilingual speech pathologist. But my communication skills and natural people skills led me to take a few journalism classes. By the end of the first semester at the University of Central Florida's Nicholson School of Communications, I was hooked and knew that nothing else would suit me better than broadcasting."

Lindsay begins her workday at about 1:30 P.M.—"usually," she says, "to a newsroom of chaos, as reporters are making phone calls, the scanner is buzzing with breaking news, and our assignment editor and early show producer are trying to fit it all in. I usually start off my day by checking the wires, seeing if there's something we might be missing and just doing an overall checkup on what's been going on all day." Lindsay then tapes a few afternoon cut-ins, as well as 60-second radio spots with her coanchor. "I then begin working on producing the 10 P.M. show while balancing other little tasks such as helping a reporter write a story, editing tapes for someone running behind, and consulting with our promotions editors on a new TV promo. Being in such a small market with a small staff, we all take on just a little bit more than our 'title jobs.'"

Around 4 P.M., Lindsay begins touching up her makeup and fixing her hair in preparation for her anchoring the 5:30 P.M.

newscast. "By 5 P.M., I'm reading my scripts, changing copy if need be, and getting ready to sit on set. By 5:20 P.M. we are on set doing microphone checks and reading through scripts one last time before we air at 5:30 P.M. for a half hour of news."

When the newscast is complete, Lindsay tapes a few more cut-ins for prime time before grabbing a quick dinner, and then continues to work on the 10 P.M. newscast. "And then we do it again!" she says. "We're on set by 9:50, on air at 10, and off at 10:35. I usually walk out the door close to 10:45 P.M., pending scanner traffic. Not on a regular basis, but every once in a while, I report, whether it's spot

To Be a Successful Radio or Television Anchorperson, You Should . . .

- be able to handle deadline pressure and be able to "wing it" or improvise when necessary

- have a mastery of the English language, including good diction, correct grammar usage, and pronunciation

- have a pleasant speaking voice, and if on television, a professional appearance

- be creative, curious, and aggressive—yet know how to meet and interact with people in a friendly manner

news or a specific story on which I've been working."

DO I HAVE I WHAT IT TAKES TO BE AN ANCHOR?

Aspiring radio and television anchorpeople must have a mastery of the English language—both written and spoken. Their diction, including correct grammar usage, pronunciation, and no regional dialect, is extremely important. Anchorpeople need to have a pleasing personality and voice, and, in the case of television anchorpeople, they must also have a pleasing appearance.

Besides being knowledgeable, television news anchors must also look the part. Meeting with clothing consultants, having makeup done, and paying careful attention to physical appearance are all part of the job.

Anchorpeople must be able to handle deadline pressure and be able to "wing it" or improvise when necessary.

Anchorpeople need to be creative, inquisitive, aggressive, and should know how to meet and interact with people. They need to be able to build a network of people and news sources that they can use to help them report their stories.

HOW DO I BECOME A RADIO OR TELEVISION ANCHOR?
Education
Lindsay earned a degree in broadcast journalism (with a minor in Spanish) from the

University of Central Florida. "During my junior year," she recalls, "I interned at CBS affiliate WKMG in Orlando for eight months—four with news, four with sports. During my final semester in college I landed a job as the weekend assignment editor at ABC affiliate WFTV in Orlando, and worked there for a year before coming to South Dakota. While at both stations I took the time to closely watch, study, and imitate on-air talent. I read the scripts, watched the videos—paying close attention to detail. Having the hands-on experience at both WKMG and WFTV is something school couldn't teach me. Prepare me for, yes, but teach, no."

High School

In high school, you should focus on a college preparatory curriculum. You should learn how to write and use the English language in literature and communication classes. Subjects such as history, government, economics, and a foreign language are also important.

Even at the high school level, it's a good idea to explore opportunities to work during the summers at local radio or television stations or to job-shadow an anchor or reporter for a day.

Postsecondary Training

A strong liberal arts background with emphasis in journalism, English, political science, or economics is advised, as well as a telecommunications or communications major, will prepare you for this field. It might also be helpful to earn a second degree—for example in biology or science—if you want to break in as a health or science reporter.

Internships and Volunteerships

Participation in an internship is key to landing a position in the field. Many news anchors get their first jobs directly from their internship assignments, and it is important to choose your internships carefully to make sure that they offer many opportunities for hands-on experience in writing and editing.

Labor Unions

Depending on the size of the market in which you work, you may be required to join the American Federation of Television and Radio Artists (AFTRA). AFTRA, which is made up of dues-paying announcers, newscasters, editors, writers, directors, actors, DJs, and vocalists, has more than 70,000 members throughout the country.

Advancement Possibilities

Producers plan each aspect of the newscast, from the writing to the direction and set design.

Press secretaries serve as spokespeople for political figures and other celebrities.

News directors supervise on-air "talent," producers, reporters, editors, and other newsroom staff. They decide which news events will be covered and assign staff to gather information and report on them.

WHO WILL HIRE ME?

Most radio and television news anchors do not begin their careers with that title. They begin as reporters or writers.

Once you have the college degree and some experience, finding work means sending out tapes and résumés. According to the National Association of Broadcasters (NAB), there are more than 1,000 broadcast television stations and more than 11,500 radio stations in the United States. While that may seem like a large market for your job search, the competition for anchor jobs is keen.

The NAB maintains a list of current job and internship openings, and with the boom of cable and satellite television, there are now more stations at which to apply.

Lindsay is unsure of her career plans in the next 5 or 10 years. "I keep changing my mind," she says. "I'd love to end up on MSNBC or CNN as a daytime anchor. Then again, I'd like to plant my roots and grow old with one town where local news is all that matters. Where you can really connect with an audience. Where what's really going on doesn't get 'lost' in the midst of a broadcast."

WHERE CAN I GO FROM HERE?

Most successful anchors advance from small stations to large ones. Experienced anchors usually have held several jobs. The most successful anchors may be those who work for the networks. Usually, because of network locations, anchors must live in or near the country's largest cities.

Related Jobs

- columnists/commentators
- continuity writers
- copy writers
- critics
- editorial writers
- newswriters
- reporters
- script readers
- technical writers
- writers

Some careers lead from announcing to other aspects of radio or television work. More people are employed in sales, promotion, and planning than in performing; often they are paid more than anchors. Because the networks employ relatively few anchors in proportion to the rest of the broadcasting professionals, a candidate must have several years of experience and specific background in several news areas before being considered for an audition. These top anchors generally are college graduates.

WHAT ARE THE SALARY RANGES?

According to a 2006 Salary Survey conducted by the Radio-Television News Directors Association (RTNDA) and Ball State University, salaries for radio news anchors are lower than for television news anchors. Also, larger stations and larger markets pay more than smaller stations and smaller markets. For radio anchorpeople, salaries range from a low of $8,000 to a high of $120,000 with a median salary of $23,500. For television anchorpeople, salaries range from a low of $13,000 to a high of $1,200,000 with a median salary of $58,500. For television anchors in larger markets, salary negotiations might include such extras as a clothing allowance.

WHAT IS THE JOB OUTLOOK?

Competition for radio and television anchor jobs is high because the number of people who want to become anchors is much greater than the number of jobs available. While small radio stations and television stations are more likely to hire beginners, the pay is low and the hours are long.

Anchorpeople who have a variety of broadcast experience and expertise in other areas such as business, sports, or health may have an advantage over others. Most openings in the field will occur due to workers leaving the workforce or transferring to another field.

Reporters and Correspondents

SUMMARY

Definition
Television and radio reporters and correspondents write and record the daily news segments for broadcast. They conduct on-air interviews, edit recorded footage, and report live from remote sites. They may also work as anchors, introducing news segments and reading news briefs to radio and TV audiences. Foreign correspondents report on news from countries outside of where their newspapers, radio or television networks, or wire services are located.

Alternative Job Titles
Broadcast journalists

Salary Range
$18,000 to $46,000 to $150,000+

Educational Requirements
Some postsecondary training

Certification or Licensing
None available

Employment Outlook
More slowly than the average

High School Subjects
English (writing/literature)
Geography/social studies
Government
Journalism
Speech

Personal Interests
Broadcasting
Current events
Film and television
Photography
Writing

Flames lick the dark sky. Water from hoses guided by firefighters arcs over the house. A family, in tears, stands in the street. Tom Elser, a reporter for KETV in Omaha, Nebraska, sits in the newsroom and hurries to complete his script and voice-over, which will be combined with the aforementioned video and brief sound bites from interviews with eyewitnesses and firemen to create a narrative of the fire and its effect on residents of the destroyed home. He's careful to remain sensitive to the family's privacy, while also providing the viewing audience with information about the fire and how it started. He uses his natural curiosity to cover all the bases, to ask all the questions. How did the fire get started? How soon will the fire be contained? Where will the family spend the night? What will they do next?

With the news package complete and ready for broadcast in a half hour, Tom rushes back to the scene. The fire still smolders, but is under control. The wet street reflects the streetlights and the faces of worried neighbors up and down the block. Tom listens to his earphone, and stands before the camera, poised and ready to go live with the report.

WHAT DOES A REPORTER AND CORRESPONDENT DO?

You're a reporter and you hear a rumor. Something about a corrupt politician, a casino, dirty money. Something about cops on the payroll, a suspicious suicide, a convict's loose lips. What do you do? It's almost instinctual—you sniff around for information. You make phone calls, then more phone calls, looking for leads. "Do you know anybody who knows anybody . . . ?" You use your contacts, and you call in favors. You accumulate information, studying documents and reports. Then maybe, with camera and microphone in hand, you pay somebody a surprise visit. If you're lucky, your interview subject will spill the beans, or at least sweat heavily and blink a lot. And once you have some cold, hard facts, you can edit the story into a nice news "package" to deliver to the folks watching the 10:00 news.

Or, it might go something like that—your work won't always be so dramatic. You won't always be reporting on scandals, and you won't always have time for the amount of investigation needed to break open a controversial story. There aren't enough reports about shady politicians and corrupt corporations to fill the daily newscasts of the thousands of stations across the country. For every big story, there are several small stories: reports about local businesses, home safety, schools, regional sporting events, and other subjects of interest to your community.

Americans spend more than three hours a day listening to the radio; 70 percent of us rely on TV as our main source of news. With this kind of demand for programming, reporters must work hard to come up with story ideas, quickly gather the information, and report while the information is still news. They work with producers and other reporters to exchange ideas and discuss the most newsworthy concerns. After deciding on the stories for that day's newscasts, the reporters will then pursue leads and gather information. Once they have reliable information, they begin to prepare the news package (the videotaped news segment).

Preparing the package involves videotaping interviews and relevant footage. TV reporters may shoot the footage themselves or bring a camera operator to the scene. Radio reporters also typically work alone on the news scene, though they may be assisted by engineers. It is important for radio and TV reporters to understand the latest video and audio equipment. After taping an interview, the reporter will then review the material and determine which information is most significant to the story, as well as edit the material according to the time allotted for the report. The TV reporter looks for the most interesting quotes from the interview subject, and the most relevant visuals and sounds. Often, reporters go live to the scene; the reporter will then introduce the news segment during the newscast and answer questions from the anchor about the story.

Reporters may have specific areas, or "beats," to cover, such as a police station or city hall. Or they may be assigned specific regions within the viewing area. Though most reporters, particularly in radio, are required to cover all the news stories, some stations and newscasts have reporters who focus on particular subject matters—a reporter may specialize in reports on crime, technology, health care, entertainment, or business. Most reporters only report on that day's news, but, in some cases, a reporter may spend several days with a particular news story, such as on a news magazine program. An investigative report might also be broadcast as a series within a daily newscast.

The three major networks (ABC, CBS, and NBC) offer daily news coverage of events of national interest; there are also cable channels (such as CNN, FOX, and MSNBC) that provide around-the-clock news information. With bureaus in Washington, D.C., New York, and other cities, the networks provide job opportunities for many reporters. These positions are highly competitive, however; most broadcast reporters work in cities all across the country for network affiliates, local cable news channels, or radio news stations.

Some reporters gather and report news in foreign countries. This type of reporter is called a *foreign correspondent*. Foreign news can range from the violent (wars, coups, and refugee situations) to the calm (cultural events and financial issues). Although a domestic correspondent is

---

Lingo to Learn

composition In photography, the arrangement of subjects and camera angles into a series of shots.

copy The text for a news report; information considered printable and newsworthy.

electronic media Broadcasting companies that transmit information electronically, such as TV and radio stations, cable networks, and news services.

sound bite A brief recorded statement or catchy comment (as by a public figure) broadcast on a radio or TV news program.

wire services News organizations, such as United Press International and the Associated Press, that provide TV and radio stations with information on the latest news.

---

responsible for covering specific areas of the news, like politics, health, sports, consumer affairs, business, or religion, foreign correspondents are responsible for all of these areas in the country where they are stationed. A China-based correspondent, for example, could spend a day covering the new trade policy between the United States and China, and the next day report on the religious persecution of Christians by the Chinese government.

A foreign correspondent often is responsible for more than one country. Depending on where he or she is stationed, the foreign correspondent might have to act as a one-person band in gathering and preparing stories.

WHAT IS IT LIKE TO BE A REPORTER OR CORRESPONDENT?

Tom Elser, a TV reporter for KETV in Omaha, Nebraska, works what is called the "nightside shift" Monday through Friday, from 1:30 P.M. to 10:30 P.M. (unless late-breaking news keeps him working into the night). His reports are aired on KETV's NewsWatch at 10:00 P.M. Tom has worked at KETV for more than eight years.

To ensure that important news issues are covered effectively, most reporters are typically assigned a "beat." They became experts in this area and are responsible for checking with sources and contacts within that beat. "My beat," Tom explains, "includes a local law enforcement agency and city council.

"My day begins on the phone," Tom says. "After walking in the door, I typically check e-mails, the Associated Press wires, and earlier newscasts. I then start calling contacts and following up on recent stories."

After gathering story ideas, Tom heads to an afternoon meeting, which includes producers, nightside reporters, news managers, and promotion employees. In this meeting, Tom and his colleagues brainstorm ideas and discuss the most important story possibilities. "As a group, we decide what stories we should pursue," Tom explains. "After getting my assignment, I pick up the phone again and start pursuing interviews. I spend most of the time on the phone," Tom says. "The hardest part is getting interviews. If all goes well, I will be assigned a photographer and we'll start shooting the story. Many times the story will change because of breaking news or because the assigned story isn't working. Sometimes it takes several hours to get all the material we need for the story.

"On the way back to the station, I talk with the photographer about the best video and ask for any suggestions for the story. Throughout the day I check in with the 10 P.M. producer about the progress of the story and the focus. Normally, I complete my script one hour before the newscast. I voice the story and hand it off to the photographer. He/she will edit the story together. About 20 minutes before

To Be a Successful Reporter or Correspondent, You Should . . .

- be levelheaded and able to remain calm during stressful situations

- have a strong knowledge of current events, history, geography, and the workings of each level of government

- have good writing and speaking skills

- be curious about the world around you and willing to learn

- be assertive and able to ask direct, straight-to-the-point questions

- be ready to travel and work odd hours, including holidays and weekends

the newscast, I head out the door to do the 'live' shot. Afterwards, I come back to the station and write any follow-up notes for the next day. I also write a shorter version of the story for the morning show."

DO I HAVE WHAT IT TAKES TO BE A REPORTER OR CORRESPONDENT?

Reporters are levelheaded and able to keep calm in stressful situations. In most situations, reporters going live are required to think on their feet. Reporters must also have a good understanding of topical issues, history, geography, and government. And reporters must write and speak well.

Sue Kopen Katcef, lecturer/executive producer at the University of Maryland's Philip Merrill College of Journalism/UMTV, stresses the importance of a reporter's desire to learn. "You have to learn quickly," she says, "and respond quickly. And you should also ask straightforward, to-the-point questions." Assertiveness is also important in getting the interview and the answers to your questions. "You can't be a wallflower in the line of duty."

Tom Elser's curiosity helps him in his work. "I like to know things right when they're happening," he says. "I want to meet people and talk to them. I'm not shy." This helps him to get the interviews he needs. "It can be difficult getting people to talk," he says. "People have become very media shy."

Compassion is another important skill for reporters, especially when they must interview people who have suffered a tragedy. Tom recalls an early story in his career, talking to the family of a murder victim on the day of the crime. "You have to detach yourself from the tragedy," he explains. "You can be compassionate and do your job at the same time."

Asked to name one of the drawbacks of his career, Tom says that he would prefer more time to prepare stories. "The work is highly intense," he says. "I'm a perfectionist, but on some days you only have a short amount of time to get the story on the air. You do the best you can with the amount of time and information that is available."

HOW DO I BECOME A REPORTER OR CORRESPONDENT?
Education
High School

You should take courses in journalism, English, history, geography, and political science. Working for your high school newspaper or radio station will provide you with valuable experience interviewing, editing, and writing. Try out for a speech team to hone your speaking, debating, and research skills. Also, become familiar with video and recording equipment by working for your high school's media department. Contact a local reporter and ask to spend a few days shadowing him or her to get a sense of the work involved. "If you have an opportunity to get involved with television production at your high school or when you get to college, do it," says Sarah McCurdy, a reporter for KVLY/KXJB in Fargo,

North Dakota. "That will help you. Also, many stations will hire younger people to do production work or answer phones, those are great ways to network and get familiar with the newsroom. Always pay attention to what's going on in the world around you. To be a reporter you have to be up on current events and you have to know how to look for story ideas."

Postsecondary Education

Reporters can sometimes find work without a journalism degree, but a good school can provide you with professional contacts and internship opportunities. Some students even pursue master's degrees in journalism. Broadcast programs require students to take courses like reporting, photography, ethics, and broadcast history. Many schools also have TV and radio stations that either employ students or offer students credit for their work. The Accrediting Council on Education in Journalism and Mass Communications (ACEJMC) can provide you with information on journalism schools at its Web site http://www2.ku.edu/~acejmc/.

Internships and Volunteerships

Tom Elser says that his internship experience was pretty extensive. "I interned for a radio station," he says, "which led to an internship at a TV station, KMTV. I interned at KMTV for more than two years. I learned a lot and was even put on the air to report. I believe internships are the only way to get a job in television. They provide students with contacts and lots of real-world experience."

Sarah McCurdy agrees with Tom. "An internship is a very important part of

Moments in Broadcast Reporting History

May 6, 1937, Lakehurst, New Jersey

Reporter Herb Morrison was covering the mooring of the *Hindenberg* (an early passenger zeppelin) for later radio broadcast. Though expecting to do simple coverage of the landing, Morrison watched and reported as the Hindenberg burst into flames, creating one of the most famous radio broadcasts in history.

jumping into this profession. You can do an internship in a large market station or a smaller market station. Oftentimes you can get more hands-on experience in a smaller market station. It's a way to learn how the news is put together. This is how you get your foot in the door, so to speak, and see if it's really something you want to pursue."

Your college journalism program will direct you to internship programs. Some colleges bring in recruiters from the networks, and from TV and radio stations in major markets. Paid internships with TV and radio stations are highly competitive, but they're also the most valuable. Unpaid interns are restricted in the amount of work they are allowed to do for a station, and therefore receive only limited experience. Some internships may be available in your local area, and others will require you to move; internships are also advertised in newspapers and on Web pages, and listed with various professional organizations. The Society of Professional Journalists (http://www.spj.org) offers some annual internship opportunities. The Minorities in Broadcasting Training Program (http://www.the-broadcaster.com) provides opportunities for college graduates with journalism backgrounds to train as radio or TV reporters.

Labor Unions

In most smaller markets, reporters aren't required to belong to the American Federation of Television and Radio Artists (AFTRA); the networks and the TV and radio stations in larger cities do require union membership. AFTRA, comprising dues-paying actors, announcers, DJs, newscasters, editors, writers, directors, and vocalists, has more than 70,000 members across the country. The union acts as an advocate for better wages, working conditions, and benefits. It isn't necessary to join AFTRA until you have hired on with a station that requires membership.

WHO WILL HIRE ME?

Experienced reporters are in demand throughout the country, in small markets and large. Positions are usually advertised in the local newspapers, or on the job lines of broadcast stations. You may have to submit tapes of your work along with a résumé; you should also be persistent in getting your work reviewed for consideration. By doing an online search of broadcasting job listings, you're likely to bring

up a number of Web sites with descriptions of available positions.

Tom's internship led to full-time work, but only after he left the Omaha station for a CBS affiliate in nearby Lincoln. As a regional reporter, Tom covered the news within 100 miles of the city. "There I shot the stories and edited them," he says. "Now I work with a photographer." After eight months as a regional reporter, Tom returned to work in Omaha.

WHERE CAN I GO FROM HERE?

For those willing to relocate, advancement means moving up into a larger market, or into network news. Within a local TV or radio station, a reporter may eventually move on to another area of broadcasting, such as directing or producing a newscast. Reporters also become anchors, who are better paid and more prominent in the newscast. Many more people are

Advancement Possibilities

News anchors host newscasts on television and radio. They read news copy and introduce live and taped news segments.

Station managers oversee the daily operation of radio and television stations. They supervise all the station departments, such as sales and marketing, management, technical, and on-air "talent."

employed in sales, promotion, and planning than are employed in reporting and anchoring; and people in sales and management positions often draw a better salary than the journalists.

WHAT ARE THE SALARY RANGES?

As with any broadcasting position, the salary for a reporter varies according to the size of the TV or radio station, the size of the audience, and the reporter's experience. Some reporters in the country make less than $20,000 a year, while some star reporters in major markets may be able to demand over $150,000 (though such salaries for reporters are rare). According to the U.S. Department of Labor, reporters and correspondents had earnings that ranged from less than $18,340 to $68,880 in 2004. Reporters and correspondents employed in radio and television had mean annual earnings of $46,290 in 2004.

Salaries for foreign correspondents vary greatly depending on the network or station, the cost of living, and the tax structure where foreign correspondents work. Generally, salaries range from $50,000 to an average of about $75,000 to a peak of $100,000 or more. Some media will pay for living expenses, such as the cost of a home, school for the reporter's children, and a car.

WHAT IS THE JOB OUTLOOK?

Newsrooms provide TV stations with healthy profits every year, and this is not

Related Jobs

- columnists/commentators
- copy writers
- disc jockeys
- editorial writers
- editors
- interpreters
- news directors
- newspaper reporters
- newswriters
- online producers
- producers
- screenwriters
- sportscasters
- technical writers
- traffic reporters
- weather forecasters

expected to change. TV reporters will continue to be in demand, although the number of news departments and news staff is expected to grow more slowly through 2014, according to U.S. Department of Labor. There are currently more than 200 broadcast journalism programs in the country, and their students don't account for all the reporters seeking work in broadcasting; because news directors hire graduates from many different programs (and some prefer to hire graduates with a liberal arts degree), there's growing competition for the available positions.

Salaries are likely to stay low for broadcast reporters. With the large number of applicants for reporting positions, news directors can have their choice of the best without having to pay much. News directors are still not entirely happy with the graduates of broadcast journalism programs: studies done by such organizations as the Society of Professional Journalists and the Freedom Forum report that news directors believe today's reporters can't write well and don't have sufficient understanding of current affairs, history, and geography. Studies such as these may result in radical changes in journalism education, and also in news department hiring practices.

Technology has a big impact on the way news is reported. The development of satellite technology and portable video cameras has revolutionized broadcast journalism over the last 25 years, and new developments over the next 20 years will likely have the same powerful effects. As the Internet competes for TV's viewers and radio's listeners, look for newsrooms to make better use of the technology. Many radio stations are broadcasting over the Web, and many TV stations have Web pages that feature up-to-the-minute local news coverage.

Sue Kopen Katcef agrees that rapid changes in technology will change broadcast journalism and the role of reporters. "Broadcast journalists will continue to be asked to do more—possibly with less," she predicts. "Even now 'just' being a broadcast news reporter—or anchor—is pretty much a thing of the past. The broadcast journalist, because of the evolving nature of the business, must be able to take digital photos, get them on to a Web site, and download audio (including podcasts), in addition to the 'usual' responsibilities that come with being a broadcast journalist."

Screenwriters

SUMMARY

Definition
Using dialogue, images, and narration, screenwriters write scripts for dramas, comedies, documentaries, adaptations, and educational programs. They may write complete original scripts, or work on assignment by a producer or director. Screenwriters either work freelance or as part of a staff of writers.

Alternative Job Titles
Scriptwriters

Staff writers
Story editors

Salary Range
$23,000 to $80,000 to $200,000

Educational Requirements
High school diploma

Certification or Licensing
None available

Employment Outlook
About as fast as the average

High School Subjects
English (writing/literature)

History
Journalism
Theater

Personal Interests
Entertaining/performing
Film and television
Photography
Reading/books
Selling/making a deal
Theater
Writing

Screenwriters write scripts for entertainment, education, training, sales, television, and films. They may choose themes themselves, or they may write on a theme assigned by a producer or director, sometimes adapting plays or novels into screenplays. Screenwriting is an art, a craft, and a business. It is a career that requires imagination and creativity, the ability to tell a story using both dialogue and pictures, and the ability to negotiate with producers and studio executives.

WHAT DOES A SCREENWRITER DO?

Suppose you have an idea for a science fiction TV movie—your movie, set in the not-so-distant future, concerns green martians. With a powerful telescope, the U.S. government has been watching these green martians plowing the red dust of their planet for several years; then one day, without warning, the green martians turn a shade of purple, a kind of pale fuchsia, and the world panics. You tell your friends about your brilliant idea for a TV movie—they all think it's stupid, but you don't care. You think it's brilliant. This confidence and love for your work, and your fearlessness in the face of rejection, are possibly your most important assets in your career as a writer for television.

Your idea for a TV-movie will, if you're lucky, be the first step in a long trek to seeing the show on the air. You must not only be good at writing—characterization, plot, dialogue, and the many other techniques of storytelling—but also be a good salesperson; you'll be expected to represent your work, defend it, and promote it. And although the idea formed in the privacy of your own head, you'll be collaborating on the movie with many professionals. Depending on your involvement with the project, you may be working directly with producers, directors, editors, and other writers. You may be required to be on the set during filming, and you may be expected to make revisions at the drop of a hat. And if the movie is being filmed by a small production team, you may be involved in casting, finding locations, and even promoting the film.

So, you have your purple martian idea. What's next? There are various ways that writers get their work produced. Some writers compose entire scripts, sitting alone in their homes with their computers. They pay close attention to the elements of the story, developing interesting characters and situations. They come up with the lines the characters will say to each other. All of this requires not just talent, but also an understanding of how

a story moves forward. Writers gain this understanding by watching movies and TV shows, and reading short stories and novels. They also read published scripts of well-written films. In composing your martian script, you must format it properly as well, with proper spacing for cues, directions, and spoken lines.

Then comes the next step: selling the script. This can be the most frustrating and difficult aspect of writing for television. Thousands of people are trying to sell their scripts to TV and the movies. Selling your script requires a contact within the TV industry. Some writers have many connections with producers and directors; they've gained these connections by living in Los Angeles, the base for television production. These writers promote themselves and their work. They may take entry-level jobs with production companies and get to know the people who make decisions on scripts. Many writers also have agents; for a percentage of the money you make from the script, an agent will use his or her connections in the industry to get the script read and considered for production. But the services of an agent can be as difficult to obtain as a reading by a producer. And even if you do sell your martian script, there's no guarantee that the script will ever be produced. Some writers have made whole careers from selling their ideas and treatments for films that ultimately are never made.

Or maybe you think your martian story would make for a good episode of a science fiction TV series. If you've established yourself in the industry, and have made valuable connections, you can get meetings with producers. Even without a fully written script in hand, you can "pitch" your ideas. With a complete understanding of the series and its characters, you can describe your idea to the producer; but be prepared to have other ideas, in case the producer doesn't like the first one.

Most network TV series have writing staffs, as well. As a staff writer for a series, you're expected to work long hours, and to collaborate with the other writers, the producers, directors, and actors. Writers for daytime soap operas are often the most diligent of all TV writers—a new episode of a soap airs every day, even in the summer when other series writers can take a break.

OK . . . so maybe you've convinced yourself that the purple martian idea is a bad one. Dramatic television isn't the only outlet for TV writers. Practically everything that airs on network TV or cable starts with a written script. Documentaries, sitcoms, newscasts, and educational programs are just some of the television projects that require the work of writers. And not all writers work in Los Angeles; freelance screenwriters can be found all across the country. TV series are frequently filmed outside of Los Angeles, so series staff writers may find themselves in New York, Canada, and even Baltimore. And with the number of new cable channels developing with headquarters in various cities across the country, writers can make successful careers outside of Los Angeles and apart from the networks.

Lingo to Learn

agent A person with connections in the industry; for a percentage of the final sale of a script, an agent will represent a writer, showing the script to producers and directors.

draft A complete written script, either revised or unrevised. A "rough" draft is an initial version of a script; a "final" draft is a script ready for production.

pitch A description of an idea, usually verbal, presented to a producer or director. A writer pitches screenplay ideas hoping to be hired to write the entire script.

reader An entry-level position in a production company; a reader reads scripts submitted to the company, analyzes them, and determines which are worthy of being passed on to producers.

treatment A written proposal for a script; between 3 and 15 pages. A treatment offers a plot summary.

WHAT IS IT LIKE TO BE A SCREENWRITER?

Ellen Sandler has been a screenwriter/producer for 25 years. She has worked as a writer/producer for many network television comedies including *Coach*, *Taxi*, and *Everybody Loves Raymond*, for which she was nominated for an Emmy for her work as co-executive producer. In addition, Ellen teaches sitcom writing at the Writer's Program at the University of California–Los Angeles and Television Writing for Playwrights at the Herbert Berghof Studio in New York City.

Ellen began her career working in theater. "I was a theater director and writer in New York," she recalls, "which had always been my dream, but I was not making very much money. Then a play that I cowrote and directed in Los Angeles got noticed by Jim Brooks who, at the time, was the executive producer of *Taxi*. He liked what he saw and hired me and my then partner to write an episode for *Taxi*. After that, other people were interested in hiring us—TV writing paid a lot better than the theater and it was fun besides. I had to learn a whole lot of new skills and that was an exciting, if sometimes frustrating, challenge."

When Ellen was working on the staff of the television show *Everybody Loves Raymond*, a typical day would involve her getting up at about 6:30 A.M., taking her two children to school, and arriving at her office at Warner Brothers, the studio that produced the show, at about 8:45 A.M. "About 10:00 A.M.," she recalls, "the writers would gather in the writer's room to work on stories for future scripts or rewrites of the current episode in production. After lunch we'd do a run-through of the current show in production down on the set. We'd laugh at the jokes, make notes in our scripts about what wasn't working and what could be cut, and then we, the writers, would go back to the writer's room and wait for the executive producer to come back with the network notes. Then we'd rewrite. That could go till 6:00, 7:00, 8:00, or later.

On Fridays, it would be show night, which means after a full day of camera rehearsals and last-minute rewrites, we'd

To Be a Successful Screenwriter, You Should . . .

- be able to work on a deadline
- know how to create vivid characters, scenes, and storylines
- have strong communication skills
- have good research skills
- be aware that no show you create will last forever; you will always need to look ahead to land your next job

have a catered dinner for the entire cast and crew, and then everyone would gather on the floor of the sound stage to shoot the show with an audience of several hundred in the stands. As each scene was shot, the writer/producers would cluster around the monitors, watching closely for every detail and listening for how every line played. Then we'd shoot the scene again, correcting anything that might have been off the first time. It could get to be a pretty late night, usually ending around midnight."

DO I HAVE WHAT IT TAKES TO BE A SCREENWRITER?

As a screenwriter, you must be able to create believable characters and develop a story. Ellen Sandler says that character and motivation, as well as humor, are key to creating a well-written television comedy, "because no matter how good the jokes are," she explains, "they don't really work unless the characters' behavior is believable and their motives are clear and consistent."

You must also have technical skills, such as writing dialogue, creating plots, and doing research. In addition to creativity and originality, you need an understanding of the marketplace for your work. You should be aware of what kinds of scripts are in demand by producers. Word processing skills are also helpful.

Varied interests and curiosity are also important for screenwriters. One day you might be researching the slang used in Tombstone, Arizona, in the 1880s and the next, social customs of Elizabethan England.

In addition to the stress caused by the instability of working on a freelance basis, there's a lot of stress in the work itself. Screenwriters must meet constant deadlines. And because the process requires a great deal of collaboration, they must be ready to throw away something they have just spent a long time writing if others in their team have a different approach.

HOW DO I BECOME A SCREENWRITER?
Education
High School
Though talent plays a big part in a writer's success, technical skill is also important. Take English courses that will introduce you to both classic and contemporary works of fiction and theater. From these novels and plays, you can pick up the techniques of storytelling. In drama and theater courses, as well as drama clubs, you'll learn about dialogue and scenes; you may even have the opportunity to direct a production or to play a role. "Drama clubs and classes are great for teaching you about dramatic structure," says Ellen. "Any chance to act or do improv will be helpful if you want to be able to write believable characters and sparkling, original dialogue. Video projects will help you learn how to tell a story with pictures and movement. Also, you'll learn what goes into production, and get a sense of the collaborative nature and the economics of making film and TV."

Additionally, many schools also have speech and debate teams, as well as journalism departments, which train students in writing news and editorials, conducting research, and writing yearbook copy.

Postsecondary Training
Producers aren't generally interested in a writer's educational background—you'll be judged on your writing and ideas. But film schools will help you develop your writing skills and your understanding of filmmaking. These schools will also help you make some connections in the industry and inform you of internships, competitions, and conferences. Ellen Sandler offers the following advice to screenwriting students: "Students of writing must be committed to seeing a task through to the end, and they must be willing to hear criticism and use what they hear to improve their work; but the most important thing they must have is the courage to fail and

still continue. If they aren't willing to write badly first and then keep working to improve their writing, they will never write well. Think of your first draft as raw material, not a finished project. Good scripts evolve. They go through a long process of many drafts, so like Rocky, you've got to be able to go the distance."

Many colleges and universities have undergraduate and graduate film departments, but some of the most respected film schools are at the University of California–Los Angeles (http://www.tft.ucla.edu/ftv_mfa), the University of Southern California (http://www-cntv.usc.edu/academic_programs/writing/academic-writing-home.cfm), the American Film Institute (http://www.afi.com), and Columbia University (http://wwwapp.cc.columbia.edu/art/app/arts/film/viewProgram.jsp). Write to these schools or visit their Web pages for information about course work and faculty.

Most college theater departments offer courses in playwriting, and many English departments are developing undergraduate creative writing programs. In writing workshops, you can develop skills in dramatic and narrative structure. There are also many master of fine arts programs that allow you to further refine your abilities.

Labor Unions

TV screenwriters are usually required to join the Writers Guild of America (WGA). Those living east of the Mississippi may join Writers Guild East, while those living west of the Mississippi may belong to Writers Guild West. Members pay $2,500 annually to belong to and take advantage of health care benefits, legal assistance, and payment negotiation. To become a member, you must accumulate a certain amount of writing experience. The WGA branches maintain very informative Web pages (http://www.wga.org and http://www.wgaeast.org/) with information on agents, books on screenwriting, research aids, and many interviews with screenwriters.

Internships and Volunteerships

If you attend film school, you will probably be required to participate in an intern-

---

Advancement Possibilities

Film writers write scripts for major motion pictures; they may also be called in to revise the scripts of other writers or to write individual scenes.

Film directors are in control of the decisions that shape a film, and are responsible for a film's overall style and quality.

Film producers head productions by arranging for financial backing, as well as bringing together creative teams of directors, writers, and actors. In television, these responsibilities are typically handled by studio and network executives.

Executive producers are responsible for the decisions that shape a television show by overseeing the show's overall style and quality. He or she is often, but not always, the writer/creator of the show.

ship. This will allow you the chance to work closely with screenwriters and other television and film professionals. You might also get the opportunity to work as a screenwriter assistant, to be a script reader, or perhaps to perform clerical duties for a production company, independent screenwriter, or other employer. These employers may also offer volunteer opportunities.

WHO WILL HIRE ME?

Jobs as a screenwriter can be extremely hard to come by. Most established screenwriters credit their own persistence and assertiveness; you should be prepared to work for a while at entry-level jobs with production companies and TV series in order to get to know the people who make decisions on scripts. Only about half of the members of the WGA are actually employed, and that's an improvement over previous years. Though we occasionally hear about very young writers and filmmakers, most screenwriters have had to work for years and years in the industry before establishing themselves.

WHERE CAN I GO FROM HERE?

Competition is stiff among screenwriters, and a beginner will find it difficult to break into the field. More opportunities become available as a screenwriter gains experience and a reputation, but that is a process that can take many years. Rejection is a common occurrence in the field

of screenwriting. Most successful screenwriters have had to send their screenplays to numerous production companies before they find one who likes their work.

Once they have sold some scripts, screenwriters may be able to join the WGA. Membership with the WGA guarantees the screenwriter a minimum wage for a production and other benefits such as arbitration. Some screenwriters who write for minor productions, however, can have regular work and successful careers without WGA membership.

Those screenwriters who manage to break into the business can benefit greatly from recognition in the industry. In addition to creating their own scripts, some writers are also hired to "doctor" the scripts of others, using their expertise to revise scripts for production. If a film proves very successful, a screenwriter will be able to command higher payment, and will be able to work on high-profile productions. Some of the most talented screenwriters receive awards from the industry, most notably the Academy Award for best original or adapted screenplay.

Some screenwriters might also work in other creative genres, such as fiction writing or the theater. "Television production is demanding work, time and energy wise," Ellen says, "but I find time to do at least one small theater project each year, just because I love working in that form. It gives me some much-needed artistic balance. It's really great to get paid for writing, and I always feel blessed when I do, but money isn't everything. As a TV writer I have to concern myself with what network executives and commercial sponsors need and want, because that's who pays the bills. When I work on a play, I feel like I have a lot more control over my creativity, that it's just about the work itself, and that's always been important to me."

WHAT ARE THE SALARY RANGES?

With some TV stars making over a million dollars an episode, many aspiring writers are under the misconception that TV holds big paychecks for them, as well. But TV writers get paid a mere fraction of the salaries of on-screen talent. Typical salaries might average about $80,000 annually for screenwriters who work as staff writers for a television series. That's still a good salary, but you have to consider the nature of television—you lose your job when the series is canceled, and many new series don't make it through their first season. But if the series continues for several years, and is sold into syndication, you can look to make money from the reruns, as well.

According to the U.S. Department of Labor, writers and authors earned salaries that ranged from less than $23,700 to $87,660 or more in 2004. Writers and authors employed in television and radio broadcasting had mean annual earnings of $44,490 in 2004.

Though TV has more jobs for writers than the motion picture industry, writing for TV is not considered steady, reliable work. Many writers work freelance, so they

> ### Related Jobs
>
> - agents
> - columnists/commentators
> - copywriters
> - critics
> - directors
> - editorial writers
> - fiction and poetry writers
> - humorists
> - lyricists
> - newswriters
> - playwrights
> - producers
> - reporters
> - script readers
> - technical writers
> - theatrical writers

generally can't predict how much money they'll make from one year to the next.

Screenwriters who are members of the WGA are eligible to receive health benefits.

WHAT IS THE JOB OUTLOOK?

Writers will continue to find work with the networks, though the networks are ordering fewer new episodes of prime-time dramas and sitcoms. Viewership for network TV has decreased over the last several years due to competition from cable, DVDs, the Internet, and computer and video games. But this competition opens up opportunities for writers. Advances in technology may soon allow for 200 to 500 cable channels to be piped into your home—screenwriters will be needed to help in the production of programs for these channels.

Sportscasters

SUMMARY

Definition
Sportscasters cover sporting events for radio and TV news; they write, produce, and edit feature segments for broadcast. They anchor newscasts, providing scores and highlights.

Alternative Job Titles
Play-by-play announcers
Sports anchors
Sports directors
Sports reporters

Salary Range
$4,000 to $40,000 to $400,000

Educational Requirements
Bachelor's degree

Certification or Licensing
None available

Employment Outlook
More slowly than the average

High School Subjects
English (writing/literature)
Health
Journalism
Physical education
Speech

Personal Interests
Broadcasting
Current events
Exercise/personal fitness
Film and television
Sports
Writing

Lars Peterson's favorite sporting event to cover is the Iditarod Sled Dog Race, a 1,000-mile race from Anchorage to Nome, Alaska, where people brave the elements by riding on a sled pulled by dogs. "PETA [People for the Ethical Treatment of Animals] will tell you it's cruel to animals," says Lars, a sports anchor/reporter in Anchorage, Alaska, "but if you ask me it's cruel to people! Those mushers have to brave frigid temperatures and sleep deprivation for a purse of $65,000 and a new Dodge truck.

"As a broadcaster following the race, you get to fly from checkpoint to checkpoint on a little airplane (Cessna 185) and sleep on the floors of schools and churches. It is a very secluded two weeks considering there are no roads, hotels, or restaurants. We do our stories on portable editing machines and then send them back using cargo planes that deliver the mail to the small villages. Like the mushers, you don't get very much sleep, but at least you don't have to be outside 24 hours a day! The reward of covering the Iditarod is the chance to see rural Alaska firsthand."

WHAT DOES A SPORTSCASTER DO?

From cricket and squash to cricket squashing, most sports, no matter how unusual, have fans. These fans want information. They want to know scores and stats. They want to hear the play-by-play. They want interviews with sports figures and highlights of recent games. And they also want to learn about the many other aspects of the growing sports industry: sports medicine, fitness, and sports business have become typical subjects for reporters on nightly news programs. *Sportscasters*, as part of news anchor teams, do more than just sit behind desks and recite the scores of the local high school matches—they are active members of the sports and recreation industry, and of their news team.

If you love sports, then being a sportscaster may be your dream job. You get to know the local players and coaches, and you talk about sports on a daily basis. And you get paid for it. You can also enjoy a certain amount of local or national fame—it's your voice and personality that TV viewers or radio listeners get to know. Some people have made long careers as sportscasters, in cities large and small, and they have become as closely associated with the team as the players themselves. Sportscasters also make live appearances outside of the sports arena to promote their news teams and to get to know their audiences.

A sportscaster for a local network affiliate reports the sports live during news broadcasts—your local news may air two or three times a night. The sportscaster has a few minutes during these broadcasts to announce scores, upcoming sporting events, and to show and narrate highlights from recent games. With a broad knowledge of all kinds of sports, they prepare their segments in the hours before broadcast; they write their scripts, find the most compelling highlights, and time it all to fit within the time allotted by the producer. These sportscasters also record segments for later broadcast—these segments include on-location interviews with various sports figures. They don't just interview the members of local sports teams; they also cover charity sporting events, offer inspirational sports stories, and report on the business of sports.

Sportscasters on affiliate TV news teams don't do much play-by-play; as a matter of fact, they only occasionally

---

Lingo to Learn

conferences In professional and college football, the groups into which teams are divided (e.g., the NFL, divided into National and American Conferences).

division In college football, groups of teams, with the first division consisting of the most competitive teams, and the third division the least competitive.

franchise Enjoying membership in a professional sports league.

hat trick In a soccer or hockey game, three goals scored by a single player.

leagues Alliances of sports teams organizing the competitions.

report live from sporting events, and then only for a few minutes. To do play-by-play, your best bet may be in radio. Though radio stations employ sportscasters as part of their news teams, stations also need announcers for the live local games they broadcast—usually high school and college games. Sports teams also hire play-by-play announcers. As a member of a team's media relations department, a sportscaster puts together stats and press notes, as well as arranges for interviews to air live during the games. During the actual games, radio sportscasters rely on their knowledge and speaking skills to describe the action to listeners.

But the opportunity to do play-by-play isn't limited to radio sportscasters; cable stations in larger cities air live sporting events and rely on the talents of TV sportscasters who either work for the team or the station. National TV sports coverage also calls on the play-by-play skills of network sportscasters. These national sportscasting positions are highly competitive, and often are filled by former professional players; but as new cable channels develop, offering 24 hours of sports coverage, more opportunities will open up for sportscasters.

WHAT IS IT LIKE TO BE A SPORTSCASTER?

Lars Peterson is a sports anchor/reporter at NBC-affiliate KTUU-TV in Anchorage, Alaska. He has been a television sportscaster since 1999, but worked in radio sports and news beginning in 1997. "I grew up in a small town called Naselle, Washington," he says. "It's located at the mouth of the Columbia River and the Pacific Ocean. It's a fishing and logging community that virtually hasn't changed in 20 years. Because of that, I grew up without TV—instead I listened to the radio. One thing I have always enjoyed is basketball, so I would listen to the Portland Trailblazers [professional basketball] games. Bill Schonely, the announcer for the Blazers, sounded like he was always having fun. I thought, 'I want to have a job where you get to watch basketball and talk with the team.' That happened when I was about 12 years old, and even though I'm in television now, I'm having fun!"

Lars works 1:00 P.M. to 11:00 P.M. Monday through Friday. "In television (sports especially) you will always work nights," he says. "When I come to work, I am either sent out on assignment by the sports director (or something I have set up) or I produce the 5:00 P.M. and 6:00 P.M. sports for the sports director. Usually it involves tracking down local stories. Whether it's talking with our local college teams or our minor league hockey team, I gather a story for the 5:00 P.M., the 6:00 P.M., or the 10:00 P.M. sportscast." After the story has been shot and the interviews are gathered, Lars returns to the station, writes and edits the story, and reads the copy during the 10:00 P.M. newscast. "My main job is to anchor the 10 P.M. sports, my second is to report for the 5 P.M. and 6 P.M. newscasts. We have photographers here in Anchorage, but I shoot my own video about half the time. I do all of my own editing and writing except when I'm on a road trip with our satellite truck. In this instance, I usually have a photographer who both shoots and edits the stories."

DO I HAVE WHAT IT TAKES TO BE A SPORTSCASTER?

The basic requirement for a sportscaster is a love and enthusiasm for sports. Most viewers and listeners of sports news have this enthusiasm and demand it from their sportscasters. These audience members also want someone who is personable and trustworthy, and who can speak clearly and express him- or herself simply.

To Be a Successful Sportscaster, You Should . . .

- be a rabid sports fan
- have confidence in your abilities and never give up when trying to break into the field
- be able to speak clearly and express yourself
- be willing to work at all hours and on holidays and weekends
- be willing to travel
- have a thick skin, since fans won't always agree with your opinions or ideas

Sportscasters have the opportunity to interview and interact with well-known athletes and coaches. Despite this proximity, they need to avoid being starstruck by these professionals in order to do their jobs effectively. "I've gone fishing with Larry Csonka (a member of the 1972 undefeated Miami Dolphins and now a professional fisherman)," Lars Peterson recalls. "I shot hoops with NBA star Karl Malone when I was in Oregon, and I got to hang out with NASCAR's Dale Jarrett for a day. I'm not one to get starstruck, which probably makes me a good candidate for this type of work."

HOW DO I BECOME A SPORTSCASTER?

Education

Lars Peterson received his bachelor's degree in communications from the Edward R. Murrow School of Communication at Washington State University. "While in college," he recalls, "I took advantage of every opportunity to get hands-on experience, including doing freelance work for FOX Sports Northwest (mainly gripping for football games). That was probably the best experience because I was able to broadcast local high school football and basketball games on weekends and during the play-offs."

High School

If you want to be a sportscaster, you need to learn the basics of journalism. In addition to courses that will train you in news writing and reporting, interviewing, editing, and photography, take English courses. Physical education courses that offer course instruction in addition to exercise can help you become more familiar with the sports and recreation industry. A health class can teach you about fitness.

Though you may only really be interested in football, baseball, or basketball, in order to become a sportscaster you should learn about all kinds of sports. Watch ESPN and your local sports news, and read the newspaper's sports page to get to know as much about as many different sports as you can. Go to work for your high school newspaper or radio station, and cover the local sporting events. You may even find part-time work with the sports department of your city newspaper, or with a radio or TV station. Your guidance counselor may be able to direct you to a local mentoring program that could introduce you to professional sports journalists, allowing you the opportunity to shadow a sportscaster for a day or two.

Postsecondary Training

In recent years, broadcast journalism professionals have been debating the value of journalism schools; some believe students should pursue degrees in history and political science for a broader education. Others still stress the importance of journalism school for students wanting careers in broadcasting. Many journalism schools are offering majors in sports journalism, and even graduate sports journalism programs. But the important thing is to gain as much practical experience as you can. Look for part-time jobs with local or college radio

---

Yogi-isms

Lawrence "Yogi" Berra, a Hall of Fame catcher for the New York Yankees, has provided the sports media with some of its most amusing and memorable quotes. A term—"yogi-ism"—has evolved to describe a statement in the simple, contradictory style of Yogi Berra's quotes. Here are a few of his memorable lines:

- "You can observe a lot just by watching."

- "Baseball is 90 percent mental; the other half is physical."

- "If people don't want to come to the ballpark, how are you gonna stop them?"

- "If you can't imitate him, don't copy him."

---

and TV stations, and volunteer with sports organizations.

Internships and Volunteerships

Many TV and radio stations have internship programs, along with summer job opportunities. Most of these internships are unpaid; the paid internships offer better training, but are very competitive. If you're in a broadcast journalism program, your advisers can connect you to available internships; recruiters from network and cable sports departments may even visit your school. You can write to the networks for information on their internship opportunities.

Pete Byrne, a sports anchor/reporter for KVLY-TV in Fargo, North Dakota, interned for a production company in South Bend, Indiana, where he learned how to operate a camera, shoot interviews, and edit tape. His second internship was at WHME-FM radio, where he provided the color commentary for Notre Dame baseball. Pete encourages aspiring sportscasters to pursue an internship to prepare for a career in the field. "If you can get course credit, or get paid, great," he says. "Even if you cannot, you need to learn the business you intend to get into, and this is really the only way. Broadcasting is not like most fields of work, where you earn a degree, and then get a job based on what you accomplished in the classroom. You need experience to get hired. It's a nasty paradox of the business. That's where the internships come in handy. I learned more about what I do now in two semester-long internships than during the rest of my four years of college combined. That was my training for this career."

WHO WILL HIRE ME?

Some sportscasters get their first paying jobs from the stations for which they intern. TV and radio stations often widely advertise open positions; check your local newspaper for local positions, or consult the Internet for many job listings.

Less than six months out of college, Pete Byrne landed his first job as a producer at Midwest Sports Channel (MSC) in Minneapolis as a result of contacts he made during an internship. "After graduation," he recalls, "I took another internship, this time unpaid at KSTP-TV in the Twin Cities, and worked in the sports department a few nights a week editing and writing and occasionally interviewing local athletes. The executive producer at MSC was a former sports director at KSTP, and called there looking for a freelance producer to take on a weekly 12-episode show called *Minnesota Wrestling Weekly*—30 minutes on high school and college wrestling in the state of Minnesota. It wasn't exactly SportsCenter, but it got my foot in the door. After the 12-week show was up, they kept me on as a freelance producer, and within a year, the producer for their main show starting producing the games for the new NHL franchise Minnesota Wild, and I took over their main show. Two years after that, I decided I wanted to be in front of the camera, and took a job as the weekend sports anchor in Mankato, Minnesota (one of the

---

Advancement Possibilities

News anchors host radio and television news broadcasts. They read news copy and introduce live and taped news segments.

Producers supervise the production of newscasts, plan segments, and keep programs running on time.

General managers manage the operations of television and radio stations; they're involved in marketing, promotion, contracts, and public relations.

smallest markets in the United States). It's led me to where I am now."

WHERE CAN I GO FROM HERE?

Typically, sportscasters start in part-time positions in the smaller markets, then move up into full-time sports anchor positions. They then either advance into a top anchor position or move to a larger market. But many sportscasters work for the same radio or TV station for many years, enjoying successful careers with a local affiliate.

Unlike many who get into sports broadcasting, Lars Peterson has no interest in working for national sports networks such as ESPN. "I have no desire to do anything nationally," he says. "In fact, I would like to do what I grew up listening to, working for the Portland Trailblazers. The Blazers have both TV and radio contracts and, one day, my goal is to move to Portland and work for the team. Living in a nice place and being close to your family are more important than fame and fortune. Fame and fortune are nice, but you usually have to sacrifice the other two things in order to get to that level."

"Its hard to say where I see myself 5 to 10 years from now," says Pete Byrne. "I'm not so concerned with market size like many of my colleagues, nor am I obsessed with being on ESPN, although it would be fun. As a sports fan, I want to cover sports that I can get excited about. In my case, that likely means a larger Midwest market with a major university or professional franchises. I'm not setting my goals based

on a certain market size, but rather on a certain sports presence within a given market. If the market has big sports, I can live with that."

WHAT ARE THE SALARY RANGES?

Salaries vary according to the size of the market and newsroom and the sportscaster's experience. According to a 2006 salary survey conducted by the Radio-Television News Directors Association (RTNDA) and Ball State University, television sports anchors' salaries range from a low of $15,000 to a high of $400,000, with a median salary of $40,000. For radio sports anchors, salaries range from a low

Related Jobs

- actors
- broadcast meteorologists
- comedians
- disc jockeys
- news anchors
- public-address announcers
- public relations workers
- radio and television traffic reporters
- reporters
- show hosts and hostesses
- sportswriters
- television directors
- television producers

of $4,000 to a high of $100,000, with a median salary of $32,500.

WHAT IS THE JOB OUTLOOK?

Newsrooms provide TV stations with healthy profits every year, and this is not expected to change. Therefore, sportscasters will continue to be in demand, and news staff is expected to increase at a steady rate. But there's a lot of competition for these positions; there are many more graduates of journalism programs than there are jobs. This discrepancy may mean changes in the future of journalism education—look for programs to develop more well-rounded curricula to better prepare students for the workplace.

Sportscasters are expanding their area of coverage to include more than sports scores and highlights—their feature stories include reports on the thriving sports and recreation industry, and on health and fitness. The sports segments of newscasts may eventually move toward feature-oriented reports and away from the traditional listing of sports scores and highlights.

Television Directors

SUMMARY

Definition
Television directors control the decisions that shape a television program, from live productions and local newscasts to dramatic TV-movies and comedy series. The director is responsible for a broadcast's overall style and quality.

Alternative Job Titles
Producer/directors

Salary Range
$18,000 to $64,000 to $250,000+

Educational Requirements
Bachelor's degree

Certification or Licensing
None available

Employment Outlook
About as fast as the average

High School Subjects
English (writing/literature)

Journalism
Speech
Theater

Personal Interests
Broadcasting
Current events
Film and television
Photography
Theater

The television station is about to go live with the local news broadcast, and Richard Perry stands in the control booth, wearing a headset. He's listening, and watching, and considering. The camera operator, the anchors, the producer—they're all passing on information from the audio department, and the floor. Looking at the TV screen, Richard prepares to broadcast the first images of that evening's newscast.

Audio gives the countdown, and Richard, with his fingers touching lightly against the controls of the switcher, directs the camera operator. "A two-shot," he calls for, then, smoothly, the TV screen cuts to the two anchors on the set below. With the producer helping him to keep on time, Richard calls for a tape to be rolled, following an over-the-shoulder shot of an anchor and a graphic. After a stressful, fast-paced half hour, the whole day's work of preparing for this one program will be complete. If Richard has made all the cuts and transitions smoothly and clearly, the home audience will remain unaware of all the elements that go into a broadcast.

WHAT DOES A TELEVISION DIRECTOR DO?

Every year, thousands of young directors enlist in the filmmaking departments of schools like the University of Southern California and New York University; others max out their credit cards in hopes of making low-budget features worthy of the Sundance Film Festival. But there are thousands of directors working who have never been to film school, who don't live in Hollywood, and yet have established themselves in their profession. These people make successful careers and earn regular salaries by directing for network TV affiliates in cities both large and small; or they work for special-interest cable channels, like the Food Network and ESPN; or they work on a freelance basis, taking on a variety of projects for a number of different production companies. Directors work on local news programs, coverage of area sporting events, and commercials for local businesses. And with the development of narrowcasting (broadcasting meant for limited viewing, such as for classrooms, hospitals, or corporations), some directors create programming for very small audiences. Every television project, no matter how short or how small the intended audience, requires a director.

Your duties as a director depend on the nature and size of the project. Whether directing a rock music video or a live presentation of a symphony orchestra, a pay-per-view broadcast of a brutal boxing match or a TV-movie about a famous boxer's life, all directors have one thing in common: they direct the talents and skills of a number of professionals, bringing together all the pieces to create a complete program. The director is responsible for creating the look of a broadcast by determining camera angles and cuts. The director of a TV-movie, a documentary, or an episode of a series, will generally have more control over the material and its interpretation than the director of a news broadcast or a live event. If you're directing a movie, you're working from a script, you're rehearsing with the actors, you're shooting and reshooting scenes from many perspectives. To achieve the intended mood and tone of the piece, you carefully organize the work of screenwriters, lighting and sound technicians, camera operators, and editors. But if you're covering a baseball game, you have much less control—you get only one shot at broadcasting that game, leaving little room for error. And with reporters turning in pieces right up until the hour of a news broadcast, TV news directors don't even know the final content of the evening edition until just before it airs.

Do you thrive on stress? Are you able to make snap decisions? Do you want to take part in live events and late-breaking news? Events such as the summer and winter Olympics, professional and college football games, and awards presentations require the talent of directors; these directors work with the announcers, the camera operators, and other members of the technical crew to smoothly broadcast a live—and sometimes unpredictable—program. But you don't have to work for a network sports or news department to cover live events. For the director of the local news of a network affiliate, every day requires quick reflexes and focus. As a news director, you're responsible for getting all the news segments on the air; during a broadcast, you sit in the control room giving orders, keeping the broadcast moving smoothly from segment to segment. Wearing a headset, you receive information from the producer and technical crew. The camera operators work from your direction. But the director's job isn't limited to the actual broadcast; you must also direct promotional segments, news updates, and some video-taped segments to accompany the live reports later.

In smaller TV stations, the directors of nightly news programs may be involved in many different aspects of the production. They may create graphics and supers (short for "superimposed" words running across the screen, such as the names of interview subjects, or titles of a news segment), and pie charts and graphs and other informational pieces. In a larger station, the work is divided up among the directors, producers, editors, assistants, and technical directors. (*Technical directors* are members of the technical crew, who work directly with the cameras and other equipment.)

But maybe you're interested in working with a variety of projects—many directors work freelance. When taking on different projects for different producers, your job description changes frequently. You may work as a director on one project and as technical director on another. You may be directing actors in an original drama, or interviewing people for a documentary. Or you may take on many elements of the production, from getting funding for a project, to hiring writers and assistants, to setting up locations. You may even be involved in publicizing the film and entering the film into festivals and competitions.

WHAT IS IT LIKE TO BE A TELEVISION DIRECTOR?

The next time you watch the evening news, pay attention to the camera changes, the words that flash across the screen, and

---

Lingo to Learn

editor A member of a production team who views all the shots filmed by the director and decides which ones to use and how to use them.

over-the-shoulder In news production, a shot of an anchor with a graphic above the shoulder; in dramatic production, means a shot from behind someone, literally "over the shoulder."

super Short for "superimposed," the words that appear at the bottom of the TV screen giving an interviewers name of the title of a show's segment

two-shot A shot which features two subjects (such as actors, anchors, reporters) in one frame.

wipe An image sliding across another image, as with letters across a screen.

the graphics above the shoulder of the news anchor. You probably rarely think about these various elements, unless something goes wrong. It's Richard Perry's job to make sure all the segments of the newscast flow freely together. Richard Perry is a director/editor for a television station in Wilmington, North Carolina. Though he directs the 5:30 P.M. newscast, he reports for work at 5 A.M. to help prepare for the morning show, as well as to direct the various updates and promotions to be broadcast throughout the day.

From 5:00 A.M. to 6:00 A.M., he makes the graphics for the morning news and preps the supers. The newsroom sends a printed list of the words and titles, or supers, needed to run across the screen during the broadcast. He types the supers into the chryon (the character generator). From 6:00 A.M. to 7:00 A.M., Richard then runs the chryon for the morning show. This involves hitting the control for running the words across the screen at the right time. From 7:00 A.M. to 8:30 A.M., Richard directs the local weather and news cut-ins for broadcast during *Good Morning, America.*

Splitting his shift, Richard then leaves work at 9:00 A.M. and doesn't return until 2:00 P.M. From 2:00 P.M. to 4:00 P.M., Richard works on commercial production, then begins preproduction for the evening news. In the half hour before the evening news, Richard goes over the script. Then he begins the 5:30 P.M. broadcast—"also known as the half-hour adrenaline rush," says Richard.

Most TV stations have both a director and a technical director—the director

To Be a Successful Television Director, You Should . . .

- be able to handle stress and meet deadlines

- be a good listener who is able to incorporate the ideas of others into your work

- be a leader and be able to make intelligent snap decisions

- be able to handle occasional criticism and second-guessing from viewers and coworkers

- be ambitious and willing to work very hard to attain success

calls the shots, and the technical director makes the adjustments on the control board. But in a smaller station like Richard's, directors take on many responsibilities. "I sit in front of the switcher," Richard says, "and tell everyone what to do, and push all the right buttons at the right time so the show looks smooth." He tells the camera people what to shoot next, and calls for tapes to be played, or rolled, during the broadcast.

DO I HAVE WHAT IT TAKES TO BE A TELEVISION DIRECTOR?

As a director, you must be prepared for a lot of stress; many people, from producers, newscasters, and camera operators to the actual home audience, are relying on your talents. Because you're working with numerous professionals, you must also be good at listening, and capable of incorporating their ideas into the program or live broadcast.

"I'm a pretty good leader," Richard says, describing the skills required of a good director. "You have to be, in order to pull together so many people to this one common goal: getting the show on the air cleanly." He also has to make snap decisions when things go wrong. "I have an ability to focus on whatever is before me, and to block out everything else that is unnecessary."

Richard also points out the personality conflicts that can arise with producers and directors. "We tend to work those things out," he says. "I work with a good group of people." But the most stressful aspect of the job for Richard is the actual newscast. "Sometimes things come in late," he says, "and that causes everything to be reshuffled. It makes for a lot of chaos and it's up to the director to pull it all together."

HOW DO I BECOME A TELEVISION DIRECTOR?

Education

Richard received a bachelor's degree in speech communications from the University of North Carolina at Wilmington. He had his first opportunity to work in a control room while volunteering for a small cable outfit. He also did video work for a preacher, taping footage at a local prison and other locales. "I learned basic composition of shots then," Richard says.

High School

The sooner you can get to know a camera, and how to set up interesting shots, the better. Pay close attention to the broadcasts and programs you see on TV, thinking about them in terms of camera angles and editing. Work for the high school newspaper and you'll become familiar with reporting and deadlines, and you may have the opportunity to work as staff photographer. Some high schools even have their own TV stations that videotape original programs. Check with your high school's media department about working on the production crews that videotape school events. Plays and presentations are frequently videotaped for the library archives, and tapes of sporting events are used by coaches to review the strengths and weaknesses of the team. If you're less interested in live directing and more interested in working with actors and scripts, get involved with the drama club or the local community theater.

Postsecondary Training

Though a college degree isn't necessarily required of a TV director, it does give you an edge in the workplace. Also, many colleges have internship programs and career services that can help you get your foot in the door, and provide you with directing experience. If you're interested in working for a TV news station, you should apply to the broadcast departments of journalism schools. If you're interested in directing dramas and sitcoms for network and cable TV, you may want to enroll in a drama school to develop a theater background and experience working with scripts and actors. A number of universities and colleges also offer film studies programs. But, no matter what college program you enroll in, one of your top goals should be to develop practical experience. If your college of choice doesn't offer opportunities for learning about cameras and control rooms, you should seek out those opportunities on your own through part-time jobs and volunteerships. Many young directors develop directing skills working for ad agencies, video production companies, and local cable channels.

Internships and Volunteerships

An internship with a television news department frequently leads to full-time employment with that same department upon graduation. Because of this, internships can be highly competitive, and many students must take nonpaying internships. The paid internships, however, are the most valuable; federal law limits the amount of work unpaid interns are allowed to do for a station. Only with a paid internship can you get the full experience of working as a director for a TV newscast.

A summer fellowship at the International Radio and Television Society Foundation (http://www.irts.org) offers an all-expense-paid program, which includes career-planning advice and practical experience at a New York–based corporation. They also offer a minority career workshop, which brings students to New York for orientation in electronic media. The Alliance of Motion Picture and Television Producers and the Directors Guild of America (DGA) spon-

sors Assistant Directors Training Programs for students who meet eligibility requirements. Visit the DGA's Web site (http://www.dga.org/index2.php3?chg=) for more information.

Labor Unions

Though you can work for a small station without union membership, the networks and major markets require you to be represented by the Directors Guild of America (DGA). The DGA represents film and TV directors, assistant directors, and others. With membership, you'll have access to health care benefits and legal representation. The DGA also offers awards to members and promotes the hiring of minorities and women.

WHO WILL HIRE ME?

Richard's internship as a production assistant in his last semester of college led to his permanent position with his employer. "Honestly," he says, "I never thought I'd be able to direct; it looked so hard . . . so many things going on at once. But I gradually worked my way up through prompter, camera, tapes, audio, and finally I was a director." He worked part time for the station for three and a half years before being hired full time.

If unable to take part in an internship, you can hire on with video production companies or local network affiliates or cable stations. Freelance production companies also offer opportunities for new directors. You should be prepared to take any position that will offer hands-on experience with cameras and production,

Advancement Possibilities

News anchors oversee news broadcasts. They read reports and introduce other broadcast professionals who specialize in health, investigative reports, weather, or sports.

Film directors oversee the activities of actors and technical staff to create a motion picture.

General managers of television stations supervise sales, personnel, marketing, and technical departments, as well as on-air "talent."

Producers plan and coordinate radio and television broadcasts.

basis. TV directors are expected to pay their dues in the business and to work hard to learn about all aspects of the industry.

WHERE CAN I GO FROM HERE?

Though Richard could move into a production manager position, he's happy as director. "If I want to move up as director," he says, "I'll have to move up to a larger market. Maybe Charlotte or Raleigh." Richard advises, "Get in where you can and work your way up. You learn a lot on the way up, and there's a lot of paying of dues in this business." There's not a typical career path for directors, but Richard's advice does define the general sensibility in the television business.

Once you've worked on some productions, other opportunities will open up for you.

WHAT ARE THE SALARY RANGES?

Salaries vary greatly and are determined by a number of factors. A director of a newscast of a small TV station may receive very low pay, while a director working for a network can earn tens of thousands of dollars a year. Also, a freelance director working project to project may earn a great deal one year, and much less the following year. Payment for some projects may also involve union negotiation.

A 2006 salary survey by the Radio-Television News Directors Association

Related Jobs

- art directors
- artist-and-repertoire managers
- assistant directors
- casting directors
- directors of photography
- film directors
- film editors
- producers
- radio directors
- screenwriters
- sound editors
- stage managers

found that television news directors had salaries that ranged from $25,000 to $300,000. Their median annual salary was $75,000. Assistant news directors earned between $30,000 and $150,000. The median salary was $62,500. According to the U.S. Department of Labor, the mean yearly income for directors employed in radio and television was $55,400 in 2004.

Directors who work full time for stations or other organizations generally receive benefits such as health insurance and paid vacation and sick days.

WHAT IS THE JOB OUTLOOK?

Despite talk of the Internet decreasing TV's audiences, more TV programs are produced now than ever before, and this number of programs will only grow in leaps and bounds. New technology will allow cable stations to offer hundreds of additional channels and therefore more original programming. Also, more companies and organizations, such as NASA, recognize TV and video productions as ways to educate the public about their work, as well as to train their employees. Directors will be needed for all these projects.

Newsrooms provide TV stations with healthy profits every year, and this is not expected to change. Therefore, directors will continue to be in demand to direct newscasts.

About half of all TV directors work freelance, and that number will likely increase. As TV productions become more costly, and as smaller, less-profitable cable networks produce original programming, hiring directors on a project-to-project basis may be the most economical.

Television Producers

SUMMARY

Definition
Television producers work behind the scenes of television programs and newscasts; they write scripts, hire staff, and bring together the many different elements of production.

Alternative Job Titles
Executive producers
Producer/directors
Writer/producers

Salary Range
$26,000 to $58,000 to $200,000+

Educational Requirements
Bachelor's degree

Certification or Licensing
None available

Employment Outlook
About as fast as the average

High School Subjects
Business

English (writing/literature)
Journalism
Theater

Personal Interests
Broadcasting
Current events
Photography
Reading/books
Selling/making a deal

"I never considered being a producer until I was hired by KELO [a CBS television affiliate in Sioux Falls, South Dakota]," says executive producer Beth Jensen. "I knew I wanted to work for the station, and accepting the producer job was a way to get my foot in the door. When I was first hired, I didn't enjoy producing. I really wanted to be out gathering the news and talking with the people involved. I was fortunate enough to be able to do that for several years. But I decided that producing was a better long-term choice for me. I like the big picture thinking. It's fun to watch several stories evolve during the day, and I enjoy the challenge of seeing how they fit into different newscasts as those shows come together."

WHAT DOES A TELEVISION PRODUCER DO?

Since they're involved in writing, editing, budgeting, planning, casting, hiring—and weaving together all the different parts of a production into a complete program—a better question might be, "What doesn't a *television producer* do?" Producers oversee the production of newscasts, sporting events, dramas, comedies, documentaries, specials, and the many other programs that make up network and cable broadcasting. Because of the varied nature of television programming, a producer's role may also change from project to project. A producer on one project may only be involved in arranging financial backing and putting together the creative team of directors and actors. A producer on another project may oversee practically every detail of the production, including arranging for equipment and scheduling personnel.

Maybe your idea of a TV producer has been formed by Nick-at-Nite and its reruns of *The Mary Tyler Moore Show*— Mary and Murray dealing with the on-air antics of Ted Baxter. But a more accurate media portrayal of a producer is by Holly Hunter in the film *Broadcast News*. Ambitious, busy, and intelligent, Hunter's character literally runs the show. She comes up with ideas for stories, determines the newsworthiness of events and subjects, chooses graphics, edits taped material, and writes copy. One scene in the film shows Hunter at work during a live news-break; she quickly arranges for on-air interviews and organizes information from a variety of sources. She sets up reports from correspondents on the scene. As she speaks softly through a microphone, she directly passes on information to the anchorman through his earpiece, and the film shows us how closely connected she is to the broadcast.

Producers of the daily newscasts across the country are some of the most hardworking producers in television. They are required to have great news judgment— along with reporters, they determine which stories are worth broadcasting. They assign stories, review taped reports, and help the reporters edit the material. Paying close attention to time restraints, producers take all the elements of the newscast and piece them together. These pieces include live and taped reports, news feeds, graphics, special segments, and voice-overs. Often producers have to deal with late-breaking developments and must quickly assign reporters and photographers to a story, then weave the new report into the evening's newscast. Producers write scripts for the broadcast from information provided by wire services. The work environment for a TV newscast producer is fast paced and doesn't let up even at the end of a work-day—whenever there's news to be covered, a producer must be prepared to cover it.

Producers for documentaries and specials are also very actively involved in their productions, but they're typically allowed days, rather than hours, to complete projects. They're involved in hiring writers, directors, camera operators, and technicians. They scout out locations and interview potential subjects. With interviews and events on tape, they review the material, select the best footage, and edit it into a program of a predetermined length. As with a newscast producer, they must also weave in graphics, voice-overs, music, and other effects.

Whereas newscast and documentary producers rely upon their news judgment, producers of dramatic and comedy series rely on their sense of entertainment. They come up with ideas for programs and hire the talent who can help them execute these ideas. They write scripts from these ideas or hire freelance writers, and they audition actors and cast them in roles.

WHAT IS IT LIKE TO BE A TELEVISION PRODUCER?

Beth Jensen has worked as a television producer at KELO-TV, a CBS affiliate in Sioux Falls, South Dakota, for nine years. "I started at KELO producing the 5:00 and 10:00 P.M. newscasts," she recalls. "Then I moved to mornings. I then spent four years

reporting during the week and producing the Saturday morning show. I became a full-time producer five years ago. I started with the 10:00 newscast, moved to the 6:00, and added executive producer responsibilities. And now I don't have a regular newscast; I am executive producer and work with the producers on their shows."

Beth's workday begins as soon as she wakes up in the morning. "I watch our morning newscast to see what's happened overnight," she says, "and what stories we might be working on during the day. While I'm still at home, I also watch national news, read the local paper, and check out news Web sites to get story ideas." Beth arrives at work in time for a daily 9:00 A.M. meeting. "Reporters, photographers, production assistants, producers, and anyone else who has story ideas gather in a circle to share story ideas," she explains. "We divide our morning meeting into two rounds. First, we go around pitching what we consider to be potential lead stories. Then we go around again and pitch everything else. Reporters are given their assignments at the meeting, and we discuss the focus of their stories before they set up shoots. Then I work with reporters and producers during the day as stories develop. As it gets closer to show time, I read through the newscasts to check the content. And when all of our hard work airs, I watch the shows to see how the stories were executed."

Beth has other duties in addition to her daily responsibilities. "I work on the professional development of the producers," she says. "We meet monthly to see how we're working on our news goals. I

Lingo to Learn

AVID A brand of a popular computer editing system; allows the editor to edit film on a computer.

gaffer Working with the *grip* (the person who maintains the equipment throughout production), the technician who serves as head of the electrical department.

postproduction Editing, sound, effects, and the other work done on a project after principal photography is completed.

shot composition How all the elements in a camera shot are arranged, or composed.

stock footage Segments of film or video kept in a library and reused in various broadcasts.

talent The on-air personalities who anchor, or narrate, a broadcast; the actors and extras who appear on camera in dramatic productions.

To Be a Successful Television Producer, You Should . . .

- have well-developed writing skills
- be organized and detail oriented
- have business training so you can deal with budgets and other financial concerns
- have strong people skills
- be willing to travel and work long hours
- be able to handle stress and meet deadlines

also work with our news director on the goals of the newsroom and work toward those goals. It's also my responsibility to schedule producers and production assistants."

DO I HAVE WHAT IT TAKES TO BE A TELEVISION PRODUCER?

A producer, whether working on series television, newscasts, or specials, must have writing skills—as a producer you'll be writing news copy and scripts. Because you're responsible for bringing together many different elements of a program, you must have good organizational skills. Producers on some projects are responsible for budgeting and other financial concerns, so a head for business can be beneficial to you, as well.

Producers work with teams of professionals and must be able to bring people together to work on the single goal of completing a project. "One of the best parts of my job," Beth says, "is working with the producers on their shows. We have an extremely talented group of producers and I love watching them develop their potential."

HOW DO I BECOME A TELEVISION PRODUCER?
Education

High School
It's very important to take composition, English, and other classes that help you to develop writing skills. Journalism courses, with emphasis on news reporting, are valuable. On your high school newspaper or with a school radio station, you may be able to gain some editing and producing experience. A local radio or TV station may offer high school students part-time work or internships.

If you're less interested in news and more interested in entertainment, your drama department could provide you with valuable experience; most theatrical productions require people working behind the scenes to organize, promote, and seek funding. Such experience can give you a sense of a producer's responsibilities.

Postsecondary Training
Producers of news programs are often graduates of journalism schools. Most universities across the country have journalism, or communications, departments, and many of these departments offer

courses in broadcasting. Though a broadcast journalism degree is valuable to someone looking for work in TV news, it's not required. Actually, some news departments prefer students with a broader education; many news directors complain that today's journalism school graduates don't have an adequate understanding of history, geography, and political science.

When choosing a journalism school, make sure the school offers opportunities for hands-on experience, whether through participating network affiliates, or through its own broadcasting stations. Also, make sure the school has a good internship program, and that the school makes strong efforts to place its graduating students in jobs. Beth majored in broadcast journalism at Boston University. During this time, she interned at KDLT, an NBC affiliate in Sioux Falls, during two summers. She also spent a semester in London taking classes and interning at CNN, as well as a summer in Washington, D.C., interning on Capitol Hill. In addition to participating in internships, Beth worked at her college's TV station and daily newspaper.

For those wanting to produce series television, courses offered by a theater or film department can give you a sense of dramatic structure. At a film school, you'll learn much about the business, as well as make connections with people wanting to help young filmmakers.

Internships and Volunteerships

An internship with a television news department frequently leads to full-time employment with that same department upon graduation. Because of this, intern-

---

Advancement Possibilities

News anchors lead the broadcast on camera; they read news copy from a TelePrompTer and introduce taped and live reports on issues such as health, finance reports, weather, and sports.

News directors lead the news staff, directing the producers, reporters, and editors; determine the newsworthy events to be covered; and assign news staff to specific stories.

General managers manage the operations of TV stations; they're involved in marketing, promotion, contracts, and public relations activities.

---

ships can be highly competitive and many students must take nonpaying internships. The paid internships are the most valuable; federal law limits the amount of work unpaid interns are allowed to do for a station. Only with a paid internship can you get the full experience of working for a TV newscast. Your journalism school should have some connections to internships; some schools are visited annually by recruiters from TV and radio stations. Your local stations should also offer internship opportunities. And check the World Wide Web for internship listings from all across the country.

WHO WILL HIRE ME?

The job of producer is not an entry-level position. You will need to "pay your dues" by gaining experience working with different equipment and people. Internships are often the best way to break into the business. Interns are frequently offered paid positions after they graduate from school. This is what happened in Beth's case. She was hired after graduation as a reporter by the television station for which she had interned.

WHERE CAN I GO FROM HERE?

Within a newscast, a producer may move up to news director or into station management. Some producers for network television move on to produce their own projects for independent production companies.

WHAT ARE THE SALARY RANGES?

Though producers with their own production companies, like producers for network television, can make well over $200,000 a year, most producers working on newscasts earn considerably less. Bringing in the big paychecks as a producer for television comes from years of hard work, good luck, and well-established connections. But good producers don't generally enter the field with big money in mind—they love the work. Producers who don't make a great deal of money benefit in other ways: they often call all the shots and have control of a project. They get to make the creative decisions that shape the broadcast.

According to the U.S. Department of Labor, producers and directors earned salaries that ranged from less than $26,870 to more than $141,500 in 2005. Producers and directors employed in radio and television broadcasting earned mean annual salaries of $58,210.

Producers who are full-time, salaried employees of stations or networks typically receive benefits such as health insurance and paid vacation and sick days. Independent producers must provide these extras for themselves.

Related Jobs

- art directors
- artists and repertoire managers
- assignment editors
- assistant directors
- casting directors
- directors of photography
- executive producers
- film editors
- motion-picture directors
- news anchors
- online producers
- production managers
- radio directors
- radio producers
- reporters
- screenwriters
- sound editors
- stage managers
- television directors

WHAT IS THE JOB OUTLOOK?

New cable networks with original programming are developing at a rapid rate; and many more networks are expected to develop as technology allows for cable companies to offer more channels. Freelance opportunities will also increase as these cable companies look to independent production companies for the bulk of their programming. TV producers must keep track of advancing technology; not only will they be required to understand various computer-assisted techniques, but broadcasting is also becoming more closely involved with the Internet and interactive television.

Producers will continue to be in demand to put together newscasts: newsrooms provide TV stations with healthy profits every year, and this is not expected to change. But the number of students graduating from broadcast journalism departments is also growing. There are currently more than 200 broadcast journalism programs in the country, and their students don't account for all the people seeking work in broadcasting; because news directors hire graduates from many different programs (and some prefer to hire graduates with more well-rounded liberal arts degrees), there's growing competition for the available positions.

Weather Forecasters

SUMMARY

Definition
Weather forecasters compile and analyze weather information and prepare reports for daily and nightly newscasts. They create graphics, write scripts, and explain weather maps to audiences. They also provide special reports during extreme weather conditions.

Alternative Job Titles
Broadcast meteorologists

Weathercasters
Weather reporters

Salary Range
$25,000 to $43,000 to $300,000+

Educational Requirements
Bachelor's degree

Certification or Licensing
Voluntary

Employment Outlook
More slowly than the average

High School Subjects
Agriculture

Chemistry
Earth science
Mathematics
Speech

Personal Interests
Broadcasting
Computers
Current events
The environment
Helping people: protection
Science

Still stuck at the TV station after two full days, Ed Piotrowski wades through the constantly changing weather information transmitted from the National Hurricane Center (also known as the Tropical Prediction Center), the Storm Prediction Center (formerly known as the Severe Storms Forecast Center), and other sources. The hurricane has approached Myrtle Beach, South Carolina, and people are keeping close to their radios and TVs. They're all relying on Ed, and the other meteorologists in the region, to provide them with reliable information—listening closely to all broadcast reports to help them determine what precautions to take to protect their homes and their lives.

Interrupting regular programming, Ed broadcasts live from in front of his computer equipment. He very calmly relates the information he has analyzed, telling his viewers everything he can about the hurricane—its position, where it's expected to go, and what it will mean to the city. Though these storms are dangerous, fickle, and frightening, Ed takes it as his responsibility to inform and instruct his viewers, to keep them calm and safe.

WHAT DOES A WEATHER FORECASTER DO?

El Niño. F5-rated tornadoes storming down tornado alley. Heat waves and ice storms. Flood-started fires in North Dakota. Hurricanes Andrew, Hugo, Betsy, and Katrina. Extreme weather conditions often become national celebrities while the citizens of the threatened cities suffer. These people look to TV and radio *weather forecasters* to advise them of upcoming storms, how to prepare for them, and how to recover from them. But weather forecasters aren't just on the air during extreme conditions—they're on radio and TV broadcasts many times every day. Though one day you may be relying on your local forecaster to help you prepare for a midnight tornado, another day you may simply want to know whether to leave the house with an umbrella.

Some weather forecasters are reporters with broadcasting degrees, but more than half of TV and radio weather forecasters have degrees in meteorology. Meteorology is the science of the atmosphere, and colleges across the country offer courses and degrees in meteorology for people who want to work for broadcast stations, weather services, research centers, flight centers, universities, and other places that study and record the weather. With a good background in the atmospheric sciences, broadcast weather forecasters can make informed predictions about the weather, and can clearly explain these predictions to the public.

The weather centers of your local radio and TV stations compile data from a variety of sources. They interpret the data, and report it to the viewing and listening public. The data they receive is compiled by various weather stations around the world; even the weather conditions swirling over the oceans can affect the weather of states far inland, so your local weather forecaster keeps track of the weather affecting distant cities. Weather stations and ships at sea record atmospheric measurements, information that is then transmitted to other weather stations for analysis. This information makes its way to the National Weather Service in Washington, D.C., where meteorologists develop forecasts, which they then send on to regional centers across the country. Broadcast weather forecasters receive this data. They also read information from radar, computers, satellites, and charts.

With the aid of computers, broadcast weather forecasters turn all this data into your daily weather report. They prepare maps and graphics to aid the viewers. Broadcasting the information means reading and explaining the weather forecast to viewers and listeners. Many people look to TV and radio news for weather information to help them plan events and vacations. Farmers are often able to protect their crops by following weather forecasts and advisories. The weather forecast is a staple element of most TV and radio newscasts. Some cable and radio stations broadcast weather reports 24 hours a day; most local network affiliates broadcast

Lingo to Learn

advisory A report on weather conditions that may lead to hazards but don't pose immediate dangers.

barometer An instrument that measures atmospheric pressure.

cold front The edge of a cold air mass that moves forward and displaces warmer air, leading to dropping temperatures and humidity.

Doppler radar An electronic instrument that measures atmospheric motion of objects such as precipitation.

heat index Not the actual temperature, but a number that describes the combination of temperature and humidity.

NEXRAD Next-generation weather radar; a network of Doppler radars.

reports during morning, noon, and evening newscasts, as well as provide extended weather coverage during storms and other extreme conditions.

In addition to broadcasting weather reports, radio and TV weather forecasters often visit schools and community centers to speak on weather safety. They are also frequently involved in broadcast station promotions, taking part in community events.

WHAT IS IT LIKE TO BE A WEATHER FORECASTER?

The people of Myrtle Beach, South Carolina, look to Ed Piotrowski of WPDE-TV for information on approaching hurricanes and other weather events. "Don't go into TV weather just to be on TV," Ed advises. "You must have a passion for the weather to do a fantastic job." Ed has had this passion ever since he was a kid. "All through grade school I would run out and tell people all about the weather." This passion eventually led him to an internship that helped him realize that TV was the place for him. "I realized how cool it is to be the first person to tell everyone about weather changes." As chief meteorologist for WPDE, Ed is responsible for delivering the forecast for radio and three television evening newscasts. "I also manage a staff of three, and several interns."

His day often begins with a visit to a local school, where he talks to students about weather and safety. The visit is tape recorded for later broadcast. "I head to the weather center at around 2:00 P.M. and prepare graphics and the forecast for the nightly shows." After the newscast at 6:00 P.M., Ed takes a dinner break then returns for the 10:00 P.M. and 11:00 P.M. shows.

Preparing the forecast means interpreting a great deal of data from a variety of different sources. The station receives weather information from the National Center for Environmental Prediction, the National Hurricane Center, the local National Weather Service offices, and the Storm Prediction Center (formerly known as the Severe Storms Forecast Center). Data also comes in from many different cities around the world. "All the data collected is put into many computer programs with various scientific formulas. These programs eventually put out weather scenarios for several different times in the future. Our job is to interpret these and make our forecast accordingly."

Though Ed relies on his education and background in meteorology to work with the various tools of the weather center, he points out that weather computers vary in their operation. "Most of this is learned on the job," he says. And the technology is rapidly changing. "Doppler radar is constantly evolving. The computers are getting fancier and faster."

While presenting the forecast on the air, Ed is doing many things behind the scenes. "There's a lot of switching and moving around that the viewer doesn't see because we are masking it with graphics." The viewing audience sees Ed in front of a weather map, but actually he's just standing in front of a plain blue wall called a "chromakey." Ed watches the monitor for the visuals, and points to the map based on what he sees on the TV screen. During the forecast, the newscast producer gives Ed time cues (the amount of time left in the presentation) through an IFB—a hearing device hidden in Ed's ear.

During hurricanes, Ed has even more responsibilities—and a whole different set of rules. "People like to see someone they think is their friend. But during hurricanes, we don't want to be on TV joking around. We need to interpret the data to give people the scenario we think will play out in our area upon landfall. It could be the difference between life and death."

Adam Behrman has been a meteorologist since December 2005. He works for Wyomedia at KTWO-TV in Casper,

Wyoming. "I have been fascinated by and interested in weather since I was a little boy," he says. "I used to watch the Weather Channel when I was five years old. So it has always been my intent to go into weather in some form or another."

To prepare for his day, Adam wakes up at 2:45 A.M. and is usually at work by 3:45 A.M. "The first thing I do is create a forecast," he says. "Since Casper is the only town in Wyoming with TV stations, I forecast for the entire state. I receive all my information from the Internet. After about an hour and 15 minutes, I am done forecasting and ready to start creating graphics. I use a weather graphics program called Galileo to create and render my graphics. This usually takes about an hour to finish. This leaves me with some

To Be a Successful Weather Forecaster, You Should . . .

- have a strong interest in the weather and the environment in general

- be good at math and science and have computer skills

- speak clearly and be able to explain weather maps, conditions, forecasts, and other meteorological data

- have an outgoing personality and enjoy meeting people and participating in community-related events

time to prepare for our 6 A.M. show called *Good Morning Wyoming.*" Adam gives the weather forecast six times during the hour-long show and he also chats with the host at the beginning, middle, and end of the show. "From 7:00 to 9:00," he says, "we do *Good Morning America* inserts every half hour, during which we do a quick insert of local news and weather. At 9:00, I go to a news meeting in which all the reporters discuss which stories they are doing for the day. I usually start getting the graphics ready for the noon show by 11:15 A.M. At 12:00 P.M., I do the news and then I go home at 12:30. Throughout the day, I also update the station's Web page forecast and respond to e-mails."

DO I HAVE WHAT IT TAKES TO BE A WEATHER FORECASTER?

To be a good weather forecaster, you need to have a strong interest in weather and the environment. An understanding of math and science is important to a broadcast meteorologist because using charts and formulas is essential to predicting the weather. You should also have computer skills, as you'll be using computer data transmitted from weather centers, as well as preparing graphics for broadcast. Because you'll be on air a lot, you should have good speaking skills and be capable of clearly explaining weather maps and forecasts.

"To be successful," Ed Piotrowski says, "it's important to have an outgoing personality as well as a solid background in meteorology. You need the personality on light weather days, and you really need good meteorology skills when talking about hurricanes." Ed appreciates the opportunities to meet a lot of people and to attend many events. And he appreciates his viewers' patience with the uncertainty of weather forecasts. "You can blow the forecast and still have a job the next day!"

But Ed wishes he could have a more regular schedule; his schedule depends on the radar. "And it can be demanding with all the public appearances you make," he says.

HOW DO I BECOME A WEATHER FORECASTER?
Education

Ed Piotrowski received a bachelor of science in meteorology from North Carolina State, and then learned a great deal about TV weather from an internship with WCTI-TV in North Carolina. "It was the best thing I ever did to start my career," he says. "It taught me many things that I didn't learn in college. It was great on-the-job experience." Ed got this training on his own, by actually calling the TV station and asking if he could come in and watch the weather department at work. "Next thing you know, I was spending three to five days a week there learning all about TV weather. It was tough to understand at first, but the more I did things, the more I learned about being an on-camera meteorologist."

High School

Math and science courses will help you prepare for a college meteorology program.

Join a school science group, or organize one that focuses on atmospheric research. "If you already know you're going to be a meteorologist," says Ed Piotrowski, "it's important to take high school courses that include computers, higher levels of mathematics, chemistry, physics, geography, and even oceanography. Remember, 75 percent of the earth is water, and there is a tremendous amount of air/sea interaction when it comes to what weather will occur in your neighborhood. Additionally, if television is the way to go for you, speech classes will help with your delivery and build confidence." High school students should also take English and composition courses to develop their writing skills. Become involved with your high school newspaper or radio station to gain broadcast experience.

Ed recommends that students interested in the field should, first and foremost, call a local television station and ask the meteorologist if they can schedule a visit. "This person can answer many questions about the business. What goes on behind the scenes? How do you make forecasts? How do you make the graphics? What college would be best for me? I did exactly this and learned so much about television broadcasting. Some see this and decide it's not for them, while others quickly gain a passion for it!"

Postsecondary Training

Though a degree in meteorology isn't required of broadcast weather forecasters, it is very valuable—and you'll need such a degree to advance in the profession. Talk to your high school guidance counselor about these programs. The

Advancement Possibilities

Chief meteorologists head the weather centers of newscasts; they direct staffs of weather reporters, assistants, and interns.

News anchors host radio and television newscasts.

General managers manage the daily operations of TV and radio stations; they're involved in marketing, promotion, contracts, and public relations.

American Meteorological Society (AMS) offers a listing of schools, with extensive information about each program, at its Web site (http://www.ametsoc.org/amsu-car_curricula/index.cfm). More than 100 programs are listed at the AMS Web site, offering such courses as atmospheric measurements, thermodynamics and chemistry, radar, cloud dynamics, and physical climatology.

Certification or Licensing

The American Meteorological Society offers three certification programs: the certified broadcast meteorologist program, the seal of approval, and the certified consulting meteorologist program. In addition, the National Weather Association (NWA) also offers a seal of approval to broadcast meteorologists. Contact the AMS and NWA for information on eligibility requirements. Certification isn't required for broadcast weather forecasters to work in the business, but it will give you an edge when looking for a job.

Internships and Volunteerships

Most local radio and TV stations provide internship opportunities for student weather forecasters. While in college, Ed Piotrowski participated in an internship at WCTI-TV in New Bern, North Carolina. "Honestly," he says, "it was the best thing I ever did to kick-start my career. I learned a tremendous amount while at North Carolina State University, but much of my experience in computers, forecasting, and presentation came while interning. I had a great boss who helped me understand forecasting, gave me free reign on learning the graphics systems, and allowed me to make videotapes on the big blue wall to polish my skills. You can't buy experience like this . . . it's invaluable! An internship on your résumé looks so much better to a prospective employer than just a college degree. Keep in mind that you are normally not paid for an internship. What you don't get monetarily you more than make up for in experience!"

Adam Behrman says he landed an internship by e-mailing a lot of television stations in both the Toledo and Columbus, Ohio, areas. "I ended up getting the one I was hoping for in Toledo with WTOL-TV working for Robert Shiels," he recalls. "During my internship I would arrive at 3:00 P.M. and organize all the weather data that came in on printouts. Then I would make up a forecast, and Robert would tweak it however he saw fit. I also gained valuable experience working with the graphics system they had. Sometimes the job was a lot of fun, especially when we got to go on live shots to different locations. After the 6 P.M. show, I would practice doing the weather in front of a green screen. I got to make a tape by the end of the internship, which I used to get this job."

If your school doesn't have an internship program, contact the chief meteorologists of local stations. Internships offer valuable experience, and often lead to full-time employment. There can be a lot of competition for paid internships, however, and you may have to make do with volunteer work for a station to gain experience. Though your duties are limited in a volunteer situation, you can still learn a lot about the business and make connections. Some undergraduate programs offer students paid research opportunities, but most research and teaching assistantships are open only to graduate students.

WHO WILL HIRE ME?

Ed Piotrowski's first full-time job was with the TV station where he interned. "I was very fortunate," he says. "I showed great initiative and the weekend job opened up right around the time I graduated." Ed held the weekend position for one year, and then went to work on the station's morning newscast for two years. He's held his current position as chief meteorologist at WPDE-TV for 12 years.

If your internship doesn't lead to full-time job opportunities, you can check your local ads or job listings on the Internet. The AMS and NWA send members job listings, and also post job openings on their Web pages. Most broadcast meteorologists work for network television affiliates and local radio stations; because evening national newscasts don't have weather forecasts, there are few network opportunities for broadcast meteorologists. National cable networks like the Weather Channel and 24-hour news channels hire weather forecasters and offer internships.

With a degree in meteorology, you can work for a variety of other services as well—the U.S. government is the largest employer of meteorologists in the country. Meteorologists work for the National Weather Service, the military, the Department of Agriculture, and other agencies.

WHERE CAN I GO FROM HERE?

Someone forecasting for a network affiliate in a smaller region may want to move to a larger city and a larger audience. In many cases, though, meteorologists work up within one station. Full-time broadcast meteorologists generally start forecasting for the weekend news, or the morning news, then move up to the evening news. A meteorologist may then become chief meteorologist, in charge of a newscast's weather center and staff.

In five or 10 years, Ed Piotrowski hopes to continue working as a weather forecaster at WPDE-TV in Myrtle Beach. "I feel very comfortable here," he says, "and will continue to attend conferences around the country to stay up on cutting-edge technology and forecast techniques. My goal is to never let the competing television station beat me! It is also very important not to worry about climbing the ladder to get to the top markets for top pay. At that high level, it doesn't matter how good you are. One day you have a job, the next you could be out the door for no apparent reason. As your career unfolds, there will be a place you really like and in which you feel at home. While the pay isn't as good, there is much more stability in small markets. In small to mid-size markets, the longer you stay, the more attached people get to you and, as long as you continue to do your job well, the more likely management will be to want to keep you there. If they know you are the reason people are watching your station, they'll pay a decent salary to keep you there."

"I don't really care where I end up," says Adam Behrman, "which is a good attitude to have in this business. My only concern is that I end up at a station that doesn't encourage me to change my forecasts to get better ratings, and that I am making considerably more money than I am now."

Fast Fact

Would you believe that late night funnyman David Letterman was once a TV weather forecaster in his native Indiana? During his short career he once predicted hail the size of canned hams!

WHAT ARE THE SALARY RANGES?

In the newsroom, weather forecasters generally make more than sportscasters but less than lead anchors. The salary for weather forecasters varies greatly according to experience and region. In some of the smallest markets, a weather forecaster can expect to make around $25,000 per year; in the largest markets, a weather forecaster may make $100,000. The median for forecasters across the country is around $43,000.

In some top stations in large cities, a TV weather forecaster can become something of a local celebrity, attracting higher ratings for the station. Popular weather forecasters with large audiences have been known to command over $300,000 a year.

Related Jobs

- climatologists
- disc jockeys
- geologists
- geophysicists
- hydrographers
- mathematicians
- mineralogists
- news anchors
- oceanographic assistants
- physicists
- reporters
- seismologists
- sportscasters
- stratigraphers
- weather observers

WHAT IS THE JOB OUTLOOK?

Meteorology is greatly affected by technological advances. New tools and computer programs for the compilation and analysis of data are constantly being developed by research scientists. Future broadcast meteorologists will need a lot of technical expertise, in addition to their understanding of weather. With these projected developments, forecasters will be able to predict the weather weeks in advance, and someday, even months in advance.

Usually, meteorologists are able to find work in the field upon graduation, though they may have to be flexible about the area of meteorology and the region of the country in which they work. Positions for broadcast meteorologists, as with any positions in broadcast news, are in high demand. The number of news departments and news staff is expected to increase at a steady rate, but the growing number of graduates looking for work in news departments will keep the field very competitive. Currently about half of TV and radio weather forecasters do not hold meteorology degrees; with increased competition for work, forecasters without extensive backgrounds in the atmospheric sciences may find it difficult to get jobs.

But a national fascination with weather may lead to more outlets for broadcast meteorologists. Look for more cable weather information channels like The Weather Channel to develop. Weather disasters are requiring more coverage by news departments; in addition to forecasting, broadcast meteorologists will be involved in reporting about the aftereffects of storms and other extreme conditions. Many people look to the Internet for global and regional weather information, so look for broadcast and Internet weather resources to merge. Broadcast meteorologists are becoming more actively involved in developing and maintaining pages on the World Wide Web.

SECTION 3

Do It Yourself

"What are you going to do after high school?" How many times have you heard that question? If you haven't heard it yet, you will . . . and for a while it may seem like you hear it every five minutes. You might try these replies to shock and appall your neighbors and relatives: 1) "I'm not finishing high school," 2) "I'm supposed to do something after high school?" 3) "Spend all my time writing poetry for my Web page," or 4) "I'm going into broadcasting." Okay . . . most people won't be appalled that you want to pursue a career in broadcasting, but they probably will realize just how tough it can be to get a job in radio and television. Broadcast journalism schools are being criticized for sending graduates out into the world unprepared for the intense competition for the limited number of jobs. Ownership of radio stations is frequently changing hands, resulting in lost jobs or combined positions. News departments can't afford to hire all the reporters they need, so there are always many applicants for the few available job openings and internships. And if you want to direct, produce, or write for the major networks and cable stations, your road to success is even rockier. But enough of the doom and gloom; for the ambitious, talented, well-trained, and well-educated student of broadcasting, there are many great opportunities and potential career paths. And if you start pursuing your career while still in high school, you'll be well ahead of the game.

Once you decide to answer the world's questions with choice four—"I'm going into broadcasting"—you're likely to be met with even more questions. The creative side or the technical side? Will you work in the news division or the entertainment division? Will you work on camera or off camera? People will ask these questions because if there's one industry everybody knows about, it's the TV and radio industry. Maybe you have a good answer already. Perhaps you've been passionate about the weather since you were a kid, standing in the middle of storms, watching the movement of ominous clouds and performing rain dances. "I'll be a TV meteorologist," you say. Or maybe you've been active in sports ever since you could first lift a baseball bat, and see sports announcing in your future. Or perhaps you drove your family crazy when you were kid by playing Mom's records day and night—you're a future radio disc jockey if there ever was one. For many people, careers in radio and TV speak to lifelong passions. So why not get started as early as you can? When people start asking you, "What are you going to do after high school?", wouldn't it be great to tell them what you're doing now, while you're still in high school?

Even in the smallest towns, there are extracurricular activities that can help you develop valuable experience—school newspapers, yearbooks, and drama and media clubs. You probably even have better opportunities than high school students of 10 years ago; now, many high schools are running their own radio stations and TV video departments. And if none of these clubs and departments exist in your school? That's even better—you'll have the chance to be a pioneer in your school, setting up new programs and gaining hands-on experience. The following paragraphs provide suggestions on things you can do to experience the field of broadcasting right now while you are still in high school.

❏ READ BOOKS AND PERIODICALS

Looking for detailed information on radio and television careers? One great place to start is your local or school library. There, you'll find books and periodicals about broadcasting specialties; famous disc jockeys, actors, and directors; competitions; the history of radio and television; and almost any other broadcasting-related topic you can think of. For a great list of books and periodicals about broadcasting, turn to Section 4 and read "Get Involved" and "Read a Book."

❏ SURF THE WEB

As a tech-savvy teenager, you're probably already familiar with the Internet. You may use it to research school papers, communicate with friends, and download music. But did you know that the Web also offers a treasure trove of resources for those who are interested in broadcasting? You can surf the Web to find broadcasting associations, discussion groups, competitions, educational programs, glossaries, company information, worker profiles and interviews—and the list goes on and on. So log on and begin educating yourself about broadcasting! To help get you started, we've prepared a list of what we think are the best broadcasting sites on the Web. Check out Section 4 and consult "Surf the Web" for more info.

❏ FAMILIARIZE YOURSELF WITH THE TOOLS OF THE TRADE

If you are participating in TV club or a radio station at your high school, then you have already been introduced to some of the tools of the broadcasting trade, such as microphones, recording and lighting equipment, and broadcasting-related software and hardware. If no such program exists at your school, you can still learn about the field on your own. For example, if you are interested in broadcast engineering, you could check out basic tools used by engineers such as wire cutters, screwdrivers, and pliers. If you are interested in weather forecasting, you could learn more about how to use barometers, thermometers, and other basic weather-measuring devices. If you're interested in becoming a broadcaster, you can purchase a microphone and tape recorder, and write and record your own news, sports, or weather forecast. You get the idea.

❏ VISIT A MUSEUM

Although not as ubiquitous as art, science, or natural history museums, broadcasting museums can be an excellent way to learn more about the history of broadcasting, early and cutting-edge technology, and industry pioneers. In these museums, you can also view radio receivers, transmitters, and televisions from the early days of broadcasting, watch tapes of early television shows, and create your own radio broadcast in a workshop setting. Some broadcasting museums may offer educational programs and internship opportunities to aspiring broadcasters. This is a great way to get involved in the museum, to really learn a subject, and to meet people in the industry. Talk to one of your teachers about a field trip to the museum—maybe volunteer to coordinate a field trip with a particular lesson. Of course, you can always go on your own or with some friends on a weekend or day off. One of the best-known broadcast museums is the Museum of Broadcast Communications (http://www.museum.tv/home.php) in Chicago, Illinois, which opened a new 70,000-square-foot facility in 2006. Its collection includes more than 85,000 hours of radio and television programming; artifacts such as vintage radios and televisions, costumes, and puppets; and photographs and printed materials. The museum offers a variety of educational programs and volunteer and internship opportunities.

If you don't live near the Museum of Broadcast Communications, try to find broadcasting museums near you by contacting local chambers of commerce or visiting your town or city's Web site. For more information about broadcasting museums, you can also turn to Section 4 to read "Get Involved."

❏ JOIN AN ASSOCIATION

Many broadcasting professional associations offer membership to college students. Membership benefits include the chance to participate in association-sponsored competitions, seminars, and conferences; subscriptions to magazines that provide the latest industry informa-

tion (some of them geared specifically toward students); mentoring and networking opportunities; and access to financial aid. The Society of Broadcast Engineers (http://www.sbe.org) offers membership to college students, as well as to high school students who are active in the technical operation of a broadcast station; are involved in a broadcasting-related school club or community organization; and have a general interest in broadcast engineering. Visit the "Look to the Pros" chapter in Section 4 for more information on associations that offer student membership.

❏ MAKE THE MOST OF YOUR SUMMER VACATION

Another good way to learn more about radio and television is to participate in broadcasting-related summer programs at colleges and universities. This will give you the opportunity to meet other young people who are interested in the field and help you to learn more about career opportunities in broadcasting. Summer programs usually consist of workshops, seminars, and other activities that introduce you to broadcasting. You'll also get a chance to talk with broadcasting students and faculty—so have your list of questions about the field ready. Summer programs are covered in depth in "Get Involved" in Section 4.

❏ BROADCAST JOURNALISM IN SCHOOL

One of the easiest ways to get started in broadcasting may already exist in your own school: TV clubs and radio stations are popping up in high schools all over the country. Students are producing and directing their own programming, as well as learning how to operate cameras and other necessary equipment. For example, a high school in Dearborn, Michigan, has involved students in a video club for several years now, and alumni of the program have gone on to direct films, produce television series, and succeed in other high-profile careers in the industry.

If your school doesn't currently have such a program, try to get one started. Ask a journalism or English teacher, or any interested faculty member, for help and guidance. Research other high school broadcasting departments. Visit any local radio and TV stations, and see what instructional and financial help they can offer. Price video and other equipment, and come up with a complete proposal outlining expenses, staff requirements, and the educational benefits to the students. You may not actually see the final results while still in high school—such programs can take years to develop. But you'll still be able to learn a lot about broadcasting in the process.

It's true that your school simply may not be able to offer radio and TV clubs or classes due to the expense of broadcasting equipment or a lack of widespread interest. But virtually every high school has a school newspaper and yearbook, and you should seriously consider getting involved with the publications at your school. As a member of the staff, you will develop writing skills, which can be your most important asset in broadcast-

ing work. You'll also develop interviewing skills and be required to keep up with current events, politics, and cultural trends.

❑ PARTICIPATE IN THEATER AND DRAMA

Ever get in trouble for being the class clown? Your teachers may revise their criticism when you go on to great success as the writer for a network sitcom. Okay, that might be a long, difficult journey—or you may enjoy overnight success. That's the nature of the entertainment business—it's totally unpredictable. But if you're ready to take on the fierce competition of writing, directing, or producing for television dramas, comedies, and made-for-TV movies, there are ways to prepare while still in high school.

Just as some people are passionate about news and sports, others are passionate about performing and the arts. It's this passion that can help see the young writer/producer/director through the lean times. Without this passion, you may be better off entering a more secure profession—and becoming a doctor or a lawyer. But somebody has to create all the hundreds of episodes of soap operas, sitcoms, prime-time dramas, and other entertainment programs that air every year, so it might as well be you!

Your high school drama department can give you a taste of what goes into producing a show on a small scale. Most schools put much funding into sports programs (or even video and radio programs), leaving theater programs to struggle on their own. Actually, this creates a great chance for you to get actively involved in a production from beginning to end. You can get funding for a production by contacting local businesses for donations, or selling them ads to be placed in a playbill. Promotion can also be a big part of a radio and TV producer's job, and every high school theater department requires volunteers to publicize a production.

Your high school theater department probably offers great opportunities to young technicians interested in learning about production equipment. Lighting, sound, and set design are very important to the success of a stage play. As part of the technical crew, you'll probably also use camera, editing, and other video equipment to record the play.

You may think the drama club is only for actors, but it could give you the chance to write and direct your own plays as well. If not, propose a "junior" program to your drama club advisor—such a program can give high school students a chance to direct junior high or grade school students in original plays. Collaborate on a full-length play with other writers you know, or write your own one-act. Four or five student one-acts can make for a two-hour production, offering many student writers and directors the chance to cast their own plays, direct, and see their own projects performed for an audience.

In small towns, community theaters can always use volunteers for their productions. Or start your own community theater; the well-known playwright and director Sam Shepard honed his writing and directing skills by staging a different production every week in his own apartment.

Speech teams are often associated with high school theater departments. Whether your area of interest is news, radio, or entertainment, a speech team can help you develop speaking and writing skills. Such skills are very important to radio disc jockeys, news anchors, broadcast meteorologists, and sportscasters.

And don't forget about your community radio station; some stations are pleased to help talented young writers and performers produce original programs. Submit a script and proposal for a radio show, along with a tape of your work. When taping a radio show, you'll learn a lot about how a radio show is produced, and how a station is managed. Though the majority of radio stations today offer music-only formats, public radio stations broadcast variety shows, musical concerts, documentaries, and talk shows. Garrison Keillor started his *Prairie Home Companion* music and comedy program at Minnesota Public Radio; it is now broadcast nationally, and has spawned several books, audio recordings, and even a motion picture, *A Prairie Home Companion* (2006).

❏ BECOME AN INTERN OR VOLUNTEER

Though some high school students interested in writing, directing, and producing have their sights set high on national network jobs, others want to work in smaller cities and less stressful environments. Fortunately, many cities across the country have at least one network-affiliated TV station, and there are more than 13,000 radio stations operating in the United States. This means plenty of job opportunities for people wanting to work outside of California, New York, and Washington, D.C. It can also mean opportunities for you to learn about the industry while still in high school.

A simple way to begin exploring the radio and television industry—indeed, almost any industry—is to shadow a professional. Some schools have shadowing programs that can introduce you to a professional who will answer your questions and allow you to experience a typical day at the studio. If there is no formal program in place, perhaps a journalism teacher or guidance counselor can help you get in touch with a pro. Or ask your parents and your friends' parents if they have any contacts in the broadcasting industry. Make the effort to find a shadowing opportunity because it will show you the reality of the industry like nothing else can. Shadowing will help you make well-informed career decisions. And, if you get along well with the professional you shadow, it may lead to a volunteer, intern, or part-time position.

Volunteering and interning are crucial to securing employment in radio and television because experience counts in this competitive industry. Local stations may not have formal internship programs or they may only offer internships to college students; this is where your persistence can pay off. (Well, "pay off" in learning opportunities, not cash; you'll more than likely be working for free!) Let resistant station managers know how ambitious you are by getting to know them and making sure they know you. Send them a résumé with a list of your high school achievements, extracurricular activities, and course work. Include a cover letter that spells out exactly what kind of work you are willing to do (anything!) and when you are available (anytime outside of the school day!). Call news producers and other professionals to check with them about creating an internship position. And don't give up! Some stations initially may not be interested in training a high school student, but your determination might change a few minds.

If an internship just isn't a possibility, try to arrange a less formal position. Volunteer to come in whenever they need your help, perhaps with filing or mass mailing. Public television and radio stations frequently need volunteers to help with fund-raising and even production. While cataloguing videotapes or sorting mail is probably not your ultimate career goal, voluntarily performing such tasks clearly displays your commitment and dedication to the field. This kind of work can also help you make contacts that will prove useful when you've graduated from college and are looking for a job.

❑ CONCLUSION

Because there's so much competition for every broadcasting job available, the sooner you can get started pursuing your interests, the more experience you can gain. Your high school and your community probably already offer many programs in which you can participate.

But remember—don't be discouraged if there don't seem to be many chances to learn about broadcasting in your town. You can create your own chances by getting to know local professionals and other students who share your interests. Such efforts and persistence will lead you in the direction of a great future.

SECTION 4

What Can I Do Right Now?

Get Involved: A Directory of Camps, Programs, and Competitions

Now that you've read about some of the different careers available in radio and television broadcasting, you may be anxious to experience this line of work for yourself, to find out what it's really like. Or perhaps you already feel certain that this is the career path for you and want to get started on it right away. Whichever is the case, this section is for you! There are plenty of things you can do right now to learn about broadcasting careers while gaining valuable experience. Just as importantly, you'll get to meet new friends and see new places, too.

In the following pages you will find more than 30 programs run by organizations that want to work with young people interested in radio and television. All of them can help you turn your interest into a career, but none of them will prevent you from changing your mind or just keeping your options open. Some organizations offer just one kind of program: colleges, quite naturally, will probably offer only academic courses of study. Other organizations, such as TV stations, may offer internships and job opportunities in addition to voluntary field experiences. It's up to you to decide whether you're interested in one particular type of program or are open to a number of possibilities. The kinds of activities available are listed right after the name of the program or organization, so you can skim through to find the listings that interest you most.

❑ THE CATEGORIES

Camps

When you see an activity that is classified as a camp, don't automatically start packing your tent and mosquito repellent. Where academic study is involved, the term "camp" often simply means a residential program including both educational and recreational activities. It's sometimes hard to differentiate between such camps and other study programs, but if the sponsoring organization calls it a camp, so do we! For an extended list of camps, visit http://www.kidscamps.com.

College Courses/Summer Study

These terms are linked because most college courses offered to students your age must take place in the summer, when you are out of school. At the same time, many summer study programs are sponsored by colleges and universities that want to attract future students and give them a head start in higher education. Summer study of almost any type is a good idea because it keeps your mind and your study skills sharp over the long vacation. Summer study at a college offers any number of additional benefits, including giving you the tools to make a well-informed decision about your future academic career. Study options, including some impressive college and university programs, account for most of the listings in this section.

Competitions

Competitions are fairly self-explanatory, but you should know that there are only a few in this book because many broadcasting/journalism competitions are at the local and regional levels and would be impractical to list here. What this means, however, is that if you are interested in entering a competition, you shouldn't have much trouble finding one yourself. Your guidance counselor or journalism, broadcasting, or English teacher can help you start searching in your area.

Employment and Internship Opportunities

As you may already know from experience, employment opportunities for teenagers can be very limited. Even internships are most often reserved for college students who have completed at least one or two years of study in the field. Still, if you're very determined to find an internship or paid position in broadcasting, there may be ways to find one. See Section 3: Do It Yourself in this book for some suggestions.

Field Experience

This is something of a catchall category for activities that don't exactly fit the other descriptions. But anything called a field experience in this book provides a good opportunity to get out and explore the work of radio and television professionals.

Membership

When an organization appears in this category, it simply means that you are welcome to pay your dues and become a card-carrying member. Formally joining any organization brings the benefits of meeting others who share your interests, finding opportunities to get involved, and keeping up with current events. Depending on how active you are, the contacts you make and the experiences you gain may help when the time comes to apply to colleges or look for a job.

In some organizations, you pay a special student rate and receive benefits similar to regular members. Many organizations, however, are now starting student branches with their own benefits and publications. As in any field, make sure you understand exactly what the benefits of membership are before you join.

Finally, don't let membership dues discourage you from making contact with these organizations. Some charge dues as low as $10 because they know that students are perpetually short of funds. When the annual dues are higher, think of the money as an investment in your future and then consider if it is too much to pay.

PROGRAM DESCRIPTIONS

Once you've started to look at the individual listings themselves, you'll find that they contain a lot of information. Naturally, there is a general description of each program, but wherever possible we also have included the following details.

Application Information

Each listing notes how far in advance you'll need to apply for the program or position, but the simple rule is to apply as far in advance as possible. This ensures that you won't miss out on a great opportunity simply because other people got there ahead of you. It also means that you will get a timely decision on your application, so if you are not accepted, you'll still have some time to apply elsewhere. As for the things that make up your application—essays, recommendations, references—we've tried to tell you what's involved, but be sure to contact the program about specific requirements before you submit anything.

Background Information

This includes such information as the name of the organization that is sponsoring it financially and the faculty and staff who will be there for you. This can help you—and your family—gauge the quality and reliability of the program.

Classes and Activities

Classes and activities change from year to year, depending on popularity, the availability of instructors, and many other factors. Nevertheless, colleges and universities quite consistently offer the same or similar classes, even in their summer sessions. Courses like Introduction to Radio and Broadcasting 101, for exam-

ple, are simply indispensable. So you can look through the listings and see which programs offer foundational courses like these and which offer courses on more variable topics. As for activities, we note when you have access to recreational facilities on campus, and it's usually a given that special social and cultural activities will be arranged for most programs.

Contact Information

Wherever possible, we have given the title of the person whom you should contact instead of the name because people change jobs so frequently. If no title is given and you are telephoning an organization, simply tell the person who answers the phone the name of the program that interests you, and he or she will forward your call. If you are writing, include the line "Attention: Summer Study Program" (or whatever is appropriate after "Attention") somewhere on the envelope. This will help to ensure that your letter goes to the person in charge of that program.

Credit

Where academic programs are concerned, we sometimes note that high school or college credit is available to those who have completed them. This means that the program can count toward your high school diploma or a future college degree just like a regular course. Obviously, this can be very useful, but it's important to note that rules about accepting such credit vary from school to school. Before you commit to a program offering high school credit, check with your guidance counselor to see if it is acceptable to your school. As for programs offering college credit, check with your chosen college (if you have one) to see if the school will accept it.

Eligibility and Qualifications

The main eligibility requirement to be concerned about is age or grade in school. A term frequently used in relation to grade level is "rising," as in "rising senior": someone who will be a senior when the next school year begins. This is especially important where summer programs are concerned. A number of university-based programs make admissions decisions partly in consideration of GPA, class rank, and standardized test scores. This is mentioned in the listings, but you must contact the program for specific numbers. If you are worried that your GPA or your ACT scores, for example, aren't good enough, don't let them stop you from applying to programs that consider such things in the admissions process. Often, a fine essay or even an example of your dedication and eagerness can compensate for statistical weaknesses.

Facilities

We tell you where you'll be living, studying, eating, and having fun during these programs, but there isn't enough room to go into all the details. Some of those details can be important: what is and isn't accessible for people with disabilities, whether the site of a summer program has air-conditioning, and how modern the laboratory and computer equipment are. You can expect most program brochures and application materials to address these concerns, but if you still have questions about the facilities, just call the program's administration and ask.

Financial Details

While a few of the programs listed here are fully underwritten by collegiate and corporate sponsors, most of them rely on you for at least some of their funding. Prices and fees for 2006 are given here, but you should bear in mind that costs rise slightly almost every year. You and your parents must take costs into consideration when choosing a program. We always try to note where financial aid is available, but really, most programs will do their best to ensure that a shortage of funds does not prevent you from taking part.

Residential versus Commuter Options

Simply put, some programs prefer that participating students live with other participants and staff members, others do not, and still others leave the decision entirely to the students themselves. As a rule, residential programs are suitable for young people who live out of town or even out of state, as well as for local residents. They generally provide a better overview of college life than programs in which you're only on campus for a few hours a day, and they're a way to test how well you cope with living away from home. Commuter programs may be viable only if you live near the program site or if you can stay with relatives who do. Bear in mind that for residential programs especially, the travel between your home and the location of the activity is almost always your responsibility and can significantly increase the cost of participation.

❏ FINALLY . . .

Ultimately, there are three important things to bear in mind concerning all of the programs listed in this volume. The first is that things change. Staff members come and go, funding is added or withdrawn, supply and demand determine which programs continue and which terminate. Dates, times, and costs vary widely because of a number of factors. Because of this, the information we give you, although as current and detailed as possible, is just not enough on which to base your final decision. If you are interested in a program, you simply must write, call, fax, or e-mail the organization concerned to get the latest and most complete information available. This has the added benefit of putting you in touch with someone who can deal with your individual questions and problems.

Another important point to keep in mind when considering these programs is that the people who run them provided the information printed here. The editors of this book haven't attended the programs and don't endorse them: we simply give you the information with which to begin your own research. And after all, we can't pass judgment because you're the only one who can decide which programs are right for you.

The final thing to bear in mind is that the programs listed here are just the tip of the iceberg. No book can possibly cover all of the opportunities that are available to you—partly because they are so numerous and are constantly coming and going, but partly because some are waiting to be discovered. For instance, you may be very interested in taking a college course but don't see the college that interests you in the listings. Call their Admissions Office! Even if they don't have a special program for high school students, they might be able to make some kind of arrangements for you to visit or sit in on a class. Use the ideas behind these listings and take the initiative to turn them into opportunities!

❏ THE PROGRAMS
Academic Study Associates (ASA)
College Courses/Summer Study

Academic Study Associates has been offering residential and commuter pre-college summer programs for young people for more than 20 years. It offers college credit classes and enrichment opportunities in a variety of academic fields, including journalism, communications, and writing, at the University of Massachusetts–Amherst and the University of California–Berkeley, as well as institutions abroad. In addition to classroom work, students participate in field trips, mini-clinics, and extracurricular activities. Programs are usually three to four weeks in length. Fees and deadlines vary for these programs—visit the ASA's Web site for further details. Options are also available for middle school students.

Academic Study Associates (ASA)

ASA Programs
375 West Broadway, Suite 200
New York, NY 10012-4324
800-752-2250
summer@asaprograms.com
http://www.asaprograms.com/home/
asa_home.asp

American Collegiate Adventures (ACA)

College Courses/Summer Study

American Collegiate Adventures (ACA) offers high school students the chance to experience and prepare for college during their summer vacation. Adventures are based at Arizona State University in Tempe and the University of Wisconsin in Madison; they vary in length from three to six weeks. (Note: Study abroad options are available in Italy and Spain.) Participants attend college-level courses taught by university faculty during the week (for college credit or enrichment) and visit regional colleges and recreation sites over the weekend. All students live in comfortable en suite accommodations, just down the hall from an ACA resident staff member. Courses differ from year to year and place to place, but students interested in broadcasting can usually take TV Production and other classes involving both communications and technology. Contact American Collegiate Adventures for current course listings, prices, and application procedures.

American Collegiate Adventures

1811 West North Avenue, Suite 201
Chicago, IL 60622

800-509-7867
info@acasummer.com
http://www.zfc-consulting.com/
webprojects/americanadventures

American Institute for Foreign Study's Summer Advantage Program

College Courses/Summer Study

The American Institute for Foreign Study offers the Summer Advantage Program study abroad program for high school students who are interested in foreign language, culture, and other subjects. Applicants must be at least 16 years of age, have completed their sophomore year, and have a GPA of at least 2.5. Educational programs are available in China, England, France, Italy, Russia, and Spain. Students are immersed in the artistic and cultural history of their host countries, while taking up to eight credit hours. Contact the council for more information on program fees. Scholarships are available.

American Institute for Foreign Study

Summer Programs
River Plaza
9 West Broad Street
Stamford, CT 06902-3788
877-795-0813
accounts@acis.com
http://www.summeradvantage.com

American Meteorological Society

Employment and Internship Opportunities

The society offers links to employment and internship opportunities for aspiring meteorologists at its Web site.

American Meteorological Society

45 Beacon Street
Boston, MA 02108-3693
617-227-2425
amsinfo@ametsoc.org
http://www.ametsoc.org/
　amsstudentinfo/index.html

American Screenwriters Association

Field Experience

The association offers a high school outreach program, where students are instructed on how to write quality scripts for feature films, television, documentaries, and other media. The program is currently in development; contact the association for more information.

American Screenwriters Association

269 South Beverly Drive, Suite 2600
Beverly Hills, CA 90212-3807
866-265-9091
asa@goasa.com
http://www.goasa.com/highschool.
　shtml

Buck's Rock Performing and Creative Arts Camp

Camps

Buck's Rock Camp, about 85 miles from New York City, has been in existence since 1942. It features more than 30 different activities in creative, performing, and visual arts. The camp has its very own radio station, WBBC 89.3 FM. Here, as a radio broadcaster, you put on your own radio shows and act as a DJ for your favorite music. WBBC broadcasts news, reviews, talk shows, radio plays, and documentaries as well as music. You can work as an announcer, scriptwriter, or commentator. Experienced disc jockeys help you plan the content of your productions and understand the techniques of radio broadcasting.

Buck's Rock Camp is for 11- to 16-year-olds who are artistic, talented, and independent. At camp, you make your own schedule and participate in as many activities as you want to. You may spend all of your time at WBBC, or you may combine your broadcasting with the artistic and sports programs also on offer. Many students return to Buck's Rock year after year and go on to become counselors. If you're 16 to 18 years old, you can register for the Counselors-in-Training program and spend part of your day as a camper and part as a counselor. In this program, you receive a reduction in camp tuition.

Buck's Rock Camp has two four-week sessions and one eight-week session. Tuition for four weeks costs $5,790; the full season costs $7,960. This includes everything but transportation to the camp. Campers stay in cabins, eat in the dining room, and enjoy a full schedule of evening activities. You can get financial aid to help with tuition, and Buck's Rock likes to help as many campers as possible. To apply to the camp, you must fill out an enrollment form and attend a personal interview. To get your form, and to learn more, call, write, or e-mail the camp. You can also visit its Web site.

Buck's Rock Camp

59 Bucks Rock Road
New Milford, CT 06776-5311

800-636-5218
bucksrock@bucksrockcamp.com
http://www.bucksrockcamp.com

Camp Ballibay

Camps

Camp Ballibay, established in 1964, is accredited by the American Camping Association. It offers programs (two to nine weeks in length) in Video, Radio, Art, Photography, Theater, Music, Rock and Roll, Jazz, Horseback Riding, and Technical Theater for students ages 6 to 16. Campers in the Radio program learn about the field via classes and hands-on experience in the camp's radio studio. Campers stay in cabins and have access to a swimming pool, a riding area, tennis courts, sports fields, an infirmary, a camp store, and a dining hall. Tuition for this residential camp ranges from $1,950 to $6,250 depending on the length of the program. Contact Camp Ballibay for further information.

> **Camp Ballibay**
> 1 Ballibay Road
> Camptown, PA 18815
> 570-746-3223
> jannone@ballibay.com
> http://www.ballibay.com

Camp Chi

Camps

Camp Chi, located near the beautiful Wisconsin Dells, features many activities in the fine arts, athletics, and outdoor adventure. Included in the arts category are radio and TV broadcasting. If you are interested in radio, for example, you will spend time at the camp's radio station, WCHI, learning all about radio broadcasting: how to operate the systems, interview talk show guests, produce and direct shows, and be a DJ for your favorite music. After radio, you may choose to learn more about TV. Camp Chi has its own video studio where you can produce and direct TV shows, shoot and edit footage, and write scripts. TV and radio production is supervised by a staff member who specializes in that particular field.

In addition to all the activities, the camp, which is operated by the Jewish Community Centers of Chicago, has a heated swimming pool, a spring-fed lake with waterfront activities, a climbing and repelling wall, a roller hockey arena, rope courses, six tennis courts, and an animal farm. The staff-to-camper ratio is one to three. Camp Chi is for students ages 9 to 16. You stay in cabins with built-in bunk beds. If you're 14 to 16 years old, Camp Chi offers a separate village just for teens. Cost of the camp ranges from $1,050 to $3,995, depending on age level and program. This cost includes everything but transportation to the site. For an enrollment form, and to learn more about the camp, you can write, call, or e-mail. Visit Camp Chi's Web site, too.

> **Camp Chi**
> Summer Office
> PO Box 104
> Lake Delton, WI 53940-0104
> 608-253-1681
> info@campchi.com
> http://www.campchi.com

Winter Office
3050 Woodridge Road
Northbrook, IL 60062-7524
847-272-2301
info@campchi.com
http://www.campchi.com

Corporation for Public Broadcasting (CPB)
Employment and Internship Opportunities

The Corporation for Public Broadcasting (CPB) is a private, nonprofit organization that oversees American public radio, television, and online services. It is constantly updating its employment and internship opportunities. Most of its job openings are for adults with at least some college education, but you still might want to access the CPB Jobline on the Internet to see what opportunities are available.

Corporation for Public Broadcasting
401 Ninth Street NW
Washington, DC 20004-2129
http://www.cpb.org

Frontiers at Worcester Polytechnic Institute
College Courses/Summer Study

Frontiers is an on-campus research and learning experience for high school students who are interested in science, mathematics, and engineering. Areas of study include Biology and Biotechnology, Mathematics, Aerospace Engineering, Computer Science, Electrical and Computer Engineering, Mechanical Engineering, Physics, and Robotics. Participants

attend classes and do lab work Monday through Friday. Participants also have the opportunity to try out one of five communication modules: creative writing, elements of writing, music, speech, and theater. In addition to fulfilling the academic program, participants attend evening workshops, live performances, field trips, movies, and tournaments. Applications are typically available in January and due in March. Tuition is about $2,000; this covers tuition, room, board, linens, transportation, and entrance fees to group activities. A $500 nonrefundable deposit is required. For more information, contact the program director.

Worcester Polytechnic Institute
Frontiers Program
100 Institute Road
Worcester, MA 01609-2280
508-831-5286
frontiers@wpi.edu
http://www.admissions.wpi.edu/
  Frontiers

High School Honors Program/ Summer Challenge Program at Boston University
College Courses/Summer Study

Two summer educational opportunities are available for high school students interested in broadcasting and other majors. Rising high school seniors can participate in the High School Honors Program, which offers six-week, for-credit undergraduate study at the university. Students take two for-credit classes (up to eight credits) alongside regular Boston College students, live in dorms on campus, and participate in extracurricular activities and tours of local attractions. Recent classes included Fiction Screenwriting, Video Production, and Acting for Directors and Writers. The program typically begins in early July. Students who demonstrate financial need may be eligible for financial aid. Tuition for the program is approximately $3,750, which does not include registration/program fees ($350) or room and board ($1,701 to $1,832). Rising high school sophomores, juniors, and seniors in the university's Summer Challenge Program learn about college life and take college classes in a noncredit setting. The program lasts two weeks and is offered in three sessions. Students get to choose two seminars (which feature lectures, group and individual work, project-based assignments, and field trips) from a total of 10 available programs, including Mass Communications, Creative Writing, and Persuasive Writing. Students live in dorms on campus and participate in extracurricular activities and tours of local attractions. The cost of the program is approximately $2,750 (which includes tuition, a room charge, meals, and sponsored activities). Visit the university's Summer Programs Web site for more information.

Boston University Summer Programs

755 Commonwealth Avenue
Boston, MA 02215-1401
617-353-5124
summer@bu.edu
http://www.bu.edu/summer/high_
    school/index.html

High School Journalism Institute at Indiana University
College Courses/Summer Study

Rising high school sophomores, juniors, and seniors may participate in the High School Journalism Institute at Indiana University, a five-day residential or commuter program. Workshops are offered in Television News, Yearbook, Newspaper/News Magazine, Business/Advertising, and Photojournalism. Residential participants stay on separate floors (by gender) of Teter Residence Hall, which is air conditioned and within walking distance of most workshop sessions. Cost for the five-day session for resident participants is $295; this includes tuition, residence hall room, and most supplies. Meal debit cards of either $40 or $70 are available to purchase. Commuters pay $250 for the five-day session. Applications are typically due in June. Contact the institute for more information.

Indiana University

High School Journalism Institute
School of Journalism
940 East Seventh Street
Bloomington, IN 47405-7108
812-855-0895
ljjohnso@indiana.edu
http://www.journalism.indiana.edu/
    hsji/students.html

High School Summer Institute at Columbia College Chicago
College Courses/Summer Study

Rising high school sophomores, juniors, and seniors can take courses in one of 18 academic areas for college credit via

Columbia's five-week High School Summer Institute. Academic areas of interest to readers of this book include film and video, journalism, radio, and television. Recent classes included News Reporting Basics; Introduction to Radio Broadcasting; Introduction to Radio Sportscasting; Creating a Television Program; Advanced Television Production: AVID Editing; and Writing the TV Sitcom. All courses are taught by regular Columbia College Chicago faculty, and most include field trips and hands-on experiences. Students who successfully complete their course(s) receive college credit from Columbia. Students stay in residence halls on campus; the approximately $1,400 room and board fee includes housing, an evening meal each day, and evening and weekend activities. Tuition is $150 per credit hour; there may be an additional charge for books and other materials. A limited number of scholarships are available. Contact the institute for further details.

High School Summer Institute
Columbia College Chicago
600 South Michigan Avenue
Chicago, IL 60605
312-344-7130
summerinstitute@colum.edu
http://www.colum.edu/admissions/
   hs_institute

International Radio and Television Society Foundation Inc. (IRTS)

Membership
This society is dedicated to keeping its members informed about the increasingly complex world of electronic media. Its student programs are primarily geared toward those at the college level, but high school students can join now to gain insight into the field of broadcasting. Be advised that most of the society's activities, such as its summer fellowship program and minority career workshop, take place in the New York area. As a student, you can join the International Radio and Television Society under the "friend" membership category for about $50, a small price to pay to enjoy the benefits of this organization. Contact the society for more information on the benefits of membership.

**International Radio and
   Television Society
   Foundation Inc.**
420 Lexington Avenue, Suite 1601
New York, NY 10170-1602
212-867-6650
http://www.irts.org

Intern Exchange International Ltd.

Employment and Internship Opportunities
High school students ages 16 to 18 (including graduating seniors) who are interested in broadcasting can participate in a monthlong Career-Plus-Programmes in London, England. Options are available in Print and Broadcast Journalism, Video Production, and other areas. Students learn about these fields via hands-on experience and workshop instruction. The cost of the program is approximately $6,245, plus airfare; this fee includes tuition, housing (students live in residence halls at the University of London),

breakfast and dinner daily, housekeeping service, linens and towels, special dinner events, weekend trips and excursions, group activities including a scheduled trip to the theater, and subway fare. Contact Intern Exchange International for more information.

Intern Exchange International Ltd.

2606 Bridgewood Circle
Boca Raton, FL 33434-4118
561-477-2434
info@internexchange.com
http://www.internexchange.com

Junior Scholars Program at Miami University–Oxford

College Courses/Summer Study

Academically talented high school seniors can earn six to eight semester hours of college credit and learn about university life by participating in the Junior Scholars Program at Miami University–Oxford. Students may choose from more than 40 courses, including Introduction to Public Expression and Critical Inquiry, News Writing and Reporting for All Media, and Principles of Marketing. In addition to academics, scholars participate in social events, recreational activities, and cocurricular seminars. Program participants live in an air-conditioned residence hall. Fees range from approximately $2,063 to $3,241, depending on the number of credit hours taken and applicant's place of residence (Ohio residents receive a program discount). There is an additional fee of approximately $200 for books. The application deadline is typically in mid-May. Visit the program's Web site for additional eligibility requirements and further details.

Miami University–Oxford Junior Scholars Program

Attn: Robert Smith
202 Bachelor Hall
Oxford, OH 45056-3414
513-529-5825
juniorscholars@muohio.edu
http://www.units.muohio.edu/jrscholars

Learning for Life Exploring Program

Field Experience

Learning for Life Exploring Program is a career exploration program that allows young people to work closely with community organizations to learn life skills and explore careers. Opportunities are available in Communications and other fields. Each program has five areas of emphasis: Career Opportunities, Service Learning, Leadership Experience, Life Skills, and Character Education. As a participant in the Communication program, you will work closely with reporters, producers, directors, and other radio and television professionals and learn about the demands and rewards of careers in the field.

To be eligible to participate in this programs, you must have completed the eighth grade and be 14 years old *or* be 15 years of age but have not reached your 21st birthday. This program is open to both males and females.

To find a Learning for Life office in your area (there are more than 300 located throughout the United States), contact the Learning for Life Exploring Program.

Learning for Life Exploring Program

1325 West Walnut Hill Lane,
   PO Box 152079
Irving, TX 75015-2079
972-580-2433
http://www.learningforlife.org/
   exploring/communications/index.
   html

The Museum of Broadcast Communications

Employment and Internship Opportunities/Membership

The Museum of Broadcast Communications, which opened a new 70,000-square foot facility in 2006, offers volunteer, internship, and full-time employment opportunities for those interested in broadcasting. Volunteer opportunities are available in archives, administration, and other areas. Volunteers are asked to make a one-year commitment to the position and to work a minimum of three hours a week. Internships are available in archives, development, and retail operations. Although internships are unpaid, in some instances, student can earn credit for their work. Internships typically last 15 to 20 hours a week for 12 weeks. Contact the museum for more information on these opportunities. In addition, membership opportunities are also available at the museum.

The Museum of Broadcast Communications

400 North State Street, Suite 240
Chicago, IL 60610-6860
312-822-0511
http://www.museum.tv/home.php

The Museum of Television and Radio

Employment and Internship Opportunities/Membership

If you're interested in the history of television and radio, this could be the opportunity for you. The Museum of Television and Radio, with locations in New York City and Los Angeles, offers internships to high school students. The museums are happy to accept highly motivated students who possess a keen interest in the radio and television industry. You must have an eye for detail, some computer training, and the ability to work well with others. Interns often develop their own project or help the museum in a particular area in need of research. Internships are designed to meet the needs of individuals and their schools. How many hours you'll put in each week, and whether or not you'll receive high school credit, is something to work out with your career counselor. Most students work at the museum about eight hours a week for one semester. Full-year internships are also possible. School-to-work and work-study students are welcome. Interns commute to the museums (no residential facilities are available).

To intern at the Los Angeles museum, call the museum directly to discuss your interests and schedule. If you live in New

York City, you must submit a completed application (available at the museum's Web site), a résumé, and two letters of recommendation (either academic or professional). Visit the museum's Web site for a description of internship opportunities by department. Recent listings included internship options in the curatorial, library services, public relations, publications, and research services departments.

In addition, membership opportunities are also available at the museums.

Los Angeles Branch:

The Museum of Television and Radio
Internship Program
465 North Beverly Drive
Beverly Hills, CA 90210-4601
310-786-1025
http://www.mtr.org

New York City Branch:

The Museum of Television and Radio
Internship Program
25 West 52nd Street
New York, NY 10019
212-621-6615
http://www.mtr.org

National High School Institute at Northwestern University (NHSI)
College Courses/Summer Study

The National High School Institute is the nation's oldest university-based program for outstanding high school students. It was established in 1931. The month-long program has the following divisions: Journalism, Film and Video Production, Coon-Hardy Debate Scholars, Championship Debate, Forensics—Individual Events, Junior Statesmen, Music, and Theater. Students in the Journalism program learn reporting skills and participate in hands-on writing workshops. Students in the Film and Video Production program can choose from one of two concentrations: Production or Screenwriting. Production students take core classes in camera technology, digital editing, digital design and animation, and screenwriting. Each student completes a final short project—a narrative video, documentary video, animated short, or experimental video. Students in the Screenwriting concentration take the same core classes as Production students, but also participate in daily writing labs, receiving instruction in story structure, dialogue, and visual storytelling. For their final project, students write and produce a short video project, feature film treatment, animated short, short film script, TV sitcom script, or screenplay excerpt, and their production is shot on video. The student-to-teacher ratio for these programs is six to one. Applicants for the Journalism and Film & Video Production sections must be in 11th grade and have at least a B average (although exceptions are made). A variety of extracurricular activities are also available to students in the program, including tours, movies, shopping, singalongs, and outings to sporting and cultural events. Students live on campus in university residence halls, where they also take their meals. The cost of the program is approximately $3,650, which includes tuition, room, board, health service, field trips, and group events. Scholarships are available. Visit the program's Web site for more information.

Northwestern University
National High School Institute
617 Noyes Street
800-662-NHSI
Evanston, IL 60208-4165
nhsi@northwestern.edu
http://www.northwestern.edu/nhsi

Ohio Summer Honors Institute, Residential Camps, Residential Institutes, and the Summer Scholars Program at Wright State University
College Courses/Summer Study
Ohio residents who are entering grades 10 or 11 may participate in the Ohio Summer Honors Institute at Wright State University. The Television Production option will be of particular interest to students interested in broadcasting. Only 20 spaces are available for this residential program, so it is a good idea to apply early. The all-inclusive cost for the program is about $200.

In addition to the Ohio Summer Honors Institute, several other options are available. Students in grades five through nine can participate in weeklong residential camps. The following camps are available: Aviation, Creative Writing, Meaningful Math, Computer Connections, Space Quest, Television, Theatre Arts. One- and two-week residential institutes are available to students entering grades 10, 11, or 12. Institutes are offered in Aviation Trends and Technology; Creative Writing; Psychology; Leadership; Forensic Science; and other areas. Finally, high school juniors and seniors with a GPA of at least 3.25 can participate in the Summer Scholars Program. Students have the opportunity to take a variety of classes during this one-month program, including biology, chemistry, communications, computer science, economics, English, French, geology, German, history, and mathematics. For further details on these programs, contact the Office of Pre-College Programs.

Wright State University
Office of Pre-College Programs
120 Millett Hall, 3640 Colonel Glenn
   Highway
Dayton, OH 45435-0001
937-775-3135
precollege@wright.edu
http://www.wright.edu/academics/
   precollege

Pre-College Program at Johns Hopkins University
College Courses/Summer Study
Johns Hopkins University welcomes academically talented high school students to its summertime Pre-College Program. Participants live on Hopkins' Homewood campus for five weeks beginning in early July. They pursue one of 27 programs leading to college credit; those interested in broadcasting should strongly consider enrolling in the Film and Media Studies and the Professional Communication

programs. All participants in the Pre-College Program also attend workshops on college admissions, time management, and diversity. Students who live in the greater Baltimore area have the option of commuting. Applicants must be at least 15 by July 1 of the summer in which they hope to enroll, have completed their sophomore, junior, or senior year, and have a minimum GPA of 3.0. All applicants must submit an application form, essay, transcript, two recommendations, and a nonrefundable application fee (rates vary by date of submission). Contact the Office of Summer Programs for financial aid information, costs, and deadlines.

Pre-College Program
Johns Hopkins University
Office of Summer Programs
Wyman Park Building, Suite G4
3400 North Charles Street
Baltimore, MD 21218-2685
800-548-0548
summer@jhu.edu
http://www.jhu.edu/~sumprog/index.
    html

SkillsUSA
Competitions
SkillsUSA offers "local, state and national competitions in which students demonstrate occupational and leadership skills." Students who participate in its SkillsUSA Championships can compete in categories such as 3-D Visualization and Animation, Electronics Applications, Electronics Technology, Prepared Speech, and Television (Video) Production. SkillsUSA works directly with high schools and colleges, so ask your guidance counselor or teacher if it is an option for you. Visit the SkillsUSA Web site for more information.

SkillsUSA
PO Box 3000
Leesburg, VA 20177-0300
703-777-8810
http://www.skillsusa.org

Society of Broadcast Engineers (SBE)
Membership
The society offers youth membership ($10) to high school students who are active in the technical operation of a broadcast station, are involved in a school club or community organization such as an amateur radio club, or have a general interest in broadcast engineering. Youth members receive the *Youth Member Newsletter*, the opportunity to interact with a mentor, and information on careers, education, scholarships, and internships. Contact the society for more information.

Society of Broadcast Engineers
9247 North Meridian Street,
    Suite 305
Indianapolis, IN 46260-1946
317-846-9000
mclappe@sbe.org
http://www.sbe.org

Summer College for High School Students at Cornell University
College Courses/Summer Study
Cornell University's Summer College is a program that allows high school students completing their sophomore, junior, or senior year to explore potential career

paths while earning college credit and experiencing campus life. Students live on campus for three or six weeks during the summer, taking two courses for credit and one noncredit Exploration Seminar for insight into a specific career. The Exploration Seminar in Communication is perfect for those considering a career in broadcasting or in the related fields of journalism, publishing, and public relations. Two options are available: Careers in Communication (a six-week program) and On Camera: Studies in Film Analysis (a three-week program). When the seminar meets, twice each week, participants meet communications professionals, visit newspaper offices and radio and TV stations, and learn how to produce a show on public access television. To complement this seminar, students choose at least one course in communications: Contemporary Mass Communication and Oral Communication are excellent options. You may choose your second course from any of the classes available. The courses are taught at a college level, so be prepared for challenging material and a heavy workload. A little time management, however, will give you enough free time to take advantage of the university's many cultural, sporting, and recreational events. Academic fees total about $3,400, and housing, food, and recreation fees amount to an additional $1,600. Books, travel, and an application fee are extra. A very limited amount of financial aid is available. Applications are due in early May, although Cornell advises that you submit them well in advance of the deadline; those applying for financial aid

must submit their applications by early April. Contact the Summer College for an application and further details about the courses and seminars available.

Cornell University
Summer College for High School
    Students
Summer College
B20 Day Hall
Ithaca, NY 14853-2801
607-255-6203
http://www.sce.cornell.edu/sc/
    explorations

Summer College for High School Students at Syracuse University
College Courses/Summer Study

Students who have completed their sophomore, junior, or senior year of high school are eligible to apply to the Summer College for High School Students at Syracuse University, which runs for six weeks from early July to mid-August. The program has several aims: to introduce you to the many possible majors and study areas within your interest area; to help you match your aptitudes with possible careers; and to prepare you for college, both academically and socially. Students attend classes, listen to lectures, and take field trips to destinations that are related to their specific area of interest. All students are required to take two courses during the program and receive college credit if they successfully complete the courses.

Students interested in broadcasting can explore the field via the program's Public Communications option, in which students study journalism, television and cable, radio, the music industry, public relations, advertising, and film.

Admission is competitive and is based on recommendations, test scores, and transcripts. The total cost of the residential program is about $5,600; the commuter option costs about $4,375. Some scholarships are available. The application deadline is in mid-May, or mid-April for those seeking financial aid. For further information, contact the Summer College.

Syracuse University
Summer College for High School
   Students
111 Waverly Avenue, Suite 240
Syracuse, NY 13244-2320
315-443-5297
sumcoll@syr.edu
http://summercollege.syr.edu

Summer Journalism Institute at the University of Florida
College Courses/Summer Study

Rising 10th, 11th, and 12th graders may participate in the Summer Journalism Institute at the University of Florida. Students learn about broadcasting, writing, editing, photography, and web publishing during this six-day residential program. The cost of the workshop is $360, which includes instruction, housing, and meals. Visit the program's Web site to download an application.

University of Florida
College of Journalism and
   Communications
Summer Journalism Institute
1000 Weimer Hall, PO Box 118400

Gainesville, FL 32611-8400
http://www.jou.ufl.edu/sji

Summer Journalism Institute for High School Students and the Summer Broadcast Institute for High School Students at Arizona State University
College Courses/Summer Study

High school students interested in journalism and broadcasting can participate in two interesting programs at Arizona State University. Students in the two-week, residential Summer Journalism Institute receive instruction in journalistic techniques, concepts, and philosophies at the Walter Cronkite School of Journalism & Mass Communications, produce a laboratory newspaper at campus daily paper, and learn about broadcast news at KAET-TV, the university's public television station. Students also interact with professional journalists and college academic advisers. Students in the Summer Broadcast Institute learn about radio and television via lectures, in-class discussions (many involving guest speakers and video presentations), and field trips. They also write news copy, learn the fundamentals of field production and electronic newsgathering, and are provided with an overview of the innerworkings of the radio and television industries. Students complete the program by producing a television newscast. Students in both programs stay in university dormitories, where they also eat their meals. Be sure to apply for these programs early, as enrollment is limited to 16 students per program. Applicants must be Arizona residents. Contact the university for more information on program costs, deadlines, and eligibility requirements.

Arizona State University

Summer Journalism Institute for
   High School Students/Summer
   Broadcast Institute for High
   School Students
Walter Cronkite School
   of Journalism and Mass
   Communication
PO Box 871305
Tempe, AZ 85287-1305
480-965-5011
jtschool@asu.edu
http://cronkite.asu.edu/
   specialprograms.html

Summer Scholars Program at Washington and Lee University

College Courses/Summer Study

Washington and Lee University, which created the nation's very first journalism program back in the 1860s, offers a journalism curriculum for rising seniors in its Summer Scholars Program. Participants in this residential program spend four weeks in July studying all aspects of today's mass media: legal and ethical issues; writing and marketing; techniques and problems of broadcast management, operations, and programming; and general history. In the program, participants spend three hours each weekday in class and visit both a major newspaper and a TV station. Students are also responsible for running a newspaper and operating a campus AM/FM radio station. Only 20 students are accepted into the journal-

ism curriculum each year; the competition is strong but those admitted benefit from individualized attention. There is time to take advantage of the fine computer, library, and athletic facilities at Washington and Lee University, and to participate in group excursions and activities on the weekends. Applicants must submit a form, standardized test results, and the recommendation of a teacher or counselor. Program fees, including room and board, total about $2,700; textbooks, travel, and personal expenses are extra. A limited amount of financial aid is available to those who demonstrate need as well as high academic standing. For further details and an application form, visit the program's Web site.

Washington and Lee University

Summer Scholars Program
Hill House, 218 West Washington
   Street
Lexington, VA 24450-2116
540-458-8722
summerscholars@wlu.edu
http://summerscholars.wlu.edu

Women's Technology Program at the Massachusetts Institute of Technology (MIT)

College Courses/Summer Study

This residential summer program, sponsored by the Massachusetts Institute of Technology's Department of Electrical Engineering and Computer Science, seeks to introduce high school girls to electrical engineering and computer science. Students who have completed the 11th grade are eligible to participate in the four-week program, which includes classes in computer science, electrical engineering, and mathematics taught by female Ph.D. candidates; to hear guest speakers; and to participate in lab tours, hands-on experiments, and team-based projects. Forty participants are selected each year. Students are expected to be able to handle college-level material, but they do not have to have prior experience in computer programming, physics, or engineering. The cost of the program is approximately $3,000, which includes books, lab materials, food, and housing. Transportation to and from MIT is not covered. Financial aid is available.

Massachusetts Institute of Technology
Women's Technology Program
Attn: Director
MIT Room 38-491
77 Massachusetts Avenue
Cambridge, MA 02139-4301
617-253-5580
wtp@mit.edu
http://wtp.mit.edu

Young Scholars Program: Journalism at the University of Maryland
College Courses/Summer Study

Motivated high school juniors and seniors may participate in the Young Scholars Program, a three-week exploration of journalism at the University of Maryland. Each July, participants learn more about journalism, interact with teachers and other professionals, and take a college-level course. College credit is awarded to students who satisfactorily complete the course. Participants live in the residence halls at the University of Maryland and take their meals on campus or in selected College Park restaurants. A commuter option is also available. To apply, you must submit an application form, an essay, two letters of recommendations, a current transcript, and an application fee of $55 by mid-May. Admissions decisions are based primarily on the recommendations, a GPA of 3.0 or better, and overall academic ability. Cost for the residential option is approximately $2,719; cost for the commuter option is $1,719. For further details and an application form, visit the Web site listed below or contact the Summer Sessions and Special Programs staff.

University of Maryland
Summer Sessions and Special
   Programs
Mitchell Building, 1st Floor
College Park, MD 20742
877-989-7762
http://www.summer.umd.edu/
   youngscholars

Read a Book

When it comes to finding out about radio and television, don't overlook a book. (You're reading one now, after all.) What follows is a short, annotated list of books and periodicals related to radio and television. The books range from personal accounts of what it's like to be a screenwriter to professional volumes on specific topics, such as TV commercials or the history of television. Don't be afraid to check out the professional journals, either. The technical stuff may be way above your head right now, but if you take the time to become familiar with one or two, you're bound to pick up some of what is important to radio and television personnel, not to mention begin to feel like a part of their world, which is what you're interested in, right?

We've tried to include recent materials as well as old favorites. Always check for the latest editions, and, if you find an author you like, ask your librarian to help you find more. Keep reading good books!

❏ BOOKS

Abramson, Albert. *The History of Television, 1880 to 1941.* Jefferson, N.C.: McFarland, 1987. Provides a detailed overview of the key developments that played a role in the development of television. Topics discussed include early inventions, early camera tubes, the kinescope, the iconoscope, and more.

———. *The History of Television, 1942 to 2000.* Jefferson, N.C.: McFarland, 2003. In this follow-up book to the author's previously published book of the same name covering the 1880–1941 era, a technological history of inventions, advancements, and progress in electronic media is addressed. These developments have led to electronic and print media as we know them today.

Berland, Terry, and Deborah Ouelette. *Breaking into Commercials: The Complete Guide to Marketing Yourself, Auditioning to Win, and Getting the Job.* New York: Penguin, 1997. An inside look at the TV industry and commercial acting written jointly by a woman who runs a casting company and an award-winning photographer/writer.

Boyd, Andrew. *Broadcast Journalism: Techniques of Radio and TV News.* Burlington, Mass.: Focal Press, 2000. A manual for would-be journalists in radio and TV, including news gathering, writing, interviewing, recording, and editing.

Cowgill, Linda J. *Writing Short Films: Structure and Content for Screenwrit-*

ers. Los Angeles: Lone Eagle, 2005. An acclaimed screenwriter and teacher, Cowgill cites numerous examples from films short and long to stress strategies for keeping a script on track, developing strong characters, and using compelling writing.

Crouch, Tanja L. *100 Careers in Film and Television.* Hauppauge, N.Y.: Barrons Educational Series, 2002. Focusing on behind-the-scenes positions as camera operators, film editors, art directors and more, the author talks to real-world film workers about their chosen careers.

Dominick, Joseph R., et. al. *Broadcasting, Cable, the Internet and Beyond: An Introduction to Modern Electronic Media.* New York: McGraw-Hill, 2003. This textbook for students beginning their study of electronic media is written by some of the leading practitioners and/or professors in the field.

Dunne, John Gregory. *Monster: Living Off the Big Screen.* New York: Random House, 1997. A mordantly funny insider's look at working in Hollywood and getting your scripts written, bought, and produced.

Edwards, Bob. *Edward R. Murrow and the Birth of Broadcast Journalism.* Hoboken, N.J.: John Wiley, 2004. The history of broadcast journalism could not be told without a detailed account of the pioneering contributions of Edward R. Murrow. Journalism students and non-journalism students alike will benefit from learning about the life of this esteemed, groundbreaking journalist.

Ellis, Elmo. *Opportunities in Broadcasting Careers.* New York: McGraw-Hill, 2004. As part of a career series, this resource book for anyone interested in learning about job prospects in broadcasting contains information on necessary education and training, salary statistics, and professional resources.

Engel, Joel. *Screenwriters on Screenwriting: The Best in the Business Discuss Their Craft.* New York: Hyperion, 1995. Using a question-and-answer format, this book presents many of the finest screenwriters in the film and TV business discussing the tricks of their trade. A fine guide to the realities of the business, including tips for creating the best screenplays.

England, Gary. *Weathering the Storm: Tornadoes, Television and Turmoil.* Norman, Okla.: University of Oklahoma Press, 1997. A veteran weathercaster describes his career, which paralleled many of the changes and advances in the science of meteorology.

Finer, Abbey, and Deborah Pearlman. *Starting Your Television Writing Career: The Warner Bros. Television Writers Workshop Guide.* Syracuse, N.Y.: Syracuse University Press, 2004. This concise resource book for aspiring television writers offers advice for novice and experienced writers who are having difficulty breaking into the business. The authors describe how to clean up and successfully present your scripts to executives and also provide examples of what a completed manuscript should look like.

Fischer, Walter. *Digital Television: A Practical Guide for Engineers.* New York: Springer, 2004. Modern methods of television transmission are discussed in this resource book for engineers. With a technological focus on concepts that electronic engineers would be familiar with, this book primarily serves individuals with a relevant background or those studying to become engineers.

Freedman, Wayne. *It Takes More Than Good Looks To Succeed at TV News Reporting.* Los Angeles: Bonus Books, 2003. This anecdotal book is written by a veteran television news reporter who offers an inside look at how he attained success in this highly competitive field. As such, aspiring broadcast reporters will take away many important concepts to apply to their own future careers.

Hedrick, Tom. *The Art of Sportscasting: How to Build a Successful Career.* South Bend, Ind.: Diamond Communications, 2000. Written by a veteran sportscaster and college professor, this book provides a peek into the highly competitive world of sportscasting. Students considering the field, as well as industry insiders, will benefit from the advice and expertise of the author.

Hewitt, Don. *Tell Me a Story: Fifty Years and 60 Minutes in Television.* New York: PublicAffairs, 2003. As creator and producer of *60 Minutes*, the author describes American television programming from its early days through modern times by chronicling the storytelling efforts of his highly successful, still-going-strong television news program.

Hilliard, Robert L. *Writing for Television, Radio, and New Media.* 8th ed. Belmont, Calif.: Wadsworth, 2003. This all-inclusive textbook covers newswriting, scriptwriting, sportswriting, and more. Providing examples of how to organize your content through effectively formatting your texts for each medium and subspecialty, this book covers all of the necessities for beginning and intermediate writers.

Hilliard, Robert L., and Michael C. Keith. *The Broadcast Century and Beyond: A Biography of American Broadcasting.* 4th ed. Burlington, Mass.: Focal Press, 2004. This comprehensive resource provides a complete history of American broadcasting—from the invention of radio through modern technological advances in television broadcasting. Readers will find many timelines and much factual information as well as social commentary on how broadcasting has effected our development as a society.

Holan, Tomlinson. *Sound for Film and Television.* 2nd ed. Burlington, Mass.: Focal Press, 2001. A technical guidebook to film and television sound, this textbook is a valuable tool for individuals who are interested in acoustic engineering for the film or television media.

Iglesias, Karl. *The 101 Habits of Highly Successful Screenwriters: Insider's Secrets from Hollywood's Top Writers.* Cincinnati, Ohio: Adams Media, 2001. Modeling oneself after successful screenwriters—that is, paying most attention to the habits and processes of such individuals—is the focus of this book. Aspiring writers will not get advice on how to write a script, but they'll receive suggestions and guidance on how to transform themselves into business people who can then become successful screenwriters.

Keith, Michael C. *The Radio Station.* 6th ed. Burlington, Mass.: Focal Press, 2003. Providing a comprehensive introduction to the inner workings of a radio station, this textbook is appropriate for students who want to learn about everything from job opportunities in radio, to recent technological advances, to the latest governmental regulations. This guidebook provides a complete overview of the industry, with a focus on the everyday, behind-the-scenes goings-on of a radio station.

Keller, Teresa, and Stephen A. Hawkins. *Television News: A Handbook for Writing, Reporting, Shooting, and Editing.* Scottsdale, Ariz.: Holcomb Hathaway, 2001. Focusing on how one facet of the broadcast editorial process affects the others, this textbook for beginning broadcast communications students offers a dynamic look at the combination of writing, reporting, shooting, and editing needed to produce a complete, organized news broadcast.

Kisseloff, Jeff. *The Box: An Oral History of Television 1920–1961.* New York: Penguin, 1997. A fascinating look at the beginnings of television, from the pioneering inventor Philo Farnsworth through the news, comedy, and drama creators in the early days of the medium. Intertwined throughout a chronological narrative are 300 interviews with those involved in the business, technological, and entertainment sides of the industry.

Lutgens, Frederick K., Edward J. Tarbuck, and Dennis Tasa. *The Atmosphere: An Introduction to Meteorology.* 9th ed. New York: Prentice-Hall, 2003. This introductory text to the field of weather forecasting gives an in-depth treatment that is accessible to the beginner in the field. Enhanced with full color photographs, maps, charts, and interactive CD-ROM.

McLeish, Robert. *Radio Production: A Manual for Broadcasters.* 4th ed. Burlington, Mass.: Focal Press, 1999. Covering various areas of radio production—from music to news and more—this book provides both historical commentary on radio production as a medium of communication to advice on how to interview people for radio. Industry insiders and students will find this a useful tool to turn to with questions.

Nisbett, Alec. *The Sound Studio: Audio Techniques for Radio, Television, Film and Recording.* Burlington, Mass.: Focal Press, 2003. A textbook for audio engineers, directors, writers, performers, and students, that emphasizes general principles and promotes an understanding of the importance of each operation and innovation in sound recording.

Richards, Andrea. *Girl Director: A How-To Guide for the First-Time, Flat-Broke Film and Video Maker.* Berkeley, Calif.: Ten Speed Press, 2005. Championing the female film director—from historical pioneers to tomorrow's leaders—this book encourages women of all ages to take their ideas to the next level by writing and directing their own work. With particular emphasis on teaching amateurs the step-by-step process involved in developing ideas, finding funding, and ultimately producing their own low-budget films, the book defines a wealth of essential industry terminology while highlighting examples of meaningful female contributions to this field.

Schultz, Bradley. *Sports Broadcasting.* Burlington, Mass.: Focal Press, 2001. This overview of the field of sports broadcasting offers students a complete outline of the industry—from historical moments of importance to social commentary on sports today. Details of job responsibilities of individuals working both behind the scenes and in front of the camera or microphone make this an important book for students who have not yet decided to which role they aspire.

Shook, Frederick. *Television Field Production and Reporting.* 4th ed. Boston: Allyn & Bacon, 2004. This highly respected text focuses on the importance of storytelling in television reporting and production. Considered appropriate reading for individuals at all levels within the industry, the book provides an insightful exploration of the development of exceptional reporting and producing.

Trottier, David. *The Screenwriter's Bible: A Complete Guide to Writing, Formatting, and Selling Your Script.* 4th ed. Los Angeles: Silman-James Press, 2005. Everything you need to know to write, submit, and sell a successful screenplay is included in this all-inclusive book appropriate for beginners through accomplished screenwriters. Formatting tips, marketing advice, character development, and a wealth of other topics are covered.

Webber, Marilyn. *Gardner's Guide to Television Scriptwriting: The Writer's Road Map.* Washington, D.C.: Garth Gardner, 2002. Anyone with an idea for a television show will benefit from this guidebook, which covers all of the basics of the art and business of television scriptwriting—from character development and scene construction through formatting your script and selling it.

Zager, Michael. *Writing Music for Television and Radio Commercials: A Manual for Composers and Students.* Lanham, Md.: Scarecrow Press, 2003. Appropriate for the beginning music student who dreams of composing for television, this book touches on the creative abilities needed for success in this field as well as the business know-how to successfully break into the business.

Zettl, Herbert. *Television Production Handbook.* 8th ed. Belmont, Calif.: Wadsworth, 2002. This well-respected textbook serves as an essential handbook for students entering the field of television production. Covering not only all the latest technological advancements in the field, but also all the camera, equipment, and editing basics, this best-selling book offers real-world advice from an industry veteran.

❏ PERIODICALS

Animation Magazine. Published monthly by Animation Magazine Inc. (30941 West Agoura Road, Suite 102, Westlake Village, CA 91361-4637, 818-991-2884, info@animationmagazine.net, http://www.animationmagazine.net), this magazine covers all genres in which animation is used—movies, television, commercials, and more. Also included are school and job listings, making a subscription to this Web site/magazine invaluable to animation career seekers as well.

Broadcast Engineering. Published monthly by Primedia Business Magazines and Media (PO Box 2100, Skokie, IL 60076-7800, 866-505-7173, gics@pbsub.com, http://www.broadcastengineering.com). Providing news, new product reviews, system design and integration updates, and more, this magazine for engineers, managers, and industry insiders covers the technological aspects of broadcast engineering. Sample articles are available online.

Broadcasting and Cable. Published weekly by Reed Business Information (PO Box 5655 Harlan, IA 51593-1155, 800-554-5729, BCBcustserv@cdsfulfillment.com, http://www.broadcastingcable.com). A major trade publication for anyone affiliated with the TV, radio, or cable broadcasting fields. Includes Nielsen ratings, job listings, personality profiles, advertising, and marketing.

CinemEditor Magazine. Published quarterly by American Cinema Editors Inc. (100 Universal City Plaza, 2282 Verna Fields Building, Room 190, Universal City, CA 91608-1002, 818-777-2900, http://www.ace-filmeditors.org/newace/mag_Main.html), this magazine highlights goings-on in the field of film editing (also of interest to editors working in television). Recent issues include career achievement award-winner profiles, an article about the editing of a film classic (the 1933 *King Kong*), book reviews, and career profiles.

Communicator. Published monthly by the Radio-Television News Directors Association (1600 K Street NW, Suite 700, Washington, DC 20006, 202-659-6510, http://www.rtnda.org), this journal covers issues in news gathering, management, and production for major networks as well as local broadcasting stations throughout the country.

Current. Published biweekly (6930 Carroll Avenue, Suite 350, Takoma Park, MD 20912-4493, 301-270-7240, http://www.current.org), this is a journal for and about people involved in public radio and public television, from producers to station employees. Includes interviews, programming, and news items on the Public Broadcasting Service and National Public Radio, plus a classifieds section posting jobs in public broadcasting.

Daily Variety. Published by Reed Business Information (5700 Wilshire Boulevard, Suite 120, Los Angeles, CA 90036-3644, 866-MY VARIETY, VTC-Custserv@cdsfulfillment.com, http://www.variety.com), this show-biz publication covers the latest-breaking news in the entertainment industry and is delivered in hard-copy format daily.

Directors Guild of America Magazine. Published quarterly by the Directors Guild of America (7920 Sunset Boulevard, Los Angeles, CA 90046-3304, 310-289-5333, http://www.dga.org), this publication includes in-depth articles on areas of interest to film and television directors. Articles include director profiles, technology news, historic accomplishments in the field, and important trends to watch. Sample articles are available online.

Emmy. Published bimonthly for members of the Academy of Television Arts and Sciences (5220 Lankersheim Boulevard, North Hollywood, CA 91601-3107, 818-754-2800, http://www.emmys.com/emmymag/index.php), this journal will interest general readers who seek profiles of people in the news and articles on trends and topics in the world of television.

The Hollywood Reporter. Published daily by VNU eMedia Inc. (5055 Wilshire Boulevard, Los Angeles, CA 90036-4396, 888-900-3782, mailbox@hollywoodreporter.com, http://www.hollywoodreporter.com/thr/index.jsp), this industry news source has provided up-to-date information to industry professionals for more than 75 years, covering all topics related to the entertainment industry. The publication is available in print and/or online subscriptions.

The Hollywood Scriptwriter. Published bimonthly (PO Box 10277, Burbank, CA 91510-0277, http://www.hollywoodscriptwriter.com), this trade magazine for anyone writing for film or television, or for anyone who works closely in dealing with scriptwriters, provides insightful articles on related film industry happenings. Also included in the publication are listings of recommended books as well as contests and festivals for scriptwriters.

Inside Radio. Published daily Monday through Friday by M Street Publications (365 Union Street, Littleton, NH 03561-5619, 800-248-4242, info@insideradio.com, http://www.insideradio.com), this industry publication is available by subscription and delivered via fax or Web. *Inside Radio* provides the most up-to-date information on station ownership, executive hirings and firings, job opportunities, format counts, and more.

Journal of the Atmospheric Sciences. Published monthly by the American Meteorological Society (45 Beacon Street, Boston, MA 02108-3693, 617-227-2425, amsinfo@ametsoc.org, http://www.ametsoc.org/pubs/jour-nals/jas/index.html), this research journal covers all aspects of the science of meteorology. It is available by subscription only to both members and nonmembers of the American Meteorological Society. Articles are research based and of interest to professionals in the field or anyone studying meteorology.

Journal of Broadcasting and Electronic Media. Published quarterly by the Broadcast Education Association (1771 N Street NW, Washington, DC 20036-2800, 202-429-5355. http://www.beaweb.org/publications.html), this journal covers all aspects of how media affects the social sciences. Each article is preceded by an abstract, making it easy to browse.

Journal of Popular Film and Television. Published quarterly by Heldref Publications (Helen Dwight Reid Educational Foundation, 1319 Eighteenth Street NW, Washington, DC 20036-1802, 202-296-6267, http://www.heldref.org/jpft.php). Scholarly title that emphasizes U.S. popular film with a sociocultural analysis of film theory and criticism.

Mediaweek. Published weekly by VNU eMedia Inc. (770 Broadway, New York, NY 10003, 646-654-7601, http://www.mediaweek.com/mw/index.jsp). All aspects of network television, cable, radio, and magazine publishing are included in this information-packed journal. Features include personality profiles, news items, job listings, and analysis articles.

On Writing. Published "occasionally" by the Writers Guild of America, East (555 West 57th Street, Suite 1230, New York, NY 10019-2925, 212-767-7800, http://www.wgaeast.org/newsletter_and_publications/2005/10/27/on_writing), this publication for writers contains articles, essays, and commentary on the art of writing. The guild represents writers who write for film, television, radio, and news, and the publication caters to such writers. Issues may be downloaded for free as PDF files from the organization's Web site.

Popular Communications. Published monthly by CQ Communications (25 Newbridge Road, Hicksville, NY 11801, 516-681-2922, cq@cq-amateur-radio.com, http://www.popular-communications.com). Articles cover radio history and nostalgia, amateur radio, VHF scanners, short-wave receivers, and antenna technology. Monitors virtually all aspects of communications technology.

Quill. Published nine times annually by the Society of Professional Journalists (Eugene S. Pulliam National Journalism Center, 3909 North Meridian Street, Indianapolis, IN 46208-4011, 317-927-8000, http://www.spj.org/quill_list.asp). Covering the state of journalism in the United States, this publication offers resources of interest to professional journalists, students, and educators in the field. It is available by subscription, and sample issues can be downloaded as PDF files.

Radio & Records. Published weekly (2049 Century Park East, 41st Floor, Los Angeles, CA 90067, 310-553-4330, subscribe@radioandrecords.com, http://www.radioandrecords.com). Containing the latest ratings, news, and format updates, this industry publication provides articles and items of interest to industry insiders. The publication is available by subscription and can be packaged in varying combinations with additional daily or weekly news e-mail or fax updates.

Radio & Television Business Report. Published monthly (2050 Old Bridge Road, Suite B-01, Lake Ridge, VA 22192-2484, 703-492-8191, http://www.rbr.com). Targeted toward business executives in the industry, this magazine provides in-depth articles and interviews that provide pertinent information on what is happening in the business world of television and radio. *Radio & Television Business Report* is available by subscription only, but a sample issue is available for download.

Script Notes. Published biweekly by the American Screenwriters Association (269 South Beverly Drive, Suite 2600, Beverly Hills, CA 90212-3807, 866-265-9091, asa@goasa.com, http://www.asascreenwriters.com/script-notes.shtml). If you're looking for a place to sell your script, recent job openings in Hollywood, or simply news on what kinds of scripts have been bought and sold recently, this free e-newsletter will advise you of all of this and more. Visit the association's Web site to register to receive the free e-newsletter.

TALKERS Magazine. Published monthly (650 Belmont Avenue, Springfield, MA 01108-2443, 413-739-8255, http://www.talkers.com). Covering all aspects of the television and radio talk media industry, this publication serves professionals working in managerial, technical, and legal positions within this evolving industry. Current developments in satellite, Internet, and podcast distribution are covered, as are more traditional talk media distribution avenues.

Television Quarterly. This quarterly publication of the National Academy of Television Arts and Sciences (111 West 57th Street, New York, NY 10019, http://www.tvquarterly.net/index2.html) focuses on articles that "discuss the social, political, economic, and technological issues of the medium."

Variety. Published weekly by Reed Business Information (5700 Wilshire Boulevard, Suite 120, Los Angeles, CA 90036-3644, 866-MY VARIETY, VTC-Custserv@cdsfulfillment.com, http://www.variety.com), this showbiz magazine covers everything from film, music, theater, and television, and includes the latest promotions and hirings within the industry, technology-related articles, and job listings. Appropriate for anyone interested in the business of show business, this magazine provides respected, up-to-date entertainment news.

Videomaker. Published monthly (PO Box 4591, Chico, CA 95927-4591,

530-891-8410, http://www.video-maker.com/scripts/index.cfm), this magazine is written for beginners and professional technicians with an emphasis on camcorders, desktop video, copywriting, animation software, reviews, and much more. Intended for those using video in hobbies, business, or education.

Weather and Forecasting. Published bimonthly by the American Meteorological Society (45 Beacon Street, Boston, MA 02108-3693, 617-227-2425, amsinfo@ametsoc.org, http://www.ametsoc.org/pubs/journals/waf/index.html). Providing the latest research and technological updates, this publication highlights the latest case studies and state-of-the-art analysis techniques for scientists working in the field of weather forecasting.

Surf the Web

You must use the Internet to do research, to find out, to explore. The Internet is the closest you'll get to what's happening now all around the world. This chapter gets you started with an annotated list of Web sites related to broadcasting. Try a few. Follow the links. Maybe even venture as far as asking questions in a chat room. The more you read about and interact with those in the field of broadcasting, the better prepared you'll be when you're old enough to participate as a professional.

One caveat: You probably already know that URLs change all the time. If a Web address listed below is out of date, try searching the site's name or other key-words. Chances are, if it's still out there, you'll find it. If it's not, maybe you'll find another site just like it or even better.

❏ THE LIST

About.com: Radio
http://radio.about.com

Everything you ever wanted to know about radio—from today's headlines to radio's history to how to break into the business—is available on this appropri-ately named Web site. Visit the Radio A-Z directory of information to find just about any topic related to radio you can imagine. The Radio Glossary section will help novices learn the terminology and jargon of the field. A useful feature for students is the Free Online Tutorials section for individuals who want to learn the basics about how to get into the field, how to create your own Internet radio station or podcast, or how to edit audio. Career-minded individuals can also scan the Careers, Jobs, and Schools section to read about how and where to receive a radio education and in what capacities professionals are in demand in the field. You might also want to sign up to receive radio headlines sent to your e-mail to keep abreast of the goings-on in the industry. For those looking for a bit of fun, visit the Fun Radio Things to Do section, where you can find downloads, games, and cur-rent music charts. And if you are wonder-ing what satellite radio is all about, take a tour of the XM and SIRIUS Satellite Radio Hardware and Receiver Product Tours or read the XM and SIRIUS Features Com-parison. In the Forums section, Web site visitors can register to participate in con-versations with others interested in learn-ing about the industry.

ASNE High School Journalism
http://www.highschooljournalism.org

Students who are studying broadcast journalism in high school, and those who wish their school offered a more intense broadcast journalism curriculum, should visit this Web site sponsored by the American Society of Newspaper Editors (ASNE) and tell their teachers about it as well. Though the site combines print and broadcast journalism topics, it is easy to navigate and has separate information on each. Though educational and easy to understand for students, this site is particularly geared toward high school educators who want to stay up to date on the latest opportunities for their students. New to the site is a listserv for educators, to help journalism teachers stay connected to one another. The site offers many training resources, including information on how to apply for grant money to improve or start an electronic journalism program in your school. Links to training workshops and summer camps specializing in electronic journalism are available for teachers and students alike.

Broadcast Education Association (BEA)
http://www.beaweb.org

If you're interested in learning about the business of broadcasting, this professional trade association's Web site is a great place to start. The Broadcast Education Association's mission is to prepare students for jobs in the industry and to provide useful information for professors as well. At its Web site, you can learn more about scholarships and other types of financial aid available to broadcasting students, review course syllabi from selected postsecondary broadcasting programs, and get the lowdown on student membership.

Broadcast Employment Services
http://www.tvjobs.com/index_a.htm

If you're looking for information about finding a job in television broadcasting, you'll find it here. This site is great for job seekers, but it also provides solid information and resources for students who are just considering the field. The site is divided into the broad areas of Employment, Reference, Education, Networking, Quick Links, Salary Info, Professional Development, and Miscellaneous. In the Networking section, there's a place to connect with other students to talk about your career pursuits. The Education section is another good place to visit. A list of internships includes offerings by television stations and college campuses across the United States. Another useful feature in the Education section is a list of broadcasting schools and colleges. Under Employment, you'll find bulletin boards, job banks, and job lines, all packed with available positions. This is a great place to sneak a peek at other people's résumés to get ideas. The Professional Development section provides information on tape critique services as well as résumé tape services. If you're looking for a discussion forum, be sure to spend some time in the Open Mic section of Networking. Here, you can browse through topics of discussion, ask questions, and receive responses from those working in the field.

Broadcasters Training Network (BTN)
http://www.learn-by-doing.com

If you're unsure about how to get started as a broadcaster, this site claims that it "can make it happen for you!" The core of the Broadcasters Training Network (BTN) is an apprenticeship program at local radio stations for students fresh out of high school. The program matches each student with an instructor already working at the station. For instance, if you want to become a disc jockey or a sports broadcaster, you'll work with someone who's currently performing that job in your area. This site thoroughly explains how the program works, complete with testimonials. The careers described in greatest detail are disc jockey, news reporter, talk show host, sportscaster, production engineer, and voice-over artist. Apprentices pay a hefty placement fee for the program, which is completed in six months. The philosophy of BTN is that your money and time are better spent on this intensive training program than on a liberal arts diploma. That's something you can evaluate for yourself by comparing BTN's fee to other training options, such as paid internships, volunteering, or a college degree.

CineMedia
http://www.cinemedia.org

This Web site serves as a directory for more than 25,000 media-related Web sites. A search engine allows you to search by word or phrase, linking you to an endless supply of information on all subjects that involve anything to do with film, music, or media. If you have a Web site you want to submit, you can do that as well.

Electronic Field Trip to the National Weather Service
http://www.ket.org/trips/weather

This Web site offers middle and high school students a video tour of everything that goes into forecasting the weather—from the professionals who work behind the scenes and in front of the camera to the technology and equipment used to track weather. It also describes how information gets disseminated from a weather center to the public via radio and television. The glossary link on the left-hand side of the page offers useful terminology definitions for those who think they might be interested in pursuing a career in this exciting field.

ESPN SportsZone
http://espn.go.com

When it comes to sportscasting, ESPN is head and shoulders above the competition—on the Web as well as on TV. This site covers baseball, football, hockey, soccer, golf, basketball, auto racing, tennis, and more. It is arranged in a dynamic, easy-to-navigate style, with a column on the left-hand side of the page listing each sport ESPN covers in detail, as well as fantasy sports. Also listed are resources such as ESPN wireless, podcasts, and a searchable database of leagues and sporting activities to join. Once you're finished checking the latest scores, click on Join Our Team for actual career-related information. At the time of review, ESPN Studios was hiring for a vast range of job titles including event production coordinator, associate producer, and media associate. You can even fill out and send an application online. Students will want to spend some time reviewing the College Relations section of Join Our Team to learn about and apply for internship opportunities with ESPN.

How Stuff Works
http://www.howstuffworks.com

If you spend a lot of time wondering how stuff you use or see every day actually works, then this site should be on your short list of Web sites to explore, as it covers how "stuff"—as varied and timely as tsunamis, identity theft, and satellite radio—works. Complex concepts are carefully broken down and examined, including photos and links to current and past news items about the subject. Topics of interest to those interested in broadcasting careers include "How Internet Radio Works," "How The Radio Spectrum Works," "How Satellite Radio Works," "How Radio Works, and How Podcasting Works."

Imagine
http://www.jhu.edu/~gifted/imagine

Imagine is a bimonthly journal produced by the Center for Talented Youth at Johns Hopkins University. It is designed for the go-getter high school student with his or her eye on the future. Its tagline, "Opportunities and resources for academically talented youth," says it all.

If you're always searching for good academic programs, competitions, and internships, this publication can keep you well informed on what's available and when you need to apply. There's an entertaining College Review series in which student contributors evaluate individual colleges and universities and also a Career Options series featuring interviews with professionals.

Along with the current issue, selected portions of back issues can be read online. Previous issues have included articles about the performing arts and broadcasting, as well as general tips on entering art competitions and choosing summer programs. For $30 a year, you can subscribe and get the printed journal delivered to your home—or for free, you can just read back issues online.

Museum of Television and Radio (MT&R)
http://www.mtr.org

The Museum of Television and Radio offers a wealth of television and radio programming—radio shows, television programs, and commercial advertisements—at its locations in Los Angeles, California, and New York City. Visit its Web site for information on exhibitions and educational programs available to visitors, as well as to read a weekly blog that explores themes related to television and radio.

Peterson's Education Portal
http://www.petersons.com

This site offers anything you want to know about surviving high school, getting into college, and choosing a graduate degree. Check out the College and Graduate School sections, which offer school directories searchable by keyword, degree, location, tuition, size, GPA, and even sports offered. While this site is not devoted to broadcasting schools, it is comprehensive; school listings offer the usual basics plus details on financial aid, school facilities, student government, faculty, and admissions requirements.

Princeton Review
http://www.princetonreview.com

Similar to the Peterson's Education Portal, Princeton Review is a great site to find comprehensive college reviews and information. Unique to this site are actual student comments about the school, which offer refreshingly honest opinions about the institution and its student body. Check out the site's annual rankings to read how schools stack up in academics, social scene, diversity, and other areas. Under the Students Tell All section, read about what students have to say about their college experience.

RadioSpace™
http://www.radiospace.com

If you're working at your school's radio station, you're probably operating on a shoestring budget. RadioSpace could be a great resource for you. It's a radio broadcasting agency that provides news and programming services to radio stations, thanks to the assistance of corporations, government agencies, and nonprofit organizations. Choose from headlines under the topics of current events and public affairs; consumer, business, and general interest; entertainment and sports; and health and medicine. You can download download (for free) fully produced radio reports in a choice of formats, or read through the written transcript to use portions of the story. For example, Americans for Fair Trade provided several stories, sound bites, and interviews with members of Congress over the controversial Central American Free Trade Agreement. Another story, provided by the Advancement Project, focuses on the effects of a zero-tolerance discipline policy in the country's schools. The Programming Resources page offers links to resource sites, station listings and directories, specialty resources, associations and regulatory agencies, and industry news. Click on the History section if you want to locate everything from a site on early American radio to one stocked with nifty sound effects.

Radio-Television News Directors Association (RTNDA)
http://www.rtnda.org

This Web site is hosted by an organization that serves electronic journalists in more than 30 countries. While very little of this site is aimed directly at students, once you dip into the text, you'll find plenty to absorb. Start by reading RTNDA's online *Communicator* magazine, which offers in-depth features on topics that include the impact of technology on electronic journalism, staffing and managing a news bureau, and cultural diversity in the field. Look for valuable information about scholarship programs under the Membership Benefits section. The RTNDA annually awards multiple undergraduate and graduate scholarships, awards, fellowships, and internships. The RTNDA'S job bulletin offers a free search for jobs as well as current research on salaries and articles on a variety of topics such as women and minority representation in the newsroom.

Screenwriter's Utopia
http://www.screenwritersutopia.com

Want to get creative feedback from your peers regarding the television script on which you've been working? This Web site offers workshops and consultations on how to improve your work and how to better market it. Web site users will need to register (free) to gain access to the many features of this useful site. Along with news, forums, and contests, this Web site offers surveys, reviews, and suggestions for television (and movie) scriptwriters of all levels of experience. The Script Swap section allows you to read and comment on others' work and to get feedback on your own. Any serious wannabe television writer should visit this Web site to gain a better perspective on what is currently going on in the business. And if you find that you have questions that are not answered by the Web site, you can even send an e-mail to a "Hollywood creative executive."

Television and Radio News Research
http://www.missouri.edu/~jourvs

A professor at the renowned Missouri School of Journalism created this site in order to offer a behind-the-scenes glimpse of television and news broadcasting. He has conducted a number of national surveys on topics such as newsroom profitability, salaries, staff diversity, and the use of interns. The text looks honestly at some of the less glamorous aspects of the industry. For instance, one chapter studies how broadcast news salaries have kept up with inflation. Another chapter con-

siders the inadequacy of staff benefits at American TV and radio stations. Yet another examines how minorities and women fared in the TV news work force during the 1990s. You'll definitely want to click on "TV and Radio News Careers," a lengthy, well-written article that can help you decide whether this is the right career path for you. Here, you can compare your personality traits and career values to those of people who are working in the field.

Yahoo!: Radio
http://dir.yahoo.com/News_and_
    Media/Radio

It might seem odd to include the popular search engine Yahoo! among a list of broadcasting Web sites, but it won't seem so after you've visited it. If you're hungry for more after visiting the sites listed in this appendix, pull up a chair at Yahoo!'s feast. Yahoo! has done a tremendous amount of legwork for you. For example, if you're interested in amateur and ham radio, then scan through the more than 1,200 sites currently included here. Additionally, if you want to search for radio-oriented sites or information in your city or state, a directory lets you sort more than 4,200 sites in the United States alone. If it's radio personalities you would like to research, this new section has more than 220 listings. Even podcasting and audioblogging are included. Not sure exactly what these terms mean? This search engine is a useful starting point for Web research about radio and its emerging technologies.

Ask for Money

By the time most students get around to thinking about applying for scholarships, they have already extolled their personal and academic virtues to such lengths in essays and interviews for college applications that even their own grandmothers wouldn't recognize them. The thought of filling out yet another application form fills students with dread. And why bother? Won't the same five or six kids who have been fighting over grade point averages since the fifth grade walk away with all the really good scholarships?

The truth is, most of the scholarships available to high school and college students are being offered because an organization wants to promote interest in a particular field, to encourage more students to become qualified to enter it, and finally, to help those students afford an education. Certainly, having a good grade point average is a valuable asset, and many organizations granting scholarships request that only applicants with a minimum grade point average apply. More often than not, however, grade point averages aren't even mentioned; the focus is on the area of interest and what a student has done to distinguish himself or herself in that area. In fact, frequently the only requirement is that the scholarship applicant must be studying in a particular area.

❑ GUIDELINES

When applying for scholarships, there are a few simple guidelines that can help ease the process considerably.

Plan Ahead

The absolute worst thing you can do is wait until the last minute. For one thing, obtaining recommendations or other supporting data in time to meet an application deadline is incredibly difficult. For another, no one does his or her best thinking or writing under the gun. So get off to a good start by reviewing scholarship applications as early as possible—months, even a year, in advance. If the current scholarship information isn't available, ask for a copy of last year's. Once you have the scholarship information or application in hand, give it a thorough read. Try to determine how your experience or situation best fits into the scholarship, or if it even fits at all. Don't waste your time applying for a scholarship in literature if you couldn't finish *Great Expectations*.

If possible, research the award or scholarship, including past recipients and, where applicable, the person in whose name the scholarship is offered. Often, broadcasting scholarships are established to memorialize a well-known broadcaster or an individual who played a key role in a particular field. In those cases, try to get a feel for the spirit of the person's work. If you have any similar interests or experiences, don't hesitate to mention them.

Talk to others who received the scholarship, or to students currently studying in the area or field of interest in which the scholarship is offered, and try to gain insight into possible applications or work related to that field. When you're working on the essay asking why you want this scholarship, you'll have real answers: "I would benefit from receiving this scholarship because studying journalism and Urdu will help me prepare to be a successful foreign correspondent in Pakistan."

Take your time writing the essays. Be certain that you are answering the question or questions on the application and not merely restating facts about yourself. Don't be afraid to get creative; try to imagine what you would think of if you had to sift through hundreds of applications. What would you want to know about the candidate? What would convince you that someone was deserving of the scholarship? Work through several drafts and have someone whose advice you respect—a parent, teacher, or guidance counselor—review the essay for grammar and content.

Finally, if you know in advance which scholarships you want to apply for, there might still be time to stack the deck in your favor by getting an internship, volunteering, or working part time. Bottom line: The more you know about a scholarship and the sooner you learn it, the better.

Follow Directions

Think of it this way: many of the organizations that offer scholarships devote 99.9 percent of their time to something other than the scholarship for which you are applying. Don't make a nuisance of yourself by pestering them for information. Simply follow the directions you are given. If the scholarship information specifies that you should write for information, then write for it—don't call.

Pay close attention to whether you're applying for an award, a scholarship, a prize, or financial aid. Often these words are used interchangeably, but just as often they have different meanings. An award is usually given for something you have done: built a park or helped distribute meals to the elderly; or something you have created: a design, an essay, a short film, a screenplay, an invention. On the other hand, a scholarship is frequently a renewable sum of money that is given to a person to help defray the costs of college. Scholarships are given to candidates who meet the necessary criteria based on essays, eligibility, grades, or sometimes all three.

Supply all the necessary documents, information, and fees, and make the deadlines. You won't win any scholarships by forgetting to include a recommendation from your teacher or failing to postmark the application by the deadline. Bottom line: Get it right the first time, on time.

Apply Early

Once you have the application in hand, don't dawdle. If you've requested it far enough in advance, there shouldn't be any reason for you not to turn it in well in advance of the deadline. You never know, if it comes down to two candidates, your timeliness just might be the deciding factor. Bottom line: Don't hesitate.

Be Yourself

Don't make promises you can't keep. There are plenty of hefty scholarships available, but if they all require you to study something that you don't enjoy, you'll be miserable in college. And the side effects from switching majors after you've accepted a scholarship could be even worse. Bottom line: Be yourself.

Don't Limit Yourself

There are many sources for scholarships, beginning with your guidance counselor and ending with the Internet. All of the search engines have education categories. Start there and search by keywords, such as "financial aid," "scholarship," and "award." But don't be limited to the scholarships listed in these pages.

If you know of an organization related to or involved with the field of your choice, write a letter asking about scholarships. If the organization doesn't offer scholarships, don't stop there. Write another letter, or better yet, schedule a meeting with the president or someone in the public relations office and ask them if they would be willing to sponsor a scholarship for you. Of course, you'll need to prepare yourself well for such a meeting because you're selling a priceless commodity—yourself. Don't be shy; be confident. Tell the addressee all about yourself, what you want to study and why, and let him or her know what you would be willing to do in exchange—volunteer at a favorite charity, write up reports on your progress in school, or work part time during school breaks or full time during the summer. Explain why you're a wise investment. Bottom line: The sky's the limit.

❏ THE LIST

Academy of Television Arts and Sciences

5220 Lankershim Boulevard
North Hollywood, CA 91601-3109
818-754-2830
http://www.emmys.org/foundation/
collegetvawards.php

The academy offers the College Television Awards and the Fred Rogers Memorial Scholarship.

The College Television Awards competition rewards excellence in college (undergraduate and graduate) student film/video productions in the following categories: nontraditional animation (computer-generated), traditional animation, children's programs, comedy, documentary, drama, magazine shows, music programs, and newscasts. All entries must have been made for college course credit between September 1 and December 15 to qualify. Entries longer than one hour will not be accepted. News, sports, and magazine shows, children's, and comedy entries must not exceed 30 minutes. Entries can be submitted on Beta, Beta SP, DVD, or VHS video. First-place winners receive $2,000; second-place winners, $1,000; and third-place winners, $500.

College students who are pursuing degrees in early childhood education, child development/child psychology, film/television production, media arts, music, or animation may apply for the $10,000 Fred Rogers Memorial Scholarship. Applicants must have the ultimate goal of working in the field of children's media. Particular attention will be given to student applicants from inner city or rural communities.

Air Force ROTC

Scholarship Actions Branch
551 East Maxwell Boulevard
Maxwell AFB, AL 36112-5917
866-423-7682
http://www.afrotc.com

The Air Force ROTC provides a wide range of four-year scholarships (ranging from partial to full tuition) for high school students planning to study engineering, meteorology, computer science, and other technical fields in college. Scholarships are also available to college and enlisted students. Visit the Air Force ROTC Web site to apply.

American Legion Auxiliary

777 North Meridian Street, 3rd Floor
Indianapolis, IN 46204-1420
317-955-3845
alahq@legion-aux.org
http://www.legion-aux.org/
    scholarships/index.aspx

Various state auxiliaries of the American Legion, as well as its national organization, offer scholarships to help students prepare for various careers. Most require that candidates be associated with the organization in some way, whether as a child or spouse of a military veteran. Interested students should contact the American Legion for further information.

American Meteorological Society (AMS)

45 Beacon Street
Boston, MA 02108-3693
617-227-2425
amsinfo@ametsoc.org
http://www.ametsoc.org/
    amsstudentinfo/scholfeldocs/
    index.html

The society offers a variety of scholarships to high school seniors and undergraduate students who are interested in studying the atmospheric and related sciences. AMS/Industry Minority Scholarships ($3,000 per year for two years) are available to minority (especially Hispanic, Native American, and black/African-American) students who are entering their freshman year. Freshman Undergraduate Scholarships (ranging from $2,000 to $3,000 a year) are also available to students entering their freshman year. Undergraduate Scholarships (amount varies) are available to college students entering their final year of undergraduate study. The society also offers fellowships to graduate students.

American Radio Relay League Foundation (ARRL)

225 Main Street
Newington, CT 06111-1400
860-594-0200
foundation@arrl.org
http://www.arrl.org/arrlf

Members of the league who are majoring in engineering, science, or related fields are eligible for a variety of scholarships. Awards range from $500 to $10,000. Contact the foundation for more information.

American Women in Radio and Television (AWRT)

8405 Greensboro Drive, Suite 800
McLean, VA 22102-5120
703-506-3290
info@awrt.org
http://www.awrt.org

AWRT provides a variety of scholarships via its regional chapters to college students interested in broadcasting. Applicants should visit AWRT's Web site to locate contact information for their local chapter.

Army ROTC

800-USA-ROTC
http://www.goarmy.com/rotc/
scholarships.jsp

Students planning to begin or currently pursuing college study may apply for scholarships that pay tuition and some living expenses; recipients must agree to accept a commission and serve in the army on Active Duty or in a Reserve Component (U.S. Army Reserve or Army National Guard).

Asian American Journalists Association (AAJA)

Attn: Scholarship Committee
1182 Market Street, Suite 320
San Francisco, CA 94102-4919
415-346-2051, ext. 102
brandons@aaja.org
http://www.aaja.org

The Asian American Journalists Association offers scholarships to Asian-American high school seniors and college students who are preparing for a career in journalism. Applicants for all scholarships must have a commitment to the field of journalism, possess sensitivity to Asian-American and Pacific Islander issues as demonstrated by community involvement, have journalistic ability, and demonstrate financial need.

Applicants for the AAJA/Cox Foundation Scholarship (up to $2,500) must be full-time high school seniors or undergraduate students.

Applicants for the AAJA/S.I. Newhouse Foundation Scholarship (up to $5,000) must be high school seniors or college students. While the scholarship is open to all students, the AAJA especially encourages applicants from historically underrepresented Asian Pacific American groups, including Vietnamese, Cambodians, Hmong, and other Southeast Asians, South Asians, and Pacific Islanders. S.I. Newhouse Foundation Scholarship winners will be eligible for summer internships with a Newhouse publication.

Applicants for the $2,000 Mary Moy Quan Ing Memorial Scholarship must be high school seniors who plan on being full-time students.

Applicants for the $2,000 Minoru Yasui Memorial Scholarship must be high school seniors or college students. This scholarship is awarded to a promising male Asian-American broadcaster.

Visit the association's Web site for more information on these scholarships.

Association on American Indian Affairs

Scholarship Coordinator
966 Hungerford Drive, Suite 12-B

Rockville, MD 20850-1743
240-314-7155
general.aaia@verizon.net
http://www.indian-affairs.org

Undergraduate and graduate Native American students who are pursuing a variety of college majors can apply for scholarships ranging from $500 to $1,500. All applicants must provide proof of Native American heritage. Visit the association's Web site for more information.

Association for Women in Sports Media (AWSM)

Attn: Rachel Cohen, Scholarship
    Coordinator
PO Box 11897
College Station, TX 77842-1897
rcohen@dallasnews.com
http://www.awsmonline.org

Full-time undergraduate and graduate female students pursuing careers in sportswriting, copyediting, public relations, broadcasting, Internet, or photography may apply for $1,000 Association for Women in Sports Media Scholarships and Internships. Visit the association's Web site for more information about internship options in various categories.

Broadcast Education Association (BEA)

1771 N Street NW
Washington, DC 20036-2891
888-380-7222
beainfo@beaweb.org
http://www.beaweb.org

An association of university broadcasting faculty, industry professionals, and graduate students, BEA offers more than 10 annual scholarships (ranging from $1,250 to $5,000) in broadcasting for college students. Applicants must be able to demonstrate superior academic performance and a dedication to a career in broadcasting.

CollegeBoard.com

http://apps.collegeboard.com/
    cbsearch_ss/welcome.jsp

This testing service (PSAT, SAT, etc.) also offers a scholarship search engine at its Web site. It features scholarships (not all broadcasting-related) worth more than $3 billion. You can search by specific major and a variety of other criteria.

CollegeNET

http://mach25.collegenet.com/
    cgi-bin/M25/index

CollegeNET features 600,000 scholarships (not all broadcasting-related) worth more than $1.6 billion. You can search by keyword (such as "radio," "television," or "broadcasting") or by creating a personality profile of your interests.

Daughters of the American Revolution (DAR)

Attn: Scholarship Committee
1776 D Street NW
Washington, DC 20006-5303
202-628-1776
http://www.dar.org/natsociety/
    edout_scholar.cfm

General Scholarships are available to students who have been accepted to or who are currently enrolled in a college or university in the United States. Selection criteria include academic excellence, commitment to a field of study, and financial need; applicants need not be affiliated with DAR. A scholarship program is also available for Native American students. Contact the Scholarship Committee for more information.

FastWeb

http://fastweb.monster.com

FastWeb is one of the largest scholarship search engines around. It features 600,000 scholarships (not all broadcasting-related) worth more than $1 billion. To use this resource, you will need to register (at no charge).

Foundation for the Carolinas

PO Box 34769
Charlotte, NC 28234-4769
704-973-4500
infor@fftc.org
http://www.fftc.org

The foundation administers more than 70 scholarship funds that offer awards to undergraduate and graduate students pursuing study in the arts, business, engineering, and other disciplines. Visit its Web site for a searchable list of awards.

Golden Key International Honor Society

621 North Avenue NE, Suite C-100
Atlanta, GA 30308-2842
800-377-2401
http://www.goldenkey.org

Golden Key is an academic honor society that offers its members "opportu-

nities for individual growth through leadership, career development, networking, and service." It awards more than $400,000 in scholarships annually through 17 different award programs. Membership in the society is selective; only the top 15 percent of college juniors and seniors—who may be pursuing education in any college major— are considered for membership by the organization. There is a one-time membership fee of $60 to $65. Contact the society for more information.

GuaranteedScholarships.com

http://www.guaranteed-scholarships.com

This Web site offers lists (by college) of scholarships, grants, and financial aid (not all broadcasting-related) that "require no interview, essay, portfolio, audition, competition, or other secondary requirement."

Hawaii Community Foundation

1164 Bishop Street, Suite 800
Honolulu, HI 96813-2817
scholarships@hcf-hawaii.org
http://www.hawaiicommunityfoundation.org/scholar/scholar.php

The foundation offers a variety of scholarships for high school seniors and college students planning to or currently studying journalism, communications, and other majors in college. Applicants must be residents of Hawaii, demonstrate financial need, and plan to attend a two- or four-year college. Visit the foundation's Web site for more information and to apply online.

Hispanic College Fund (HCF)

1717 Pennsylvania Avenue NW,
 Suite 460
Washington, DC 20006-4629
hcf-info@hispanicfund.org
http://www.hispanicfund.org

The Hispanic College Fund, in collaboration with several major corporations, offers many scholarships for high school seniors and college students planning to begin or currently attending college. Applicants must be Hispanic, live in the United States or Puerto Rico, and have a GPA of at least 3.0 on a 4.0 scale. Contact the HCF for more information.

Illinois Career Resource Network

http://www.ilworkinfo.com/icrn.htm

Created by the Illinois Department of Employment Security, this useful site offers a great scholarship search engine, as well as detailed information on careers (including those in radio and television). You can search for broadcasting scholarships based on majors (such as broadcast journalism, radio and television, and radio and television broadcasting technology) and other criteria. This site is available to everyone, not just Illinois residents; you can get a password by simply visiting the site. The Illinois Career Information System is just one example of sites created by state departments of employment security (or departments of labor) to assist students with financial and career-related issues. After checking out this site, visit your state's department of labor Web site to see what it offers.

Indiana Broadcasters Association (IBA)

3003 East 98th Street, Suite 161
Indianapolis, IN 46280-2907
800-342-6276
indba@aol.com
http://www.indianabroadcasters.org

The IBA offers scholarships to high school seniors and undergraduate students interested in broadcasting careers. Applicants for the IBA Scholarship for High School Seniors must be second-semester seniors at Indiana high schools, have a GPA of at least 3.0, be residents of Indiana, and plan to attend an Indiana postsecondary institution that is an IBA member college/university. They also must plan to major in broadcasting, electronic media, telecommunications, or broadcast journalism; be actively participating in a high school broadcasting facility or working or interning for a commercial broadcasting facility; and have received credit in a high school broadcasting, electronic media, telecommunications, or broadcast journalism course.

Applicants for the IBA Scholarship for College Students must be undergraduate students, Indiana residents, and currently attending IBA-member colleges/universities majoring in broadcasting, electronic media, telecommunications, or broadcast journalism. They also must be actively participating in a college broadcasting facility or working or interning for a commercial broadcasting facility. Visit the association's web site to download an application and request form.

Indianapolis Association of Black Journalists (IABJ)

PO Box 441795
Indianapolis, IN 46244-1795
317-388-8163
http://www.iabj.net

African-American high school graduates in Indiana who plan to enroll as communications or journalism majors in an accredited college or university or current college students attending Indiana colleges or universities majoring in communications or journalism may apply for the $1,000 Lynn Dean Ford/Indianapolis Association of Black Journalists Scholarship. Visit the association's Web site to download an application.

Institute of Electrical and Electronics Engineers (IEEE)

1828 L Street NW, Suite 1202
Washington, DC 20036-5104
ieeeusa@ieee.org
http://www.ieee.org

The institute offers a variety of scholarships and fellowships to its student members who are pursuing education in electrical and electronic engineering and computer science. Applicants must be undergraduate or graduate students. Contact IEEE for more information.

Iowa Broadcasters Association (IBA)

PO Box 71186
Des Moines, IA 50325-0186
515-224-7237
iowaiba@dwx.com
http://www.iowabroadcasters.com/
   scholar.htm

Applicants for the Quarton-McElroy/IBA Scholarship must be residents of Iowa, have graduated from or be about to graduate from an Iowa high school, and be enrolled in or enrolling full time in a broadcasting program at an IBA-approved two- or four-year college/university in Iowa. Visit the association's Web site to view a list of IBA-approved colleges/universities and to download an application.

Kansas Association of Broadcasters (KAB)

Scholarship Committee
1916 Southwest Sieben Court
Topeka, KS 66611-1656
785-235-1307
harriet@kab.net
http://www.kab.net/Default.aspx

Kansas residents attending or planning to attend a postsecondary institution in Kansas and pursue full-time study in broadcasting or a related curriculum may apply for the association's Broadcast Scholarship Program. Applicants must maintain at least a 2.5 GPA. Visit the association's Web site to download an application.

Marine Corps Scholarship Foundation

PO Box 3008
Princeton, NJ 08543-3008
800-292-7777
mcsf@marine-scholars.org
http://www.marine-scholars.org

The foundation helps children of marines and former marines with scholarships of up to $5,000 for postsecondary study.

To be eligible, you must be a high school graduate or registered as an undergraduate student at an accredited college or vocational/technical institute. Additionally, your total family gross income may not exceed $63,000. Contact the foundation for further details.

Michigan Association of Broadcasters Foundation (MAB)

819 North Washington Avenue
Lansing, MI 48906-5135
800-YOUR-MAB
mabf@michmab.com
http://www.michmab.com/MABF/
index_mabf.html

The MAB Foundation offers the following $1,000 scholarships in cooperation with local television stations: the MABF/abc12 Broadcasting Scholarship, the MABF/WOOD-TV8 Educational Scholarship, and the MABF/WXYZ-TV Broadcasting Scholarship. Applicants for all scholarships must be college students currently pursuing study in a broadcasting-related field in the state of Michigan. Contact the association for more information.

Missouri Broadcasters Association

1025 Northeast Drive
Jefferson City, MO 65109-2579
573-636-6692
http://www.mbaweb.org/mc/page.do

Graduating high school seniors who are planning to study broadcasting may apply for the Missouri Broadcasters Association Scholarship. Applicants must be Missouri residents who are planning to attend or are currently attending a Missouri college, university, or accredited vo-tech school. They also must be full-time students and maintain at least a 3.0 GPA. Contact the association to request an application.

National Association of Black Journalists (NABJ)

NABJ Scholarship Program
8701-A Adelphi Road
Adelphi, MD 20783-1716
301-445-7100, ext. 108
http://www.nabj.org/programs/
scholarships/index.html

Applicants for NABJ scholarships must be pursuing study in broadcast or print journalism, be members of the NABJ, demonstrate financial need, be African-American, and demonstrate a dedication to the field of journalism. Contact the association for more information.

National Association of Farm Broadcasters (NAFB)

Attn: Terry Henne
WSGW Radio
1795 Tittabawassee
Saginaw, MI 48604-9431
989-752-3456
terry.henne@gte.net
http://nafb.com/DesktopDefault.
aspx?tabid=26

College juniors who are actively pursuing a degree in communication or journalism, with a specialty in agricultural broadcasting, may apply for the NAFB College Scholarship, which ranges from $2,500 and $3,000. Visit the association's Web site to download an application.

National Endowment for the Arts (NEA)

1100 Pennsylvania Avenue NW
Washington, DC 20506-0001
202-682-5400
http://arts.endow.gov/grants

The NEA was established by Congress in 1965 to support excellence in the arts. It offers grants to artists and arts organizations working in the following art disciplines: arts education, design, folk and traditional arts, media arts, multidisciplinary, and visual arts. Visit the NEA Web site for a detailed list of available programs.

Navy: Education: Earn Money For College

http://www.navy.com/education/
    earnmoneyforcollege

The navy offers several funding programs for college study. Students who receive money to attend college are typically required to serve a specific number of years in the navy after graduation. Other students take advantage of programs that allow them to join the Navy and complete their degrees during their service obligation. Contact your local recruiter or visit the navy's Web site for details.

Oklahoma Association of Broadcasters (OAB)

6520 North Western, Suite 104
Oklahoma City, OK 73116-7334
405-848-0771
info@oabok.org
http://www.oabok.org/Careers/
    scholarships.html

The Oklahoma Association of Broadcasters offers two scholarships to college students. Applicants for scholarships of up to $250 from the Ken R. Greenwood Student Assistance Fund must be broadcast students who are attending a college/university in the state of Oklahoma. They also must demonstrate financial need. Applicants for the $1,000 OAB Education Foundation Scholarship must be juniors or seniors who are enrolled in an Oklahoma college or university broadcasting program and majoring in broadcasting. They also must maintain a minimum B average in all courses, take at least 12 academic hours of course work during the scholarship year, and plan to enter the broadcasting profession upon graduation. Visit the association's Web site for more information.

Overseas Press Club of America

40 West 45th Street
New York, NY 10036-4202
212-626-9220
foundation@opcofamerica.org
http://www.opcofamerica.org

College students who aspire to become foreign correspondents may apply for the $2,000 Overseas Press Club Foundation Scholarship. Visit the foundation's Web site for further information.

Radio-Television News Directors Foundation (RTNDF)

Attn: Irving Washington
RTNDF Scholarships
1600 K Street NW, Suite 700
Washington, DC 20006
202-467-5218

irvingw@rtndf.org
http://www.rtnda.org/asfi/index.asp

The foundation offers a variety of scholarships to college students.

Applicants for the $6,000 George Foreman Tribute to Lyndon B. Johnson Scholarship must be enrolled full-time sophomores, juniors, or seniors at the University of Texas–Austin and interested in pursuing a career in electronic journalism.

Applicants for the $1,000 Lou and Carole Prato Sports Reporting Scholarship must be full-time college sophomores, juniors, or seniors who are studying radio or television sports reporting.

Applicants for the $2,500 Presidents' Scholarship must be enrolled full-time college sophomores, juniors, or seniors who are studying radio and television news.

Applicants for the $1,000 Mike Reynolds Journalism Scholarship must be enrolled full-time college sophomores, juniors, or seniors who have good writing ability, excellent grades, a dedication to the news business, a strong interest in pursuing a career in electronic journalism, and a demonstrated need for financial assistance.

The foundation also offers several scholarships for minorities. Minority students whose career objective is electronic journalism (radio or television) and have at least one full year of college remaining are eligible to apply for the Carole Simpson Scholarship ($2,000), the Ed Bradley Scholarship ($10,000), and the Ken Kashiwahara Scholarship ($2,500). Applicants must attend college full time.

High school seniors may also apply for these scholarships.

Sallie Mae

http://www.collegeanswer.com

This Web site offers a scholarship database of more than 2.4 million awards (not all broadcasting-related) worth more than $14 billion. You must register (free) to use the database.

Scholarship America

1 Scholarship Way
St. Peter, MN 56082-1693
800-537-4180
http://www.scholarshipamerica.org

This organization works through its local Dollars for Scholars chapters in 41 states and the District of Columbia. In 2003, it awarded more than $29 million in scholarships to students. Visit Scholarship America's Web site for more information.

Scholarships.com

http://www.scholarships.com

Scholarships.com offers a free college scholarship search engine (although you must register to use it) and financial aid information.

Scholastic

c/o Alliance For Young Artists And
   Writers Inc.
555 Broadway
New York, NY 10012
212-343-6493
a&wgeneralinfo@scholastic.com
http://www.scholastic.com/
   artandwritingawards

Student-artists and -writers in grades 7 through 12 are eligible to apply for Scholastic Art and Writing Awards of up to $10,000. Art categories for graduating high school seniors include animation, art portfolio, ceramics and glass, computer art, design, digital imagery, drawing, mixed media, painting, photography, photography portfolio, printmaking, sculpture, and video and film. More than $20 million in scholarships have been awarded since the awards were founded in 1923. Visit Scholastic's Web site for a detailed overview of the various awards, competition levels, and application instructions.

Scripps Howard Foundation
PO Box 5380
312 Walnut Street
Cincinnati, OH 45201-0311
513-977-3035
http://foundation.scripps.com/
    foundation/programs/scholarships/
    scholarships.html

The foundation offers scholarships to undergraduates and graduate students who are interested in journalism or graphic arts (as applied to the newspaper industry). Contact the foundation for eligibility requirements and participating schools.

Society of Broadcast Engineers (SBE)
c/o Ennes Educational Foundation
    Trust
9247 North Meridian Street, Suite 305
Indianapolis, IN 46260-1946
317-846-9000
mclappe@sbe.org
http://www.sbe.org

The trust awards the following scholarships to students who aspire to a career in the technical aspects of broadcasting: Harold E. Ennes Scholarship, Robert D. Greenberg Scholarship, and Youth Scholarship. Applicants must have a career interest in the technical aspects of broadcasting and be recommended by two members of the Society of Broadcast Engineers. Preference will be given to members of the SBE. Applicants for the Ennes and Greenberg Scholarships are those who have some experience in the industry, and who are interested in pursuing continuing education. The Youth Scholarship is open to high school seniors who plan to pursue education in broadcast engineering. Scholarships range from $1,000 to $3,000, depending on the availability of funds. Contact the society for more information.

Society of Motion Picture and Television Engineers (SMPTE)
3 Barker Avenue
White Plains, NY 10601
914-761-1100
http://www.smpte.org

Undergraduate or graduate students pursuing study in motion pictures and television, with an emphasis on technology, may apply for the $2,000 Lou Wolf Memorial Scholarship. The society also offers an award to a student member who submits the best technical paper. Contact the society for more information.

Society of Professional Journalists–Mid-Florida Pro Chapter

Attn: Dr. Bonnie Jefferis, Coordinator of Mass Communications
St. Petersburg College
2465 Drew Street
Clearwater, FL 33756-2816
JefferisB@spcollege.edu
http://www.spj.org/midflorida/danielleinfo.htm

The Society of Professional Journalists–Mid-Florida Pro Chapter offers the $1,000 Danielle Cipriani TV News Scholarship to television news or television production majors at a Florida college or university. Applicants must be residents of the Mid-Florida Pro Chapter region (between Gainesville and Sarasota). Visit the society's Web site to download an application.

Society of Satellite Professionals International (SSPI)

The New York Information Technology Center
55 Broad Street, 14th Floor
New York, NY 10004
212-809-5199
http://www.sspi.org/displaycommon.cfm?an=1&subarticlenbr=56

The SSPI encourages high school seniors and undergraduate and graduate students interested in the field of satellite technology to apply for a variety of scholarships (ranging from $2,000 to $5,000). Contact the society for eligibility details.

United Negro College Fund (UNCF)

http://www.uncf.org/scholarships/index.asp

Visitors to the UNCF Web site can search for thousands of scholarships and grants, many of which are administered by the UNCF. High school seniors and undergraduate and graduate students are eligible. The search engine allows you to search by major (such as communications, journalism, and television production), state, scholarship title, grade level, and achievement score.

Look to the Pros

The following professional organizations offer a variety of materials, from career brochures to lists of accredited schools to salary surveys. Many of them also publish journals and newsletters that you should become familiar with. Some also have annual conferences that you might be able to attend. (While you may not be able to attend a conference as a participant, it may be possible to "cover" one for your school or even your local paper, especially if your school has a related club.)

When contacting professional organizations, keep in mind that they all exist primarily to serve their members, be it through continuing education, professional licensure, political lobbying, or just "keeping up with the profession." While many are strongly interested in promoting their profession and passing information about it to the general public, these busy professional organizations are not there solely to provide you with information. Whether you call or write, be courteous, brief, and to the point. Know what you need and ask for it. If the organization has a Web site, check it out first: what you're looking for may be available there for downloading, or you may find a list of prices or instructions, such as sending a self-addressed stamped envelope with your request.

Finally, be aware that organizations, like people, move. To save time when writing, first confirm the address, preferably with a quick phone call to the organization itself: "Hello, I'm calling to confirm your address. . . ."

❏ **THE SOURCES**

Accrediting Council on Education in Journalism and Mass Communications

University of Kansas School of Journalism and Mass Communications
Stauffer-Flint Hall, 1435 Jayhawk Boulevard
Lawrence, KS 66045-7575
785-864-3973
http://www.ku.edu/~acejmc/ STUDENT/PROGLIST.SHTML

Visit the council's Web site for a list of accredited programs in journalism and mass communications.

American Meteorological Society

45 Beacon Street
Boston, MA 02108-3693
617-227-2425
amsinfo@ametsoc.org
http://www.ametsoc.org/AMS/ amsedu/index.html

Contact the society for information on postsecondary educational programs, scholarships, summer opportunities, certification, and membership for college students. In addition, the society offers *A Career Guide for the Atmospheric Sciences* at its Web site.

American Cinema Editors (ACE)

100 Universal City Plaza
Verna Fields Building 2282, Room 190
Universal City, CA 91608-1002
818-777-2900
http://www.ace-filmeditors.org/
  newace/home.html

The ACE offers career and education information at its Web site, along with information about internship opportunities, competitions, and sample articles from *Cinemeditor Magazine.*

American Screenwriters Association

269 South Beverly Drive, Suite 2600
Beverly Hills, CA 90212-3807
866-265-9091
asa@goasa.com
http://www.asascreenwriters.com

This organization provides membership and resources to aspiring screenwriters. It offers career information, competitions, and a high school outreach program.

American Women in Radio and Television (AWRT)

8405 Greensboro Drive, Suite 800
McLean, VA 22102-5120
703-506-3290
info@awrt.org
http://www.awrt.org

Contact AWRT for information on careers in radio and television, as well as scholarships and internships.

Association for Education in Journalism and Mass Communication

234 Outlet Pointe Boulevard
Columbia, SC 29210-5667
803-798-0271
aejmchq@aejmc.org
http://www.aejmc.org

This organization provides general educational information on all areas of journalism, including newspapers, magazines, television, and radio.

Broadcast Education Association (BEA)

1771 N Street NW
Washington, DC 20036-2891
888-380-7222
beainfo@beaweb.org
http://www.beaweb.org

An association of university broadcasting faculty, industry professionals, and graduate students, BEA offers annual scholarships in broadcasting for college juniors, seniors, and graduate students. Visit its Web site for useful information about broadcast education and the broadcasting industry.

Directors Guild of America (DGA)

7920 Sunset Boulevard
Los Angeles, CA 90046-3304
310-289-2000
http://www.dga.org

Visit the guild's Web site to learn more about the industry, to find out about DGA-sponsored training programs, and to read selected articles from *DGA Magazine*.

National Association of Broadcasters
1771 N Street NW
Washington, DC 20036-2891
202-429-5300
nab@nab.org
http://www.nab.org

The association provides information on broadcast education, scholarships, and useful publications at its Web site.

National Association of Broadcast Employees and Technicians
nabet@nabetcwa.org
http://nabetcwa.org

Contact the association for information on union membership.

National Association of Farm Broadcasting
PO Box 500
Platte City, MO 64079-0500
816-431-4032
info@nafb.com
http://nafb.com

Contact the association for information on membership for college students, scholarships, and farm broadcasting.

National Cable and Telecommunications Association
1724 Massachusetts Avenue NW
Washington, DC 20036-1903
202-775-3550
http://www.ncta.com

Visit the NCTA's Web site for information on careers in the cable industry.

Producers Guild of America (PGA)
8530 Wilshire Boulevard, Suite 450
Beverly Hills, CA 90211-3115
310-358-9020
info@producersguild.org
http://www.producersguild.org

Visit the PGA's Web site for information about career options for producers.

Radio-Television News Directors Association and Foundation (RTNDA)
1600 K Street NW, Suite 700
Washington, DC 20006-2838
202-659-6510
rtnda@rtnda.org
http://www.rtnda.org

Visit this organization's Web site to access scholarship and internship information, high school journalism resources, useful publications, and salary and employment surveys. The Radio-Television News Directors Association and Foundation also offers membership to college students.

Society of Broadcast Engineers
9247 North Meridian Street, Suite 305
Indianapolis, IN 46260-1946
317-846-9000
mclappe@sbe.org
http://www.sbe.org

Visit the society's Web site for information on membership for high school and college students, scholarships, certification, education programs, and professional publications.

Society of Motion Picture and Television Engineers

3 Barker Avenue
White Plains, NY 10601
914-761-1100
http://www.smpte.org

Visit the society's Web site for information on scholarships, membership for college students, and links to useful resources.

Society of Professional Journalists

Eugene S. Pulliam National
    Journalism Center
3909 North Meridian Street
Indianapolis, IN 46208-4011
317-927-8000
http://spj.org

Contact the society for information on student chapters, scholarships, educational information, discussion groups, and much more.

TV Jobs/Broadcast Employment Services (BES)

PO Box 4116
Oceanside, CA 92052-4116
800-374-0119
http://www.tvjobs.com

BES is an online service that provides job listings, employment-wanted notices, and information on scholarships, internships, and careers in television broadcasting.

Writers Guild of America, East

555 West 57th Street, Suite 1230
New York, NY 10019-2925
212-767-7800
http://www.wgaeast.org

To learn more about the film industry, to read interviews and articles by noted screenwriters, to access screenwriter's tools and resources, to read copies of *On Writing*, and to find links to many other screenwriting-related sites on the Internet, visit the guild's Web site.

Writers Guild of America, West

7000 West Third Street
Los Angeles, CA 90048-4321
800-548-4532
http://www.wga.org

To learn more about the film industry, to read interviews and articles by noted screenwriters, to access screenwriter's tools and resources, and to find links to many other screenwriting-related sites on the Internet, visit the guild's Web site.

Index

Entries and page numbers in **bold** indicate major treatment of a topic.

A

AAJA. *See* Asian American Journalists Association
ABC network 6, 8, 52
About.com:Radio 140
ACA. *See* American Collegiate Adventures
Academic Study Associates (ASA) 114–115
Academy of Television Arts and Sciences 148–149
Accrediting Council on Education in Journalism and Mass Communications (ACEJMC) 55, 160
ACE. *See* American Cinema Editors
ACEJMC. *See* Accrediting Council on Education in Journalism and Mass Communications
actors 14
actresses. *See* actors
adjacency 29
advisory 93
affiliate station 8
AFTRA. *See* American Federation of Television and Radio Artists
agent 61
aircheck 37
Air Force ROTC 149
airtime 8
Alliance of Motion Picture and Television Producers 81
All in the Family 8
AM broadcast 5, 9
American Cinema Editors (ACE) 161
American Collegiate Adventures (ACA) 115
American Federation of Television and Radio Artists (AFTRA) 40, 47, 56
American Film Institute 64
American Institute for Foreign Study 115
American Legion Auxiliary 149
American Meteorological Society (AMS) 96, 97, 115–116, 149, 160–161
American Radio Relay League Foundation (ARRL) 149
American Screenwriters Association 116, 161
American Society of Newspaper Editors (ASNE) 141
American Women in Radio and Television (AWRT) 150, 161
amplifier 20
AMS. *See* American Meteorological Society
analog 5, 20
Anchorage, Alaska 68, 70
anchorpeople 13. *See* radio anchors; television anchors

anchors. *See* radio anchors; television anchors
animators 11
Apollo 13 6
Arbitron ratings 5, 45
Arizona State University
    American Collegiate Adventures 115
    Summer Broadcast Institute for High School Students 127–128
    Summer Journalism Institute for High School Students 127–128
Army ROTC 150
ARRL. *See* American Radio Relay League Foundation
ASA. *See* Academic Study Associates
Asian American Journalists Association (AAJA) 150
ASNE. *See* American Society of Newspaper Editors
ASNE High School Journalism 140–141
Associated Press 52
Association for Education in Journalism and Mass Communication 161
Association for Women in Sports Media (AWSM) 151
Association on American Indian Affairs 150–151
associations. *See* organizations
AVID 86
AWRT. *See* American Women in Radio and Television
Axis Sally 4

B

Baird, John Logie 14
Ball State University 48
Baltimore, Maryland 61
bandwidth 20
barometer 93
BEA. *See* Broadcast Education Association
beats 52
Behrman, Adam 94, 97, 98
Berghof Studio, Herbert 61
Berra, Lawrence "Yogi" 72
BES. *See* TV Jobs/Broadcast Employment Services
best boys 12
books 2, 103, 130–135
Boston University 88, 118–119
Briggs, Tracy 35, 37–38, 40
Broadcast Education Association (BEA) 141, 151, 161
Broadcast Employment Services 141
broadcast engineers 12, **18–26**. *See also* engineers
Broadcasters Training Network (BTN) 141–142
broadcast executives 27–34
broadcasting 20

164

Broadcasting Training Program 16
broadcast journalism 5, 45
Broadcast News 85
broadcast operations directors 30. *See also* broadcast
    executives
broadcast quality 20
broadcast technicians 18–19. *See also* broadcast
    engineers
Brooks, Jim 62
BTN. *See* Broadcasters Training Network
Buck's Rock Performing and Creative Arts Camp 116–
    117
Byrne, Pete 72–73, 74

C

cable television 7, 8–9, 33
Camp Ballibay 117
Camp Chi 117–118
camps, in general 2, 110
Canada 61
careers 9–14. *See also specific career*
    off-air careers 10–13
        management 10
        preproduction, production and postproduction
            10–12
        promotions, sales, marketing, and community
            affairs 12–13
    on-air careers 13–14
cartoonists 11
Casper, Wyoming 94
casting agents 11
CBS
    affiliates 8, 47, 84, 86
    major network station 6, 52
Challenger 6
channel 20
Chicago, Illinois 20
chief engineers 12, 19. *See also* broadcast engineers;
    engineers
chief meteorologists 96. *See also* weather forecasters
chromakey 94
chryon (character generator) 79
CIA World Factbook 33
CineMedia 142
clubs 105
CNN 48, 52, 88
Coach 61
cold front 93
CollegeBoard.com 151
CollegeNET 151
college study in general 2, 110–111
Columbia 6
Columbia College Chicago 119–120
Columbia University 64
Columbus, Ohio 97
comedians 14
commentators 13
community affairs careers 12–13

community affairs directors 13, 30. *See also* broadcast
    executives; directors
community theaters 106
competitions, in general, 111
composition 52
conferences 69
Contact 4
continuity writers 11
copy 52
Cornell University 125–126
Corporation for Public Broadcasting (CPB) 118
correspondents 11, 13, **50–58**
costume designers 11
coverage 29
CPB. *See* Corporation for Public Broadcasting
Csonka, Larry 71

D

DAR. *See* Daughters of the American Revolution
Daughters of the American Revolution (DAR) 151–152
dayparts 29
Dearborn, Michigan 105
demographics 5, 37
deregulation 41
DeVry Institute of Technology 23, 24
DGA. *See* Directors Guild of America
digital 5, 20
digital broadcasting 37
directors 10. *See also* community affairs directors;
    directors of photography; lighting directors; program
    directors; technical directors; television directors; video
    directors
Directors Guild of America (DGA) 81, 161–162
directors of photography 11
disc jockeys 7, 14, **35–42**. *See also* radio producers
divisions 69
documentaries 85
Doppler radar 93, 94
draft 61
drama club 105–106

E

edit 5
editor 78
electrical technicians 12
Electronic Field Trip to the National Weather Service
    142
electronic media 52
Elser, Tom 50–51, 53–56
employment opportunities, in general 14–15, 111
engineers 8, 12. *See also* broadcast engineers; chief
    engineers; transmitter engineers
ESPN 72, 74, 77
    SportsZone 142–143
Everybody Loves Raymond 61, 62
executive producers 64. *See also* screenwriters
executives. *See* broadcast executives

F

Fargo, North Dakota 35, 37, 54–55, 72
FastWeb 152
FCC. *See* Federal Communications Commission
Federal Communications Commission (FCC)
    certification and licensing 23
    described 5
    relations with 10, 28
    responsibilities of 9
    station applications and, 6
Federal Radio Commission 9
Fessenden, Reginald A. 5
field experience, in general 111
field technicians 19. *See also* broadcast engineers
film directors 64, 82. *See also* screenwriters; television
   directors
film producers 64. *See also* screenwriters
film writers 64. *See also* screenwriters
financial aid 2, 146–159
fireside chats 4
fixed position 29
floor managers 12
floor staff 11–12
FM broadcast 5, 9
food critics 13
Food Network 8, 77
forecasters. *See* weather forecasters
foreign correspondent 52. *See also* correspondents;
   reporters
format 5
Foster, Jodie 4
Foundation for the Carolinas 152
FOX network 7, 8, 52
FOX Sports Northwest 71
franchise 69
freelance. *See* self-employment
frequency 5, 29
Frontiers at Worcester Polytechnic Institute 118

G

gaffers 12, 86
Galileo (weather graphics program) 94
game show hosts 14
general managers 10, 28, 82, 88. *See also* broadcast
   executives; television directors; television producers
general sales managers 40, 73, 96. *See also* disc jockeys;
   managers; radio producers; sportscasters; weather
   forecasters
Golden Key International Honor Society 152
Good Morning, America 79, 95
Good Morning, Wyoming 95
grants. *See* financial aid
graphic artists 10
Green Bay, Wisconsin 27, 30
grips 12, 86
GuaranteedScholarships.com 152

H

hairstylists 11
hat trick 69
Hawaii Community Foundation 152
HBO 9
HCF. *See* Hispanic College Fund
HDTV. *See* high definition television
heat index 93
high definition television (HDTV) 5
Hindenberg 55
Hispanic College Fund (HCF) 153
Hollywood, California 77
home base 21
How Stuff Works 143
Hunter, Holly 85

I

IABJ. *See* Indianapolis Association of Black Journalists
IBA. *See* Indiana Broadcasters Association; Iowa
   Broadcasters Association
IEEE. *See* Institute of Electrical and Electronics Engineers
IFB 94
Illinois Career Resource Network 153
Imagine 143
Indiana Broadcasters Association (IBA) 153
Indianapolis Association of Black Journalists (IABJ) 154
Indiana University 119
industry outlook, in general 15–16
Institute of Electrical and Electronics Engineers (IEEE)
   154
International Brotherhood of Electrical Workers 24
International Radio and Television Society Foundation
   (IRTS) 81, 120
Internet 7, 45, 103. *See also* Web sites
Intern Exchange International Ltd. 120–121
internships, in general 104, 106–107, 111. *See also specific*
   careers
Iowa Broadcasters Association (IBA) 154
IRTS. *See* International Radio and Television Society
   Foundation

J

Jarrett, Dale 71
Jensen, Beth 84, 86–88
jobs, part-time 111. *See also specific careers*
job shadow 33, 107
Johns Hopkins University 124–125

K

KAB. *See* Kansas Association of Broadcasters
Kansas Association of Broadcasters (KAB) 154
Katcef, Sue Kopen 54, 58
KDLT 88
Keillor, Garrison 106
KELO-TV 84, 86

Kennedy, John F. 6
KETV 50, 53
KMTV 55
KNBN NewsCenter1 43, 45
Kruger, Lindsay 43, 45–48
KSTP-TV 73
KTUU-TV 70
KTWO-TV 94
KVLY/KXJB 54
KVLY-TV 72

L

language 5, 7
leagues 69
Learning for Life Exploring Program 121–122
librarians. *See* music librarians
lighting directors 12. *See also* directors
London, England 14
Los Angeles, California 61–62
The Love Boat 8
Loyola University 23

M

MAB. *See* Michigan Association of Broadcasters
 Foundation
magazines. *See* periodicals
maintenance technicians 19. *See also* broadcast engineers
makeup artists 11
Malone, Karl 71
management careers 10
managers. *See* floor mangers; general managers; general
 sales managers; marketing managers; promotions
 managers; sales managers; station managers; traffic
 managers
Mankato, Minnesota 73
Marconi, Guglielmo 4
Marine Corps Scholarship Foundation 154–155
market 5
marketing careers 12–13
marketing managers 29. *See also* broadcast executives;
 managers
marketing workers 13
market number 45
The Mary Tyler Moore Show 85
Massachusetts Institute of Technology (MIT), Women's
 Technology Program 128–129
McCurdy, Sarah 54, 55
media 7
Meet the Press 6
membership, in general. *See* organizations
meteorologists. *See also* weather forecasters
Miami Dolphins 71
Miami University–Oxford 121
Michigan Association of Broadcasters Foundation (MAB)
 155
Midwest Sports Channel (MSC) 73

military 98
Minnesota Public Radio 106
Minnesota Wild 73
Minnesota Wrestling Weekly 73
minorities in broadcast industry 15
Minorities in Broadcasting Training Program 56
Missouri Broadcasters Association 155
MIT. *See* Massachusetts Institute of Technology
mixing 37
Morrison, Herb 55
movie rentals 7
MSC. *See* Midwest Sports Channel
MSNBC 48, 52
MT&R. *See* Museum of Television and Radio
museum, visiting 103–104
Museum of Broadcast Communications 104, 122
Museum of Television and Radio (MT&R) 122–123, 143
music librarians 11
"Must-See TV" 13
Myrtle Beach, South Carolina 91, 93, 98

N

NAB. *See* National Association of Broadcasters
NABJ. *See* National Association of Black Journalists
NAFB. *See* National Association of Farm Broadcasters
narrowcasting 15
NASA space program 6, 83
NASCAR 71
Naselle, Washington 70
National Association of Black Journalists (NABJ) 155
National Association of Broadcast Employees and
 Technicians 162
Communications Workers of America 24
National Association of Broadcasters (NAB) 16, 25, 33,
 48, 162
National Association of Farm Broadcasters (NAFB) 155,
 162
National Broadcasting Company (NBC) 6, 8, 52, 70, 88
National Cable and Telecommunications Association
 162
National Center for Environmental Prediction 93
National Endowment for the Arts (NEA) 156
National Hurricane Center 91, 93
National Public Radio (NPR) 7
National Weather Association (NWA) 96, 97
National Weather Service 92, 93, 98, 142
Navy: Education: Earn Money for College 156
NBC. *See* National Broadcasting Company
NBC Sports 21
NEA. *See* National Endowment for the Arts
network station 6, 8
New Bern, North Carolina 97
news anchors 7–8, 44, 56, 73, 82, 88, 96. *See also*
 correspondents; radio anchors; reporters; sportscasters;
 television anchors; television directors; television
 producers; weather forecasters
newscasts 85

news directors 28, 47, 88. *See also* broadcast executives;
    radio anchors; television anchors; television producers
newswriters 11
New York City, New York
    screenwriters 61
    television directors 81
    World's Fair 6
New York University 77
NEXRAD 93
NHSI. *See* Northwestern University, National High School
    Institute
Nick-at-Nite 85
Nielsen Media 7
Nielsen ratings 7, 8
Nome, Alaska 68
North Carolina State University 95, 97
North Dakota State University 38
Northwestern University, National High School Institute
    (NHSI) 123–124
Notre Dame University 73
NPR. *See* National Public Radio
NWA. *See* National Weather Association

O

OAB. *See* Oklahoma Association of Broadcasters
off-air careers 10–13
    management 10
    preproduction, production and postproduction 10–12
    promotions, sales, marketing, and community affairs
        12–13
Oklahoma Association of Broadcasters (OAB) 156
Omaha, Nebraska 50, 53
on-air careers 13–14
O'Neil, Peggy 14
O & O station 29
organizations 2, 104, 111, 160–163. *See also specific
    organization/association*
Orlando, Florida 47
Oswald, Lee Harvey 6
Overseas Press Club of America 156
over-the-shoulder 78

P

page 20, 21
Palos, Tony 20–25
panning 20
PBS network 6
People for the Ethical Treatment of Animals (PETA) 68
periodicals 103, 135–139
Perry, Richard 76, 79–82
PETA. *See* People for the Ethical Treatment of Animals
Peterson, Lars 68, 70–71, 74
Peterson's Educational Portal 143
PGA. *See* Producers Guild of America
Piotrowski, Ed 91, 93–98
pitch 61
playlist 7, 37

podcasts 58
Portland Trailblazers 70, 74
postproduction 86
postproduction careers 10–12
A Prairie Home Companion (motion picture) 106
Prairie Home Companion (music and comedy program)
    106
preemption 29
preproduction careers 10–12
press secretaries 47. *See also* radio anchors; television
    anchors
Princeton Review 144
producers 10, 47, 73, 82. *See also* radio anchors; radio
    producers; sportscasters; television anchors; television
    directors; television producers
Producers Guild of America (PGA) 162
production careers 10–12
professional organizations. *See* organizations
program
    descriptions, in general 111–112
        application information 112
        background information 112
        classes and activities 112
        commuter versus residential options 113–114
        contact information 112
        credit 112–113
        eligibility for programs 113
        facilities 113
        qualifications for programs 113
    listing of specific 114–129
program assistants 11
program directors 10, 28. *See also* broadcast executives
promotions careers 12–13
promotions managers, 12, 30. *See also* broadcast executives
prop workers 11
PSA. *See* public service announcement
public service announcement (PSA) 29
public service directors 30. *See also* broadcast executives

R

radio anchors 13, **43–49**
radio and television industry 4–6
    careers 9–14
        off-air careers 10–13
        on-air careers 13–14
    employment opportunities 14–15
    in general 4–7
    industry outlook 15–16
    language 5, 7
    structure of 7–9
radio commentators 13
radio producers 11, **35–42**. *See also* disc jockeys;
    producers
radio reporters 13
RadioSpace™, 144
radio stations (high school) 105
Radio-Television News Directors Association (RTNDA)
    34, 48, 74, 82–83, 144, 162

Radio-Television News Directors Foundation (RTNDF) 156–157
Rapid City, South Dakota 43, 45
ratings 5, 7, 8, 29
reader 61
remote 20
reporters 11, 13, **50–58**
restricted radio/telephone operator permit 23
Roosevelt, Franklin D. 4, 6
RTNDA. *See* Radio-Television News Directors Association
RTNDF. *See* Radio-Television News Directors Foundation
Ruby, Jack 6
rundown 20

S

sales careers 12–13
sales managers 13, 29. *See also* broadcast executives; managers
salespeople 8, 13
Sallie Mae 157
Sandler, Ellen 61–63, 65–66
satellite radio 7, 15, 37
Saturday Night Live 14
SBE. *See* Society of Broadcast Engineers
scenic designers. *See* graphic artists
Scholarship America 157
scholarships 2
Scholarships.com 157
Scholastic 157–158
Schonely, Bill 70
screenwriters 11, **59–67**
Screenwriter's Utopia 144–145
Scripps Howard Foundation 158
script 45
self-employment
    directors 8
    producers 8
    screenwriters 61, 66
    sportscasters 71
    television directors 81
    television producers 88
    writers 8
Severe Storms Forecast Center. *See* Storm Prediction Center
Shiels, Robert 97
shot composition 86
Showtime 9
The Simpsons 11
simulcast 29
Sioux Falls, South Dakota 84, 86, 88
Sirius Satellite Radio 37
SkillsUSA 125
SMPTE. *See* Society of Motion Picture and Television Engineers
Society of Broadcast Engineers (SBE) 23, 25, 104, 125, 158, 162–163
Society of Motion Picture and Television Engineers (SMPTE) 158, 163

Society of Professional Journalists 56, 58, 163
    Mid-Florida Pro Chapter 159
Society of Satellite Professionals International (SSPI) 159
sound bite 52
South Bend, Indiana 73
speech teams 106
sports anchors 44–45. *See also* radio anchors; television anchors
sportscasters 8, 14, **68–75**
spot 29
SSPI. *See* Society of Satellite Professionals International
station managers 40, 56. *See also* correspondents; disc jockeys; managers; radio producers; reporters
stock footage 86
Storm Prediction Center 91, 93
storyboard 29
structure of radio and television industry 7–9
stuntpeople 14
summer study, in general 2, 1042, 110–111
Sundance Film Festival 77
super (superimposed) 78
sweep 29
syndicated program 29
Syracuse University 126–127

T

talent 86
talk show hosts 7, 14
Taxi 61, 62
Taynton, Bill 14
technical directors 78. *See also* directors; television directors
technical stock clerks 19. *See also* broadcast engineers
telecommunications 7
Telecommunications Act 9
TelePromTer 7, 45
television anchors 13, **43–49**
Television and Radio News Research 145
television commentators 13
television directors 11, **76–83**. *See also* directors
television industry 6–7. *See also* radio and television industry
television market 7
television news anchors 40. *See also* anchorpeople; radio producers and disc jockeys
television producers 11, **84–90**. *See also* producers
television reporters 13
televisors 14
terrorist attacks 6
theater performances 105–106
tilting 20
Tokyo Rose 4
Toledo, Ohio 97
tools of the broadcasting trade 103
traffic managers 10, 30. *See also* broadcast executives
transmitter 7, 20
transmitter engineers 12. *See also* engineers
transmitter operators 19. *See also* broadcast engineers

Travel Channel 8
treatment 61
Tropical Prediction Center. *See* National Hurricane Center
TV camera 14
TV clubs 105
TV Jobs/Broadcast Employment Services (BES) 163
TV tube 14
24 8
two-shot 78

U

UNCF. *See* United Negro College Fund
unions
     broadcast engineers 23–24
     radio producers and disc jockeys 40
     radio and television anchors 47
     reporters and correspondents 56
     screenwriters 64
United Negro College Fund (UNCF) 159
United Press International 52
University of California
Berkeley 114
Los Angeles, Writers Program 61, 64
University of Central Florida, Nicholson School of
   Communication 45, 47
University of Florida 127
University of London 120
University of Maryland
   Philip Merrill College of Journalism/UMTV 54
   Young Scholars Program: Journalism 129
University of Massachusetts 114
University of North Carolina 80
University of North Dakota 38
University of Southern California 64, 77
University of Wisconsin 115
UPN network 7
U.S. Department of Agriculture 98
U.S. Department of Labor
   earnings data
broadcast engineers 25
broadcast executives 34
radio producers and disc jockeys 41
reporters and correspondents 57
     screenwriters 66
     television directors 83
     television producers 88

     employment outlook 14
     broadcast engineers 25
     broadcast executives 34
     reporters and correspondents 57

V

video directors 12. *See also* directors
video recording technicians 19. *See also* broadcast
  engineers

video-robo technicians 19. *See also* broadcast engineers
video technicians 19. *See also* broadcast engineers
volunteer positions 106–107. *See also specific careers*

W

Warner Brothers 62
The War of the Worlds 4
Washington, D.C. 88, 92
Washington and Lee University 128
Washington State University, Edward R. Murrow School
   of Communications 71
WB network 7
WCTI-TV 95, 97
WDAY-AM 37
Weather Channel 94, 98, 100
weather forecasters 13–14, **91–100**
Web sites 2, 140–145. *See also* Internet
Welles, Orson 4
WFTV 47
WGA. *See* Writers Guild of America
WHME-FM radio 73
Wilmington, North Carolina 79
wipe 78
wire services 52
WKMG 47
WLUK-TV FOX 11 30
women in broadcast industry 15
Women's Technology Program 128–129
World War II 4, 6
World Wide Web. *See* Internet; Web sites
WPDE-TV 93, 97, 98
Wright State University 124
writers 11
Writers Guild East 64, 163
Writers Guild of America (WGA) 64, 65, 66
Writers Guild West 64, 163
WTOL-TV 97
Wyomedia 94

X

XM Satellite Radio 37

Y

Yahoo!:Radio 145

Z

Zollar, Jay 27, 30–32
Zworykin, Vladimir K. 14